MANGROVE
LIGHTNING

R A N D O M H O U S E
LARGE PRINT

MANGROVE LIGHTNING

RANDY WAYNE WHITE

Published in the United States of America by Random House Large Print in association with G. P Putnam's Sons, an imprint of Penguin Random House LLC, New York.

Cover design by Nellys Liang

Cover images: (landscape) Elisabeth Pollaert Smith / Getty Images; (boat) Denis Dryashkin / Shutterstock

The Library of Congress has established a Cataloging-in-Publication record for this title.

ISBN: 978-1-5247-5625-3

www.randomhouse.com/largeprint

FIRST LARGE PRINT EDITION

Printed in the United States of America

10 9 8 7 6 5 4 3 2 1

This Large Print edition published in accord with the standards of the N.A.V.H.

For dear Rogan and Rachael

Your office sent bones in cloth bags. These bags have rotted and caused much chaos. When people came to claim them, it was not possible to identify individual sets correctly. Our hearts have no peace.

—A letter from Tung Wah Hospital,
    Hong Kong, to the Chinese Consolidated
    Benevolent Association regarding the
    repatriation of Chinese dead,
    San Francisco, 1928

[DISCLAIMER]

Sanibel and Captiva Islands are real places, faithfully described, but used fictitiously in this novel. The same is true of certain businesses, marinas, bars, and other places frequented by Doc Ford, Tomlinson, and pals.

In all other respects, however, this novel is a work of fiction. Names (unless used by permission), characters, places, and incidents are either the product of the author's imagination or are used fictitiously. Any resemblance to actual persons, living or dead, or to actual events or locales is unintentional and coincidental.

Contact Mr. White at www.DOCFORD.COM.

AUTHOR'S NOTE

AUTHOR'S NOTE

This novel is based on events that occurred in Florida and the Bahamas during Prohibition, as reported (often vaguely) by newspapers of the time. One of those events catalyzed several murders that remain unsolved, so I warn the reader in advance that I have created a solution that is wholly fictional and have changed the names of most of those involved. Details pertaining to smuggling liquor and Chinese workers are portrayed accurately, as based on those old accounts, and interviews done personally or by contemporary journalists. The same is true of Marion Ford's insights into biology, although, again, my personal suspicions creep in regarding exotics such as the invasive lionfish.

Florida was wilder than the Wild West during the turn of the previous century, and far more difficult to travel by rail or horseback. This is probably why reams were written about Tombstone, etc., but almost nothing about the cowboy smugglers who inhabited the Everglades. My interest in the topic spans forty years, so the old accounts held few surprises—until, while browsing issues of the **St. Petersburg Times**, I stumbled onto a reference to the Marco Island war of 1925.

War? This was news to me. Marco, now a prosperous coastal community, was, in those years, a Southwest Florida outpost inhabited by fewer than two hundred people, mostly fishermen and clammers.

I dug deeper, and found a series of articles on a "land war" that pitted homesteaders, squatters, and smugglers against a multi-millionaire developer, Barron Collier, who would ultimately open the region by building roads, a railroad, but first carved out his own county to provide the needed infrastructure. That infrastructure included a handpicked sheriff, the sheriff's bloodhound and bullwhip, and his loyal deputies.

The headlines in the **St. Pete Times** during the summer of 1925 were tantalizing: "Developer and Settlers Near Blows . . . Deputy Sheriff Beaten, Disappears . . . Marco Island Calm;

Collier Enlists 'Navy' . . . Governor Is Called Upon in Land War!"

The disappearance of the deputy, more than other events, struck me as a historical hub because it connected seemingly dissimilar elements: smuggling rum and Chinese workers, a developer's wealth versus inhabitants who made their own laws, and who bristled at efforts to bring law into the Everglades.

Journalist Denes Husty found this article that suggests why the deputy and his family suddenly "disappeared."

The Fort Myers Press
April 18, 1925

A large mud hole on Marco Island, from which a terrible stench arises, is being searched today [by authorities] in belief that it might possibly hold the secret of the disappearance on February 19th of Deputy Sheriff J. H. Cox, [plus his wife, and two young children] for whom a state-wide search has failed to reveal the slightest clue.

Cox is the principal witness in some 19 indictments against smugglers and bootleggers in the Marco district, and a little over a year ago was badly beaten by a mob while arresting one of their number. Prior to his disappearance he had received several threatening letters. Cox paid little heed to the threats, but his wife, who is of a nervous temperament, lived in constant fear of the ruffians, it has been revealed. Investigation at Marco has only brought the news that he [and his family] suddenly moved away [without] disposing of most of his personal property.

A reward of fifty dollars has been offered by Sheriff W. H. Maynard for news resulting in the finding of the missing deputy and his family. Deputy Cox was described by Sheriff Maynard as 50 years of age, 180 pounds, 5 feet 9 inches tall, wide face, red nose, "fighting gray" eyes and of a tall slender build.

Where Cox went and how is a mystery that Sheriff Maynard has been tireless in his efforts to unravel. Cities and ports of the state have been searched and all authorities so-titled, without the slightest clue being discovered.

Telling, huh? Years later, a deathbed confession by one of the accused smugglers confirmed that the deputy and his family hadn't just disappeared. They had been lured ashore, and murdered somewhere near a "bottomless" lake that was known, even then, as a place where saltwater fish such as tarpon could be found.

As stated, this novel is a work of fiction, but the scaffolding is based upon fact. Therefore, before thanking those who contributed their expertise or good humor during the writing of **Mangrove Lightning**, I want to make clear that all errors, exaggerations, or misstatements are entirely my fault, not theirs.

Insights, ideas, and medical advice were provided by doctors Brian Hummel, my brother Dan White, Marybeth B. Saunders, and Peggy C. Kalkounos, and my nephew, Justin White, Ph.D.

Pals, advisers, and/or teammates are always a help because they know firsthand that writing and writers are a pain in the ass. They are Gary Terwilliger, Ron Iossi, Jerry Rehfuss, Stu Johnson, Victor Candalaria, Gene Lamont, Nick Swartz, Kerry Griner, Mike Shevlin, Jon Warden, Phil Jones, Dr. Mike Tucker, Davey Johnson, Barry Rubel, Mike Westhoff, and behavioral guru Don Carman.

My wife, singer/songwriter Wendy Webb, provided not just support and understanding but is a trusted adviser. Bill Lee, and his orbiting star, Diana, as always have guided me, safely, into the strange but fun and enlightened world of our mutual friend, the Reverend Sighurdhr M. Tomlinson. Equal thanks go to Albert Randall, Donna Terwilliger, Rachael Ketterman, Stephen Grendon, my devoted

SOB, the angelic Mrs. Iris Tanner, and my partners and pals, Mark and Julie Marinello, Marty and Brenda Harrity.

Much of this novel was written at corner tables before and after hours at Doc Ford's Rum Bar & Grille, where staff were tolerant beyond the call of duty. Thanks go to: Liz Harris Barker, Greg and Bryce Barker, Madonna Donna Butz, Jeffery Kelley, Chef Rene Ramirez, Amanda Rodriguez, Kim McGonnell, Ashley Rhoeheffer, the Amazing Cindy Porter, Desiree Olsen, Gabby Moschitta, Rachael Okerstrom, Rebecca Harris, Sarah Carnithian, Tyler Wussler, Tall Sean Lamont, Motown Rachel Songalewski, Boston Brian Cunningham, and Cardinals Fan Justin Harris.

At Doc Ford's on Fort Myers Beach: Lovely Kandice Salvador, Johnny G, Meliss Alleva, Rickards and Molly Brewer, Reyes Ramon Jr., Reyes Ramon Sr., Netta Kramb, Sandy Rodriquez, Mark Hines, Stephen Hansman, Nora Billheimer, Eric Hines, Dave Werner, Daniel Troxell, Kelsey King, Jenna Hocking, Adam Stocco, Brandon Cashatt, Dani Peterson, Tim Riggs, Elijah Blue Jansen, Jessica Del Gandio, Douglas Martens, Jacob Krigbaum, Jeff Bright, Derek Aubry, Chase Uhl, Carly Purdy, Nikki Sarros, Bre Cagnoli, Carly Cooper, Andrew Acord, Diane Bellini, Jessie Fox, Justin Voskuhl, Lalo Contreras, Nick Howes, Rich Capo, Zeke

Pietrzyk, Reid Pietrzyk, Ryan Fowler, Dan Mumford, Kelly Bugaj, Taylor Darby, Jaqueline Engh, Carmen Reyes, Karli Goodison, Kaitlyn Wolfe, Alex and Eric Munchel, Zach Leon, Alex Hall.

At Doc Ford's on Captiva Island: Big Papa Mario Zanolli, Lovely Julie Grzeszak, Shawn Scott, Joy Schawalder, Alicia Rutter, Adam Traum, Alexandra Llanos, Antonio Barragan, Chris Orr, Daniel Leader, Dylan Wussler, Edward Bowen, Erica DeBacker, Irish Heather Walk, Jon Economy, Josh Kerschner, Katie Kovacs, Ryan Body, Ryan Cook, Sarah Collins, Shelbi Muske, Scott Hamilton, Tony Foreman, Yakhyo Yakubov, Yamily Fernandez, Cheryl Radar Erickson, Heather Hartford, Stephen Snook Man Day, Anastasia Moiseyev, Chelsea Bennett, Guitar Czar Steve Reynolds, and Shokruh "Shogun" Akhmedov.

Finally, thanks to my wonderful sons Lee and Rogan for helping finish another book.

—**Randy Wayne White**
Telegraph Creek Gun Club
Central Florida

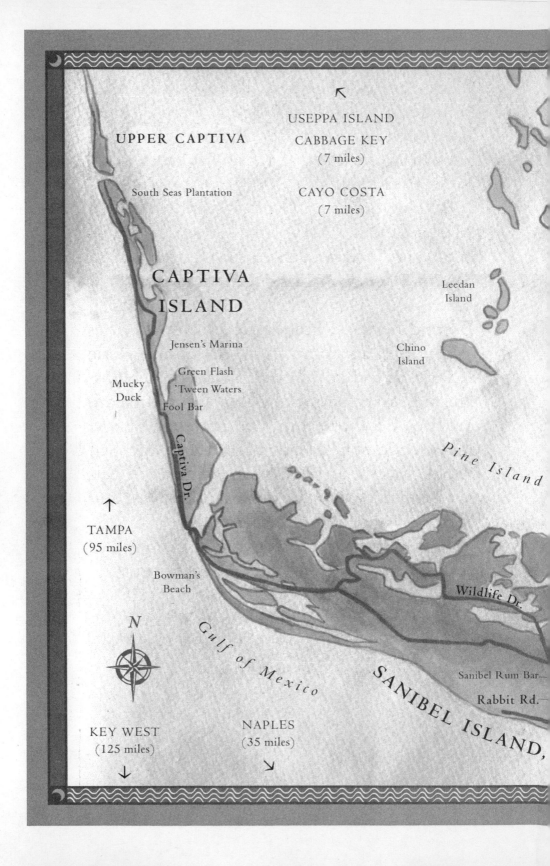

1

On the phone, Tomlinson said to Ford, "When the deputy's wife and kids disappeared, moonshiners might've dumped their bodies in the lake—it was during Prohibition. It wouldn't be the first time karma has waited decades to boot justice in the ass."

"Tootsie Barlow told you that story?" Ford, a marine biologist, was referring to a famous fishing guide who ranked with Jimmie Albright, Jack Brothers, Ted Williams, and a few others as fly-casting pioneers in the Florida Keys.

"His family was involved somehow—the Barlows go way, way back in the area. I don't know how yet, but I will. He's in bad shape, so I need to take it slow, but **you're** the one who told me about the lake—Chino Hole. That's the connection. The access road cuts through Tootsie's property."

"I had no idea. He moved to the Everglades?"

"Smack-dab in the middle. One of those little crossroads villages like Copeland or Carnestown. The property's been in his family for years. I'm driving down this afternoon. Since he quit guiding, it's probably easier for him to wake up and see sawgrass instead of the Gulf Stream. The endgame, dude, for watermen like us, it can be pretty damn sad."

"I've heard the rumor," Ford said. "As far as your story goes, I'm still lost."

"So's Tootsie. How many fishing guides put away money for retirement? He's broke, which is bad enough, but now he's afraid that God has singled out his family for punishment. Like a conspiracy, you know? Not because of something he did, more likely something his father or a relative did. The cops won't listen, his preacher doesn't believe him, so who else is he gonna call but the Right Reverend, yours truly."

Tomlinson, an ordained Rinzai Buddhist priest, seldom employed the honorific "Right Reverend." The title had been bestowed by a Las Vegas divinity mill after cashing his check for fifty bucks.

"Tootsie wants you to put in a good word

with God, I get it. I still don't see what this has to do with us . . ."

"He wants someone to convince the cops he's not crazy. And there's another connection. The deputy who disappeared was J. H. Cox. That ring a bell? It should."

"When was this?"

"Nineteen twenty-five. A few years earlier, a woman was murdered by a man named Cox. Same area; near Marco Island. I don't know if it was the same man, but your Hannah Smith is a direct descendant of the woman he killed."

Mentioning the biologist's ex-lover, Hannah, was a calculated risk to catalyze Ford's interest. In the background over the phone, Tomlinson could hear a steel drum band. "Hey, seriously, where are you?"

Ford, who was in the lobby of the Schooner Hotel, Nassau, Bahamas, said, "I'm in Lauderdale. At a convention for aquarium hobbyists. I'll get back to the lab late tomorrow. Hopefully."

"Bahia Mar, Lauderdale?"

"Close enough. Look . . . I've got a talk to give and I'm still working on my notes." As he spoke, the child-porn dealer he'd been tailing stepped to the registration desk. Ford covered the phone and moved as if getting into line.

When he rejoined the conversation, his

boat bum hipster pal Tomlinson was saying, ". . . Tootsie's story is historical fact. I've got the old newspaper stories to prove it. In August 1925, Deputy Cox, his wife, and two kids all disappeared the night before a bunch of bootleggers went on trial. Marco Island or somewhere at the edge of the Everglades—get it?—all within a few miles of Chino Hole."

"Moonshiners would need fresh water," Ford reasoned while he watched the clerk encode the porn dealer's room key.

"That's who the newspapers blamed, but there was other nasty crap going on at the time, which I'm just starting to research. You ever hear of the Marco Island war?"

"Come on, you're making this up."

"It **happened**, man. Same time period. A bunch of heavy hitters had their fingers in the regional pie—Al Capone, probably Joe Kennedy, too, but they weren't the worst. The elite rich were stealing homesteads, and smuggling in Chinese illegals to boot." Tomlinson sniffed, and added, "Lauderdale, huh? Dude, the satellite must'a stopped over Nassau, 'cause I swear can I smell jerked chicken."

Ford replied, "Call you back," and hung up as the clerk addressed the porn dealer by name for the third time—standard, in the hospitality business—then handed over a key in a sleeve with the number 803 written on it and circled.

"I'll be checking out in about an hour," Ford told the clerk when it was his turn.

There were ceiling fans in the lobby and panoramic windows, beyond which sunbaked tourists lounged by the pool. A brunette in a red handkerchief two-piece was sufficiently lush and languid to spark a yearning in the biologist—an abdominal pang he recognized as discontent.

Focus, he told himself, and returned to his encrypted notes. It became easier when the brunette stood and buttoned up her beach wrap. Every set of poolside eyes followed her to the door.

An hour later, the porn dealer reappeared in the lobby, wearing shorts and flip-flops, and exited toward the tiki bar.

Ford shouldered his computer bag, and crossed the lobby to the elevators.

From the eighth floor, Montagu Bay was a turquoise basin encrusted with slums and ox cart traffic on the eastern fringe. Spaced along the waterfront were resort compounds; postcard enclaves that were separated from Nassau's realities by armed guards and tastefully disguised concertina wire.

The biologist no longer wondered why

tourists came to places like this. People seldom traveled. Not really. Travel was too damn unpredictable. Instead, they contrived daydreams. They chose template fictions that matched, or came close enough to, the vacation they wanted to describe to their friends back home.

Near the elevator was a house phone. He dialed housekeeping, and told the woman, "I'm a dope. Can you please send someone up with a key to eight-oh-three? I locked myself out."

"Your name, sir?"

"James Lutz." That was the name the porn dealer was using.

"When security arrives," the woman added, "show them your passport, Mr. Lutz."

"Have him bring a bucket of ice, too," the biologist replied.

He was palming a twenty-euro bill when a kid wearing a name badge appeared, used a passkey, and bowed him into the room. "Hang on, I've got something for you." Inside the closet, as anticipated, was a wall safe, which he fiddled with before giving up. "Damn . . . must have punched in the number wrong. What's the default code? I need my wallet."

The kid opened the safe, and stepped back in deference to this solid-looking American who exuded confidence, but in a friendly way that suggested he was also generous.

"Thank you, Mr. Lutz," the kid said,

accepting the twenty. No eye contact; he backed out of the room.

"You're supposed to see this." The fake passport earned only a dutiful glance.

He has no future in the security trade, Ford rationalized when the kid was gone. **I did him a favor.**

On the other hand, probably not. Child pornography was a billion-dollar international industry. Nassau was the ancillary stronghold for a Russian network that branched into Haiti, Indonesia, and the Middle East, particularly Muslim regions where daughters were treated as chattel. Children provided a steady income to jihadists who enjoyed beheading infidels. When word got out that a low-level dealer had lost incriminating files while drinking at the pool bar, Jimmy Lutz, or whatever his name was, would beg first for his life, then a painless bullet.

If he lived that long.

Wearing gloves and a jeweler's eyepiece, Ford secured an adhesive keystroke transmitter to Lutz's laptop. The translucent tape was two inches long and thinner than a human hair. Once mounted on the screen's black border, it became invisible, which Ford confirmed, before returning the laptop to its case.

Next, the safe. He photographed the contents: a wallet, two passports, a bundle of cash, and half a dozen ultra-secure biometric thumb drives. Three platinum thumb drives, three stealth black. Ford's employer, a Swiss agency, had anticipated this, but had provided him with only four stealth versions. He switched out the three black thumb drives, and repositioned each exactly as he'd found it before closing the safe.

Ford had also anticipated that Jimmy Lutz was in Nassau on a working vacation. On the bed, a Dacor dive bag lay next to a leather suitcase and a valet parking ticket. He unzipped the bag and removed a buoyancy compensator vest attached to a four-hose regulator.

The gear looked new.

Using a multi-tool, he popped a pin, removed the regulator's cover; next, a lubricating seal and the main diaphragm. A stainless valve seat and plunger were cupped within. With a drop of water-soluble glue, he seated an object that would clog the system when it broke free but would dissolve without a trace within twenty minutes. He did the same to the backup regulator, then returned everything to the bag.

There was no such thing as a zero signature robbery unless the victim wasn't alive to report the crime. No guarantees when or if it would happen, but a nice touch if the man had booked an afternoon dive.

When Ford was done, he consulted photos of the room to be sure it was exactly as he'd found it, then cracked the door and eyeballed the hallway.

Damn it . . . Lumbering toward him was Jimmy Lutz after only twenty minutes at the tiki bar. Maybe he'd left his wallet, or needed cigars. Ford hurried past the bed, pocketed the valet ticket, then exited onto the balcony, closing the curtains and sliding doors.

"You . . . bastard . . . get your hands off me," a woman said from nearby. British accent. She sounded more startled than mad. A neighboring balcony was empty, but billowing curtains suggested the woman was in the adjoining suite. Ford's attention wavered until a slamming door told him Lutz was in the room. Lights came on within, then heavy feet flip-flopped toward him, as the woman, voice louder, threatened, "I'll call the police, by god, if you don't get out of here right now."

Lutz heard her; curtains parted. Ford hugged the wall while the man peered out, his face inches away through the glass. Satisfied the woman wasn't on his balcony, Lutz engaged the dead bolt and swept the curtains closed.

Ford was trapped. He waited, hearing a mix of sounds from the adjoining suite: a clatter of furniture; the woman gasping, "Damn you . . . that **hurts**," and other indecipherable noises that signaled a struggle. Or was it a kinky two-some enjoying rough love?

Inside Lutz's room, a toilet flushed. A door suctioned curtains, then banged closed.

The porn dealer was gone.

Ford grabbed his tactical bag before testing the sliding doors. Yes, they were locked. He swung a leg over the railing, ignored the dizzying distance to the beach below, and made the long step to the next balcony, which was screened by landscape foliage. A potted plant crashed to the tile when he pushed his bag through, then followed. Beyond billowing curtains, through open doors, the room went silent.

Standing, looking in, he was prepared to apologize to the couple until he accessed the scene. A fit man wearing medical whites and a name badge glared back—a massage therapist whose table had collapsed on the floor during a struggle. Askew on the table, still battling to cover her body with a sheet, was the brunette he'd seen by the pool.

"Didn't know you was there, sir," the man glowered. "She want to call the constables, fine, but what you think they'll say? She's the one requested MY services."

In Nassau, even extortion threats sounded as melodic as a woodwind flute.

"Are you hurt?" Ford asked the woman. He pushed the curtains aside and stepped in.

She was confused, and mad enough to sputter, "I want this bastard fired. If you work for the hotel, I want to file a—"

"That man don't work here," the therapist said. Until then, he'd been backing toward the door. Now, looking from Ford to the broken pottery outside, he figured out the situation. "Yeah, what the police gonna say? This guest hire me, take her clothes off, her own free accord. I already know who they gonna believe."

"You cheeky son of a bitch." The woman tried to scoot away; the sheet fell. She folded her arms to cover herself until Ford yanked the sheet free and tossed it over her. He wore a baggy white guayabera shirt, tails out to cover the waistband of his khaki slacks. Again he asked the woman if she was hurt.

"Who are you?" she demanded. "For Christ's sake, call the manager . . . or do something. This man tried to rape me."

"Naw, come on," the therapist said in a soothing way. "That ain't true. You want to know the real problem? This fella come here to rob you, that's what they'll figure out. Why else he climb over that balcony? You being such a wealthy lady, they'll know a poor boy like me wouldn't do nothing so stupid."

"Bastard," the woman said, while the man grinned.

"Ain't you the spicy one," he countered. "I'm not the type to make trouble, so tell you what. Mister, I'm willing to leave polite-like—but I want compensation for all the fun I missed, plus the coin you lost me. Sound fair?"

"Very fair," Ford said. He reached back as if for a billfold but came up with a 9mm pistol and leveled the sights at the man's nose.

"Where do you want it?" he asked.

The massage therapist, no longer smiling, said, "Shit, man. What the . . . Don't make me take that away from you, 'cause you won't like what happens next."

Staring over the sights, Ford cocked the pistol, and spoke to the woman: "Get some clothes on and call the police, if that's what you want. But not from here. There's a house phone near the elevators."

The therapist turned to her. "See there, Miz Cobourg! He plans to shoot me 'cause he don't want witnesses," while the woman asked Ford, "Is it true? The constables won't believe me?"

"Not a chance," Ford said. "You made the appointment through the concierge?"

"Of course," she said, then understood the implications. "Oh hell. Yes, it was a damn fool thing to do, I suppose." She got to her feet with the sheet around her, no longer afraid, just angry and undecided.

"It happens a lot in places like this. If you're worried about headlines, I'd pack your things now and not look back. Or just forget it."

"Who **are** you?" she asked again.

"In my bag, there's a roll of duct tape," Ford replied. Then, to the therapist, said, "Get on the floor or I'll shoot you in the knee."

The woman, kneeling over the tan tactical bag, said, "I shouldn't have come. I didn't think I'd be recognized here."

He waited for the elevator doors to close before dialing valet parking. "This is Mr. Lutz, room eight-oh-three, would you bring my car around? A lady friend will be there in a minute. Please load her bags."

When Ford stepped out into the salt-dense heat, the brunette, wearing sunglasses and a scarf, was in the left-side passenger seat of a raven blue Range Rover. He folded a twenty-euro note around the valet ticket, and confided to the attendant, "If a man shows up claiming to be me, it's the lady's husband. Understand?"

"A jealous one . . . Yes, sir," the attendant agreed.

Ford added another bill. "Can you blame him? I'll double this if you give us time for a quiet dinner."

The woman didn't speak until they were heading north on East Bay Road. "Did you shoot him?"

Puzzling, the cool way she was handling this, both now and in the room. Instead of hysterics and pointed questions about why he was armed, she remained subdued; no . . . distracted, as if she had more important matters on her mind.

"I taped his mouth, that's all. I can drop you at another hotel, but that might not be smart. Depends on how the police deal with it."

"Then what was that noise as I was walking to the elevator? I heard something, a sharp bang or thud. It came from my room. For god's sake, please tell me you didn't."

Ford pretended to concentrate on the road. "If there's no reason to stay in Nassau, there are daily flights to Cuba. It's a lot more scenic—and safer."

She lowered her window, saying, "Dear Jesus, you did. You shot him."

"You wouldn't have gotten in the car if you believed that." He looked over at her profile, the wind tangling her hair. "Or maybe you would've."

"I was unaware I had a choice. A man with a gun comes over my balcony, I assume you've been paid to shadow me. A security agent of some sort—who else carries a roll of tape and three passports in his bag?"

For a moment, she made eye contact; an up-down sweep, then was done with him. "I'll admit you don't look the part. More like a math prof I fancied at university. The type you surprise in the stacks at a library, who spills soup on his tie." She touched a button and lounged back. Her window slid into place, sealing out the monoxide din of traffic. "Aren't those always the ones who fool you?"

Ford braked left-footed, swung around a pedicab, and turned abruptly onto Baillou Hill Road, before consulting his mirror. It was four miles to the south side of the island. He drove for a while. "Cobourg—I'm not familiar with the name. What should I call you?"

"I'd prefer you didn't."

"For now, at least. He said you're wealthy. Are you an heiress or an actress?"

Cynical laughter was the response. "Come off it, please. You know precisely who I am. Who hired you?"

He'd been wrong. Her aloofness didn't signal distraction, nor was she subdued. It signaled **indifference**. A woman who didn't care what happened. It suggested she was very rich, or had powerful connections . . . or was teetering on an emotional ledge.

Ford's eyes darted from the mirror to his phone. He touched redial and handed it to her. "A friend of mine should answer. When he does, tell him to book two seats for us to Lauderdale and two seats to Havana. The earliest possible flights; doesn't matter which airlines. He's got my name and Amex number. You can text him the rest of your information. He's not the type to carry a notebook."

"Just like that, huh? Four seats, only two people. Are we traveling separately?"

"Stay in Nassau, if you want. Keep in mind police don't report sexual assaults here—not if a tourist is involved. It's bad for the local economy."

Her window scrolled halfway down, then up again. "Filthy little island, isn't it? I was shocked when that clod recognized me. I certainly didn't register under my real name." She paused. "The boy at the valet called you Mr. Lutz. I assume that's not your name. You nicked some poor fool's rental car, didn't you?"

Tomlinson's phone was ringing. Ford heard it while he studied the mirror, where a beat-up white van had joined a black Nissan.

Before putting the phone to her ear, she asked, "Why don't you speak to him? He's your friend."

"I need both hands to drive." He downshifted and accelerated; made a sharp turn onto Cowpen Road, then swung abruptly onto a sand trail that ribboned downward through a landslide of shacks, the Caribbean Sea beyond.

"We're being followed," he said. "Keep your head down while you talk. One of them has a gun."

2

Tomlinson had hoped to get his first look at the lake, Chino Hole, and Tootsie Barlow's cabin by now. Unfortunately, Tomlinson, the Zen master, was lost. Alone, too; east of Naples, off a stretch of lonely asphalt, State Route 29, that fishtailed north through sawgrass to Immokalee, then Labelle sixty miles away.

Break down out here, he thought, **something with scales will eat you.**

After a mile of cabbage palms, the sand road was blocked by a rusty chain. No room to turn around because a canal ran along one side, a deep ditch on the other.

He got out and pissed into the ditch, where

a stack of railroad ties lay among poison ivy. Beyond, through the mossy gloom, several old boxcars had been abandoned. Entangled by vines, the cars resembled huge rock formations.

An old train trestle, he realized. Beyond the chain, the road burrowed arrow-straight, but no wider than a cart path, through the trees.

Except for the chain, the area matched Tootsie's description of the road that led to his cabin. In the 1920s, Barlow's family had settled near a train outpost that had prospered until all the big timber was logged out. Then Prohibition ended. With no whiskey or cypress to haul, the Seaboard Line had gone tits-up. In this part of Florida anyway. Until then, the Barlows had been railroad gypsies. So they'd migrated south to Key Largo, learned fishing as a trade, but still owned sixty swampy acres north of Carnestown and Jerome.

Continue driving or explore on foot? Tomlinson was deciding when "Wild Thing" erupted from his phone. Ford's name flashed on the screen.

"How'd your talk go, Doc? If you **gave** a talk."

To his confusion, a woman with a silky British accent said, "Your friend would like some . . . would like . . . he'd like airline seats booked, if you please. Do you have a pen . . .

a pen and paper . . . handy?" It sounded as if she were on a roller coaster, the way her voice jumped tracks. Lots of bouncy, banging background noise as if a car were careening down a hill.

He sighed. Welcome to Marion Ford's world.

"Sure," Tomlinson said. "Let me speak to Doc."

"Who? Oh." She muffled the phone, then returned. "He's rather busy at the moment—learning to drive, I'm afraid. I'll try to make this as brief as . . . For god's sake, **do** slow down."

"Pardon me?"

"Sorry, sorry. Not you. The roads here are rubbish. Tell me something. Is your friend crooked or is he mad?"

"If you're not sure, trust me, he isn't mad. Usually, he's just . . . well, dull. Why the airline reservations? I'm not his secretary, you know."

"Has he ever killed anyone? Intentionally, I mean. Oh, brilliant . . . this should be interesting. To the left, for god's sake . . . Stay to the left!"

Tomlinson replied, "I like your style. Who are you?"

"Never mind that," she said. "He wants reservations out of Nassau." Then Ford came on the phone, saying, "This is important. She'll text you the rest. We're flying out as soon as possible."

He hung up.

Tomlinson stood there, thinking, **What the hell?**

The woman's voice was something he could fall in love with. Understated irony; an amused calm that hinted of lacy lingerie beneath a starched blouse veneer. He pictured her: black high heels and a glimpse of cleavage served with high tea.

Why the hell was she with Ford? The biologist was no barrel of laughs—well, except for the time he'd accidently eaten magic mushrooms on a piece of baked fish. Psilocybin had unleashed three hours of snappy insights and repartee from a man who'd never limboed in his life. Clearly, the two were in trouble of some type. Nothing new there, which was okay. Trouble was well within Ford's wheelhouse. He was a steady, resourceful man.

The only recourse was to stand by and await the Brit's text.

Five minutes passed, then ten. Soon Tomlinson refocused on the chain that forbade entry to the trail beyond. Keep driving or explore on foot?

He locked his van and walked.

——

After half a mile, the scent of fresh water lured him down a side trail, where a rock wall lay in shambles. The wall suggested the land had once been owned by monied gentry—an old hunting club, perhaps. On a bushy straightaway, the skeleton of a gun stand proved his paranormal powers had synced with the milieu.

Excellent.

Walking meditation is not easily practiced aboard a sailboat. Tomlinson took advantage of the terrain. Measured steps and measured breathing. He also made use of a potent doobie secreted in the pocket of his Hawaiian shirt. Soon, swamp maples; rose-colored leaves caressed the senses. Images of men in antiquated topcoats slipped past his eyes, their shotguns held as casually as umbrellas. A steam whistle howled; beneath his feet, the earth vibrated with the grinding weight of steel on steel. A passing train tugged him out of the past, through a lacy willow curtain, into the present.

And there it was: Chino Hole. The lake was a limestone sinkhole a hundred yards across, the surface glazed by a June blue sky. No remnants of a dock, no structures of any kind, yet a glowering aura clung to the trees. Dragonflies kited; mockingbirds sang. Tomlinson sensed the tranquility was as misleading as the silence that follows a sustained explosion.

Dark events . . . violence. Something wicked had been quieted here by the decades and . . . what else?

Fear. Of course. Fear was always a component. Another more subtle catalyst was also tangible yet difficult to isolate.

Tomlinson allowed his senses to blur. When he ceased seeking the truth, the truth flowed in, then through him.

Shame. That was the other component. Communal shame. Emotion is energy; ions resonated and took shape as a dome that encased the lake like a bubble. Trapped within were too many shadows to contemplate at one sitting.

He returned to the present, re-lit the joint, and let his eyes roam. The lake was a mirror, its radius halved by the reflection of shimmering cypress trees. At the center was a ring of silver-blue sky, despite squall clouds that threatened from the east. Occasionally fish breached the surface; a slow carousel of tail fins that were unmistakable.

Tarpon. Here, in this landlocked lake, thirty-some miles from saltwater, lived a population of saltwater's most coveted sporting fish.

Doc's gonna love this, Tomlinson thought. Then stiffened when, behind him, a branch snapped. Bushes rustled and crunched with momentary panic. He turned, peering through a fabric of willows. Someone . . . or something . . . had been moving quietly toward him but had stumbled.

"Hello?" He held up the joint as if it were a white flag. "Always happy to share with friends."

A rock displaced a gathering of shells. Low branches parted with the passage of someone, or something, making a careful retreat.

"Don't be afraid. Seriously, no one in their right mind's afraid of me."

Low branches paused as if to consider.

Storm clouds rumbled from the distance. Then into Tomlinson's head came a whispered, unspoken reply: **If you run . . . he will catch you.**

The shock this produced was dizzying. "Geezus, dude. That's some nasty shit to say to anybody. Why would I run? I'm just standing here smoking a jay, enjoying the fish." Nervous laughter escaped his lips. "Think those are tarpon?"

No response.

"Hey. Who's gonna catch me? Uh . . . not that I want to meet the guy. It was more of a rhetorical question."

He looked at the lake and gauged the distance in case he had to swim for his life. A windy dust devil flew toward him, crossing the water with the velocity of a wasp. Nearby, low

limbs parted with the crunch of heavy footsteps. Crows spooked into the blue, an array of
raven scars.

"Okay, okay, you win," Tomlinson hollered. "I'll be shoving off now. Sorry if I was
trespassing."

He started up the path, and made it only a
few steps, when a voice, neither male nor female, communicated from inside his skull.

Run . . . He'll make you scream.

"Enough with the bullshit! I'm about to
piss my pants as it is." He spun a slow circle
while edging his way toward the path. "Who
are you?"

Follow me, the voice demanded.

"How? I can't follow what I can't see."

You know. That's why you're here.

"The hell I do. Seriously," he muttered. He'd
been afraid something like this would happen.
On the other hand . . . He looked at the smol-
dering joint in an accusing way. Was it possible
he had imagined the voice? A mirage, perhaps,
caused by high resin content, low blood sugar,
and rumbling thunder?

For sure. There were many times he'd con-
jured a bipolar exchange with the creature
inside his brain—an evil bastard twin who delighted in mayhem.

He tugged at his hair to demand contact.
"Gemini scum. How'd you like another round

of shock therapy? If I go, asshole, **you're** stuck for the duration."

This seemed to work until the voice reached out to him from a stand of cypress:

Come. You understand.

No, Tomlinson didn't, but he followed anyway, pulled along as if on a conveyor. A path through the trees was sodden with moss, edged by roots the size of pterodactyl beaks. Temperature dropped; tendrils of mist twisted in silence. A couple of times, he called out for directions. Pointless. He was traveling parallel to the cart path, which was a comfort of sorts. The road where he'd parked the van couldn't be far.

This was true. He knew it for certain when ahead, among shadows, loomed what appeared to be massive rock formations: the old boxcars he'd seen earlier. Five of the monsters, perhaps more. They lay in a zigzag jumble beneath a cloak of cascading vines. It was if they'd been abandoned after a bad train derailment or jettisoned from the sky.

Chaos, rust, oil, decay. **Scars left from the Industrial Revolution,** Tomlinson thought. **Good riddance.**

As he drew closer, his eyes began to assemble order. Silver light filtered through the cypress dome. Details emerged. The shambles of a rock wall formed a partial circle. What might have been a fire pit appeared, then a communal sitting area. Overhead, horizontal vines turned out to be wires for battery-powered lights. No, not batteries . . . Beneath a collapsed awning were the remains of a generator.

People had lived here, he realized. Families. Railroad laborers, the poorest of the poor, had found shelter and a way to survive. Among the ferns was a rusted tin of baby formula . . . the arm off a wooden doll; a wheel with spokes; many broken bottles.

Tomlinson squatted and held up a shard of embossed glass. The color, purple amethyst, suggested the bottle was very old.

Won Ton Soy Sauce
Havana, Cuba

I'll be damned. Chinese condiments from the days before Castro. Long before. Weird. Or was it?

In the shadows, the nearest boxcar squatted on buried axles. Lettering on the side, a faded yellow, showed itself through the vines:

Sawgrass Clipper

It wasn't a boxcar. A boxcar wouldn't have been named as if it were a sailing yacht—or a double entendre. But a private car might. Yeah . . . ornate brass molding, green with age, confirmed it had been a plush custom coach. Money, big money, had once ruled this area.

He left the bottle as he'd found it and waded

through ferns for a closer look at the area near the coach. Draped above, vestiges of what might have been rags drew his attention. Not rags, really . . . more like pennants strung on wires, but the years had shredded them into streamers. In Tomlinson's mind, silence was displaced by echoes of human activity. It was like stumbling onto the remains of a birthday party decades after the candles had burned out.

Or . . . a religious ceremony. The way the pennants were strung reminded him of Tibetan prayer flags he'd seen while hiking through Nepal.

Prayer flags . . .

This possibility meshed with the soy sauce bottle he'd found. The links were Buddhism and Asia.

He felt an electric chill, and focused on the railroad car. It was the size of a semi-trailer, dwarfing him. He was that close. Nostrils flared, he waited, listened, all senses alert.

A breeze soughed to and fro through ferns and lacy cypress leaves while, overhead, the high tree canopy remained motionless.

There was no wind despite squall thermals inland. So what had caused the ferns to sway with an airless seesaw sound?

Breathing. That's what he heard. Could feel the steady inhale-exhale respirations; a pneumatic rasp amplified by steel walls.

Something was inside the railroad car, hiding. Waiting.

For the first time in many minutes, he attempted communication, backing away as he did. "Hey, man, what . . . who are you?"

A wordless rumble told him, **Open the door. Set us free.**

Tomlinson didn't speak, for there was no need. He only had to imagine his reply, which was, **Never.**

Repeating the word like a mantra, he walked backwards and sidestepped his way to the cart path but kept his eyes on the rock formation of railroad cars.

Not until his van was in sight did he run.

3

Ford told the woman, glancing at her scarf and sunglasses, "If you're going with me, you need different clothes. Shoes for walking on coral, and short pants, and a hat to keep the sun off." A moment later, he added, "Hang on."

The Range Rover was nimble; a small SUV, underpowered, but it had four-wheel drive. They drifted through a gate, downhill through an expanse of litter and weeds, past a goat staked in the shade of a mango tree. A half mile beyond was a road where a lake of slurry green leaked sewage into the Caribbean. To the west, a Delta jet was banking to land at Pindling International. But Ford wasn't headed west.

"Wait a minute. This isn't the way to the airport," the woman said.

"We're not going there. I'm not anyway, but they'll assume that's where we're headed. Yeah—" Ford consulted the mirror. "We lost the van crossing that ditch. Any idea who might want to follow you?"

"Me?" She slung her hair back and ran a finger along her lips. "Damn all . . . think I've chipped a tooth. Before you kill us both, let's get this sorted out. If not the airport, where?"

"There's a place at the bottom of the hill."

"The **ocean**? You're mad."

Ford said, "Those trees below the limestone cliff—mangroves; that swampy area. They used to run whiskey out of there during Prohibition."

"How do you know this?"

"I have friends. They said locals avoid the place because it was a quarantine station for lepers. We can hide the car there. Or you can leave me and take the car. I wouldn't advise it, though. There can't be many blue Range Rovers in the island rental fleet. You really don't know why you're being followed?"

The woman twisted around in her seat. "You're right, they're gone. I have to give you high marks for that, I suppose. Perhaps they wanted to rob us."

Ford said, "I don't think you're safe here." He looked over. "Mind telling me why? Or, at least your name."

They made solid eye contact for the first time. Regal genetics. That came into the biologist's mind while the woman thought: **Intelligent, middle-class . . . not what I expected.**

"Would I be safer with you?" She was looking at him, but a different sort of look. "Your friend called you Doc. Are you really a doctor? No more rubbish about Jimmy Lutz. I'm not a fool."

Ford wondered how she knew so much, but said, "I'm a marine biologist. It's a nickname."

"A biologist. How lovely." She didn't believe him but didn't pursue it. "Well, **Doc**, you do seem competent in a dodgy sort of way. I don't fancy speaking to police. Hmm . . . perhaps you're right."

"About Cuba?"

"Sounds quite nice, actually. Adventurous. That's what this holiday was supposed to be about—to hell with the world. That sort of thing. I didn't want to meet anyone I know. Or who knows of me."

"It'll be smoother once we get on the road," Ford replied. "Text your flight information to my friend. But only if you're not flying out on one of the main carriers."

"Whoa, whoa, whoa! That makes no sense. I thought you said—"

"I'm not taking a commercial flight. You shouldn't, either. Booking seats on two airlines is a way of throwing off the police. Or anyone else who wants to get their hands on you."

"Why do you keep saying that? A man with three passports, a bloody pistol, who's driving a stolen rental to boot. I'm inclined to think they're after you."

He said, "If you're right, we're in more trouble than you realize."

"Come again?"

Ford didn't respond.

"**More t**rouble? What, exactly, is that supposed to mean?" She sat back and reconsidered. "Wait . . . I'd prefer not to know. Send the hounds down a blind trail; clever of you. Very clever, I suppose, booking two airlines. Well, if it's adventure I was after, then, by god—" A rut bounced her head against the roof. "Ouch! **Do** be more careful. These caps cost a small fortune."

The Range Rover negotiated another ditch, then headed west onto a sandy lane, the slurry pond close enough to see terns diving among the ruins of a building that had collapsed into the sea.

"Gillian," she said. "Or Gilly. But not Jill."

It was her attempt at an introduction. Ford

glanced over while she rummaged through her purse. "What're you looking for?"

She took out an oversized phone, lowered her window, and started taking pictures. "For my scrapbook, but don't fret. I'm aware that criminals and security types don't fancy photos."

"Put that away."

"It's scenery I'm after. Not secrets." Rapid-fire, she snapped several shots, some through the windshield: the slurry pond where the collapsed structure might serve as a landmark. Then hunkered in her seat and tapped at the screen.

"You're not emailing those?"

"My mother," she replied. "If I don't post something, the poor dear will worry I've gone off on a toot—or done myself in. A few cheery pix for the mum, don't you know. Greetings from the leper colony. Like that." Her breezy manner hinted at a private darkness.

It was Ford's turn to wonder: **Who are you?**

He left the woman alone and walked to the water. The slurry pond stunk even here on Nassau's ragged windward edge. Above the mangroves, an embankment angled to a ledge where there was a sandy lane. It was a handy spot to tumble trash off trucks. Thirty feet below, a refrigerator rusted in a tide pool that bristled with sea urchins. Slabs of coral, once the walls of a building, lay in the shallows with a vague resemblance to Stonehenge.

The day before, he'd hidden a small Zodiac inflatable in the mangroves, the motor chained to a tree. As he readied the boat, he wondered, **What's taking her so long?**

Sunset was 8:20 p.m. It would be full dark by 9:15. That gave him only a few hours of daylight. Or them, if she didn't change her mind.

She might. It was a very small rubber boat. Or he might. She hadn't staged the massage incident, but the "scenic" photos were troubling.

"Oy! Oh . . . hell." The woman's voice reached him through the bushes. "Doc? Could you have a look at this? Shit . . . do hurry."

Gillian—perhaps her real name—was braced against the car, wrestling with a boot. The other boot, a sock, and a pair of jogging shoes were on the ground nearby. Not that he noticed immediately. She had changed into the red bikini top from earlier; her body lush, right there to see, long legs tan in gray hiking shorts.

"Now what?"

"I don't much care for your tone," she said, grimacing. "I stepped on something and it bloody well hurts. Do you have a first-aid kit?"

"Something went through the sole of your boot?"

"Of course not." She hopped, one-legged, to the hatch of the Range Rover and took a seat. "I was trying to put the damn thing on and lost my balance." She gazed beyond him to the water. "Where's the boat? You said you had a boat waiting."

"That is the boat."

"That's . . . You can't be serious."

"Give me your foot."

She was a woman who enjoyed pedicures. When she leaned down, glossy pink nails were only slightly darker than the cuneiform apex of her breasts. The swimsuit material was flimsy. One rosy half-moon peeked out as she watched him probe with his thumbs. Not intentionally exposing herself—Ford was alert for feigned seduction. She was in pain. No faking that. "Careful," she told him. "Like my foot's on fire."

"Could be a couple of sea urchin spines," he said. "The place is littered with the damn things. Or thorns . . . I don't know, an old stingray spine maybe. But that doesn't explain the burning sensation. At least it's bleeding a little. That's good. How do you feel?"

"Oh, just lovely, thanks." She winced; pushed her suitcase aside to make more room. "They're deadly poisonous, I suppose. A perfect fit with my trip so far."

Ford's fingers moved to her ankle. No

swelling, but her skin was warm to the touch. A varicose welt appeared to be spreading toward the calf. That didn't make sense, either. "Don't put any weight on it. I'll be right back."

"Is that bad? Hey—where are you going?"

Her phone was on the passenger seat. He swiped it open while pretending to go through his bag. The screen lock had yet to engage. This was unexpected luck, or so he believed until he tried to open recent messages, then recent calls.

Both were password-protected.

A GPS app, however, still beamed out their location. He was scanning recent address searches when he heard, "My foot's on fire, for god's sake. What are you doing?"

Ford replied, "Found it," and returned with a Gerber multi-tool he always carried and a tiny first-aid satchel from his bag.

"I'll clean it, and use some numbing spray. That'll have to do for now. We need to get moving. Or take the car. That's up to you."

"A regular Boy Scout, you are. Are they poisonous, sea urchins?"

"Hold still."

"I am. Why can't you answer the simplest of questions?"

"Ask an articulate question, I might," he said. "You mean **venomous**, not **poisonous**. Look around. In a sewage dump, everything is poisonous if you've got an open wound."

"Brilliant. A grammar lecture." She gritted her teeth, sweat beading, and leaned back with her eyes closed. "Get on with it, then, professor."

He moved to get a better angle and, for the first time, noticed dead fish littering the sand near the car. Wild cactus-like fins; their multi-colored scales faded to leather by the sun. Most had died in full defensive display, spines erect.

"Oh shit," he murmured.

"Sorry? If you've lost your nerve, throw a patch on it. I might be able to walk if you—" The woman sat up, saw Ford's expression. "Oh dear. It **is** serious."

"Lionfish," he said, motioning to the ground. "A burning sensation, I should have known. But don't panic, you'll be fine. We have to—"

"Do I look panicked?" she interrupted, calmer than she'd been moments earlier. Stared at the leathery fish a moment with bitter, bemused irony. "Ugly little brutes—and I'd been worried about sharks. Is there a chance I'll die?"

Ford, studying her, thought, **She's running from something.** But said, "No, you'd be unconscious by now. Anaphylactic shock. Those spines need to come out, though, then soak your foot in the hottest water you can stand. We have to get you to a doctor. Maybe the E.R."

"We?"

He cupped her foot in his hands; lifted the leg. "Can you move your toes?"

She did. "Isn't this where you go off and leave the troublesome toff who's slowing you down?"

"Troublesome what?"

Her eyes drifted to the ledge above the mangroves; a veiled glance as if expecting a visitor. "Go off and leave **me**. I have the car, my phone, and money—well, the last time I checked. I wouldn't blame you if— Ouch! Not so damn hard."

"Is the pain moving up your leg? Bend your knee and see how it feels."

"It bloody well hurts, I already told you."

He stepped back, hands on his hips. "Come on, I'll help you into the car. On the way, you can look up the nearest hospital. Or clinic— that would be better. Fewer people, and less chance of you being recognized." He went to open the passenger-side door.

"You're actually taking me to get help?"

"The pain'll get worse. I can't leave you like this. Some people pass out from lionfish stings. I'm not saying you will, but if you don't, you might want to. It can get that bad."

After another glance at the ledge above, she pivoted toward him. "My god . . . You were telling the truth about the massage perv, then. You didn't kill the bastard."

"I said I didn't shoot him. He's probably okay by now, but—" He shrugged, and got an arm around her waist. "Keep your foot off the ground. I'd have to clean it again, and that would—"

"Wait." She pulled away, suddenly anxious. A total change of demeanor as she faced him. "You're offering to drive me? After what you've . . . Then we were followed, for god's sake."

"I'm wide open if you've got a better idea."

"Put yourself at risk to—**why**? I wouldn't do it for you. If you expect to lure me into bed, or some sort of financial deal—" Her face contorted. "Oh hell. How much worse, the pain?"

"It varies. From mild to memorable. The sooner those spines are out—" Ford watched her eyes drift upward for a third time. Finally, he said, "Okay, out with it. Who're you working for?"

"What?"

"Drop the act. Where'd you send those photos? It wasn't to your mother."

Gillian—the name suddenly seemed to fit—started to deny what she'd done, then gave up, exasperated. "Does it really matter? Just go. Now. Oh . . . damn." She rocked back in pain. "Don't be a fool! I can bloody well manage without you mucking up my life more than it already is."

"A motorcycle," he said; paused to confirm what he was hearing. "Who's coming?"

"I don't know!"

"If they kill me, they won't leave a witness. Even if they try and miss. Understand what I'm saying? I don't care how wealthy you are."

"Bugger off," she groaned, then buckled over. "Oh god . . . I think I'm going to be sick."

Only two options, one of them too cold-blooded—she'd at least tried to warn him. He wiped down the car a final time, pocketed her phone, and loaded their bags into the Zodiac.

"We're not riding in that," she said. "It's a toy, not a boat."

Ford was carrying her; a warm, obstinate weight in his arms. "Trust me, it'll seem a hell of a lot smaller when we're twenty miles offshore. I don't suppose it's too late to call off your friends?"

Her head pivoted toward the high tree line; her body stiffened. "Hurry," she said.

Above the ruins of the leper station, a man with a rifle had appeared. He braced himself against a ledge and opened fire.

4

Tomlinson was still rattled by the voices he'd heard, the deathless breathing from inside the old railcar, when his phone bonged with a text from Marion Ford.

"I wouldn't own one of those damn things," Tootsie Barlow said from his recliner. "Don't need the clutter—not since I gave my life to the Lord." Within easy reach was his cane, a long-barreled pistol, and a fly-tying vise in a room that smelled of pine pitch and coffee. They'd been drinking beer, talking, for an hour while he tied bonefish flies for a shop on Tavernier Key.

"You don't own the poisonous bastards, they own us," Tomlinson said, and opened his phone expecting flight info. Instead, he read,

Need bio, photo of Gillian Cobourg from the UK. Unsure of E-D-A. Don't ask.

"It's from Doc—a confusing garble of bad kimchi. No telling where this madness will lead now. A woman is involved."

"Always is," the fishing guide said. Then asked, "Who you talking about?"

"Doc. Seems he's been delayed, but I can't tell if he'll be back by Monday, or next month— Hold on. What does E-D-A stand for?"

"Marion, you mean? Didn't meet him but that once, but I liked the man. He's the sort I need to convince the cops I'm not crazy. Real solid, and he knows his fish. You mentioned a woman?"

Tomlinson said, "Hope it's not the Gillian I've read about, but, god, she's got a sexy voice." A moment later, re-reading the text, he said, "Estimated **day** of arrival. Yeah, probably the woman who's been in the papers. Geezus-frogs, no telling how Doc snared a British Royal without a microscope to break the ice."

"Royal? Like she's a princess or something?"

"Could be. They tend to vacation in the Colonies. He's in Nassau. Or was—or he's in Timbuktu, for all I know," Tomlinson replied. "This morning, he pretended he was in Lauderdale."

Tootsie remarked that the best route— maybe not the fastest—from Lauderdale was inland to State Route 27, I-95 being such a nightmare, then said, "Nassau, during Prohibition, Albert—that was my daddy—he ran whiskey outta there to Palm Beach for the . . . well, let's just say, his clients. Andros was big, too, but back to what we were discussing—"

"Which ones? The Kennedys or Al Capone?" Tomlinson asked, thinking of a different sort of royalty. "The guy who built the railroad was a player, too, I've read. That's something I wanted to ask about."

"Where they loaded whiskey was near North Bight," Tootsie said, "on Nassau's windward side. There's an old leper station that kept the locals away. Spooks and dead spirits; they're scared shitless of that stuff. Many'a Chinaman was smuggled outta there, too, but they was usually dropped off around Marco—Naples had a sheriff by then. Same time period, as you say. This was after they banned slavery in Cuba."

Tomlinson was getting into the subject. "Exactly. I bet the cops did some head cracking. The first time we talked, you mentioned a deputy, a guy named Cox—J. H. Cox. Was he the same man who murdered a woman named Hannah Smith?"

"Which one?"

"The deputy who disappeared with his wife and kids. You don't remember telling me?

Supposedly, the killer was Leslie Cox, but the old records aren't worth a—"

"No, which Hannah Smith? There've been several in these parts."

"The first one, I guess, from the early 1900s. I've been researching the old newspaper files but didn't find much. She was murdered near here, and that's about it."

"Oh, that one," the old man said. "Yeah, heard about her."

Tomlinson waited, thinking there'd be more but there wasn't. "The reason I ask is, I know her great-grandniece. She's guiding now. Mostly out of Captiva, but she gets down to the Glades sometimes, too. In fact, Doc dated her for quite a spell, but I wouldn't mention that when he shows up."

"A fishing guide, you say? Seems I read something about a woman guide." Tootsie spun the fly vise, thinking back. "Yeah . . . Captain Hannah Smith. Same name as the girl what was murdered. Her grandniece, you say?"

"Four generations; they keep passing the name down. Sort of a family tradition. The fishing guide, she's Hannah number four."

Tootsie liked that. "Didn't know they was related, but I'm not surprised. The one you're talking about, this new young Hannah, she takes a nice picture. I read about her in **Florida Sportsman** and some other magazines. Mercy me, those long legs and black hair, I wished she was guiding back during my time. Want another beer?"

"Don't suppose you have a Red Stripe hidden away?"

Tootsie, using a cane to stand, said, "If money and beer grew on trees, I'd be pissing in a sink and drinking Presidente from the Dominican Republic. Now, there's a beer."

He returned with two cans of Old Milwaukee. "I've told many'a client that women come more natural to fly casting than men. It's 'cause they take advice, and don't overpower the rod."

He glanced around the room, its walls papered with photos and magazine articles from the past, most of them about him, or a famous client. "Wish I'd saved young Hannah's picture. Surprised I didn't. A woman like that, she don't need to wear a bikini to show she's something special. Marion was a fool to let her get away."

"It's not like he had a choice," Tomlinson replied, but Tootsie had already moved on, saying, "That's the problem with fishing magazines these days . . ."

He sat patiently; drank his beer, and listened. The old guide was a talker, with a high, cackling laugh. He'd spent fifty years entertaining clients during lulls fishing, and his storytelling skills were honed to rhythmical precision;

music that flowed as effortlessly as a Bach fugue.

And no less complex, Tomlinson was beginning to believe, until the topic swung back to Hannah Smith.

"The Smith family and my people, they was shipping mullet and cattle to Cuba before Miami got its first paved road. Smuggling rum and making whiskey, too. That's why I know what happened to the **first** Hannah way, way back. It worries you for some reason. Why?"

Tomlinson nodded. "You've got good instincts." It was simpler than explaining a theory he'd formulated after hearing those weird voices. It had to do with parallel universes; the repetition of concurrent lives that might unfold differently. And end differently.

"It's because I've turned my life over to the Lord," Tootsie said, "and let Him do the thinking. Big Six, is what they called her—all them Smith women were tall and rawboned. That Hannah was killed before the Hurricane of '26. Weren't but thirty years old. A man cut her throat, supposedly 'cause she was pregnant with his bastard child. Some say it was Leslie Cox. I've got my own ideas about that."

The word **pregnant** caused Tomlinson to wince. "What kind of lowlife asshole would— I can't speak for God, but a Barlow didn't murder a pregnant woman."

He was referring to the man's fear that God was punishing the Barlow family for something a relative had done years ago.

"That much is true, at least," Tootsie said.

"Spiritually speaking, that sort of shit's a deal breaker. The killer's family, on the other hand, should be dodging lightning bolts, not yours." After a thoughtful moment, he added, "The Hannah I know is pregnant, too."

"So that's what worries you."

"Don't mention it to Doc. No one's supposed to know."

"That she's pregnant? Why, because he's not the father? Or because he is?"

"I seriously doubt it, but she won't say."

The fishing guide cackled. "Just like them Smith women." His smile faded. "It weren't the deputy who kilt her. J. H. Cox come down to the islands from Tampa. John Henry, I believe his name was. A good family man. He had a young wife, a daughter, and a son just born. The Lord would want us to help them find peace."

"How?"

"Find their bodies, I guess. Do a church service, I don't know. Hell, you're the preacher, you tell me."

"If the deputy didn't kill her, who did?"

"Some say Leslie Cox. He was a drunken skunk from Georgia, but I think it was another skunk who cut her throat. Smuggling rum and making whiskey, even pot hauling, they're not so bad compared to what some men in these parts did." Tootsie Barlow, with his sun-scarred face, glanced over, a searching look. "Do you believe in Evil?"

By the way it was said, the word was capitalized.

"Does the pope wear a hat? Hell yes, and only a fool or a scientist would think otherwise."

"That's who killed her, an evil man. After cutting her throat, he cut that girl's belly open so she wouldn't float. Had a **baby** inside her, but he did it anyway, then dumped them both in the water not far from here. That was his mistake. No one should'a found the body, but they did. Them Smith girls, they was stubborn. Hannah wouldn't sink."

"Dear Jesus."

"Cruel times in a hard land. Probably best I don't say more. Not for now. Besides"—the old man reached for his cane—"I've gotta pee."

Tomlinson made a mental note: **Never mention this to Hannah.** Then wandered outside to find a shady spot of his own to piss and light another joint. He unzipped, sighed, and looked back to synchronize the landscape with what he'd learned that afternoon.

The Barlow place was a shotgun shack the
family had built after filing homesteader papers
at the county seat. It was Fort Myers in those
days, not Naples. Over the decades, the cabin
windows had anchored themselves to the view
beyond the porch: an oak hammock; domes of
cypress that mushroomed up from a sawgrass
horizon.

The big timber was gone, of course. Same
with the few houses that had sprouted around
this railroad watering stop. It was a village that
no longer appeared on modern maps as Palmetto
Station. Fifteen miles south was a Quik Stop
at Carnestown, but the nearest shopping center
was Marco Island, forty minutes away in a decent car.

Palmetto Station had become a ghost town
in the Everglades. There were a few others along
the Trail—Ochopee, Jerome, Pinecrest—where
wailing steam engines had plucked the wooded
flesh clean, then abandoned the scars to silence.

Dense, the air here. Squall clouds corralled
the heat, focusing it downward into the still-
ness of moss and mosquitoes. A sense of dread
flourished in such places.

No wonder he'd so badly misjudged Tootsie's
reasons for leaving the Keys. The old man
hated being landlocked here. Who wouldn't?
But a legal issue had forced his hand.

The family's cabin and sixty acres lay

squeezed between federally owned land. Big Cypress was to the west, Fakahatchee Preserve to the east. The feds wanted the property. Because it had been homesteaded, they had a legal right to take possession if a family member didn't maintain a "permanent residence," meaning live there nine months of the year.

Most landowners were long gone, but a few remained. They, too, were being pressured. The old man had yet to go into detail about that.

"I miss the smell of saltwater," he'd said, "but I've got no choice. Not until I find a relative crazy enough to want to live here for free. Of course, it's got to be a Barlow of legal age, who's not going to use the place to brew drugs and nonsense. That don't leave but a couple of candidates."

In January, when the feds served notice, it hadn't seemed to be a problem. Now it was. In a few short months, two of Tootsie's family members had died in freak, unrelated accidents—one struck by lightning, and, soon afterward, his grandson's wife had died when their RV caught fire. The most recent near miss was in May. A nephew, on his way to Lakeland, had been seriously injured when his truck blew a tire, or had been forced off the road.

Tootsie was unsure about that.

"We're running out of Barlows," he'd said on the phone the day after it happened. "Either

God or the Devil is behind this—maybe because of something my daddy did before I was born."

They hadn't gotten around to that, either, but had come close a few minutes earlier when Tomlinson tested the limits of weirdness by mentioning the voices he'd heard.

The old fishing guide had replied, "You heard them, too?"

"I'm not the only one?"

"Oh yeah. My grandniece, Gracie, said the same; got real excited. She's one of those kids dresses like a vampire and has tattoos. Her and her boyfriend stopped here about ten days ago, on their way north. Some boyfriend—a big fella old enough to be her daddy, or near about. I'm worried about that girl."

It was because no family member had seen or heard from Gracie since.

In the cabin, a Florida road map with markings lay on the table. "Three accidents, supposedly unrelated. I made little red stars where they happened. What do you think?" Tootsie stepped back to make room.

"Did anyone report Gracie missing?"

"Her mama, a second cousin of mine, says that's just her way—go off for weeks at a time without calling. I tried telling the cops myself, but they don't listen. Know what's strange?"

"The accidents all happened in central Florida," Tomlinson said, "but these two"—he touched the map—"are a couple hundred miles apart. No . . . it's three hundred miles to Gainesville. The voices Gracie heard, what did they say?"

"I was talking about cops. A body gets a certain age, you turn invisible. Don't matter how famous a guide I was. Used to be, a cop stopped me, he'd talk my ear off about fishing before saying, 'Have a nice day, Cappy.' Not even a warning 'cause of who I am. Or was. Oh, you'll find out. Might as well be a ghost. They stare right through you, the young ones, and don't return calls."

"Storm troopers," Tomlinson said. "I'd love to be invisible when it comes to them. Mind if I make notes while we go over this? 'Freak accidents'—tell me about those."

When they were done, and the map was folded and put away, they took another break.

Tootsie returned with a leather-bound Bible; gilded edges, very old. "No one knows what I'm about to show you." Solemn, the way he said it. Like a warning.

"I'll swear an oath, if you want."

That wasn't it. Tootsie's father, on his death-bed, had written a confession in the back of the Bible; several pages of neat block printing on lines provided for notes, or branches of the family tree.

"Do you remember when Albert died?"

"Your dad? Five years ago," Tomlinson said. "That's how we met. Well, one of the reasons."

"You wouldn't be here if I didn't trust you. It don't seem so long ago, but"—he tilted the Bible open—"read the first page of what Albert wrote. Don't skip ahead, just the first page. When the Lord tells me it's okay, you can read the rest. I got your word on that?"

"Cross my heart."

"Your heart, huh? Guess that'll have to do. I'll wait on the porch, then I 'spect you'll have to leave for home. It's almost sunset, and we'll have time tomorrow."

Tomlinson carried the Bible to a desk where light filtered in. The first page of Albert Barlow's confession was sufficient to pique his interest—an ugly, murderous admission that promised darker revelations to come.

He closed the book, thinking, **May God have mercy on their souls . . .**

5

At sunset, Ford raised Andros Island, west of Nassau, twenty miles of green water astern. By dark, he was beached in Stafford's Creek and talking to the local who'd rented him the Zodiac.

"Man! What the hell happen, she's damaged so bad?" Donell—that was the local's name—circled the boat as warily as if it were a snake. "You make the crossing from the north side, all the way, like this?"

"From the south side of Nassau," Ford said.

Donell knew he was lying. From the rocks at Small Hope Bay, he'd seen the boat surfing downwind, as boats often did after crossing from the Atlantis Hotel or possibly Chub Cay.

He let it go. "Lucky you made it, no matter

which direction. One tube, it got no air. This here other tube, she's leaking bad. What you hit?"

Ford said, "Hold the flashlight." The moon was down; coconut palms shadowed the stars. He took a seat and counted out ten stacks of hundred-dollar bills. "Will that cover the damage?"

Donell gave some thought to demanding more, but decided, **Not here. Not with him.**

He reached for the money.

Ford covered it with his hand. "When I'm sure my plane's okay, that was our deal. There are a couple of other things I want you to do."

They hiked inland. Stafford's Creek broadened, then bowed. A small seaplane floated in darkness on buoyant tethers. It was a Maule amphib with a four-cylinder turbo. The fuselage was blue on white, with leather seats inside and Plexiglas doors, but it looked silver on this tropical night with stars. The craft was designed to land damn near anywhere and equipped to make long hauls. Fully fueled, she could cruise at 160 knots for more than six hundred nautical miles.

"You leavin' tonight, sir?"

"I want to clear customs before the shift change."

"Owens Town?"

"West Palm. You told me it was all taken care of in Owens Town."

"It is, sir, I assure you of that. But why not stay? The missus, she make you a nice breakfast. Fresh kingfish and bammy bread. Or"—a smile came into his voice—"could be green turtle meat somehow got in my icebox. Believe you mentioned a fondness for that."

"Poaching turtles, Donell? I must've heard wrong. A sergeant in the Royal Police Force could lose his stripes for that."

Donell was head constable in these parts.

"Lose your stripes for all sorts of things," he countered. "Not worth it unless the pay's right. What's them other things you want me to do?"

Ford went over it, before saying, "When I'm home safe, you can stop worrying about those extradition papers. I'd hate to think of you back in Miami-Dade Correctional." He took off his shoes, ready to wade to the plane. "Get rid of the Zodiac while I make sure I've still got fuel . . . and the battery's not missing."

"Man, who you think you're dealing with?"

"Let's call it the No Gambling in Casablanca syndrome. A safety precaution, that's all."

Donell grumbled until he was out of sight and chortled on his way to the beach. Then sobered when he panned the light over the inflatable boat and, for the first time, took a close look.

Oh hell . . . What had he gotten himself into?

A deflated tube was pocked with what appeared to be bullet holes. Awash on the deck was the clotted residue of what might be blood. He knelt, tested the viscosity with his fingers, then sniffed.

Metallic, the smell. Something else: a bloody swatch of medical gauze was trapped in a scupper. When he reached for it, his eyes noticed the glitter of gold. **A bullet casing,** he thought.

No . . . When he held it to the light, it was a woman's earring.

Beautiful. The earring looked expensive, one bonny white pearl attached. He searched on hands and knees but found no mate.

What to do? If he gave it to the wife, she'd wonder why there was only one. Sell it, he might be linked to something bad; maybe even a murder charge.

It was smarter, Donell decided, to use it as proof of his integrity—and also to remind the American that blackmail could work both ways.

He hustled back to the plane, shined the light around. No sign of the man until, from somewhere nearby, Ford's voice said, "That was fast. Why don't I smell rubber burning?"

"Man, best if you take off first. A fire might draw attention. But don't you worry—"

Ford stepped clear of the shadows. "Until you get rid of that Zodiac, your money stays on the plane with me. Oh, another thing. Careful when you wade out, there're lionfish all over the place. I've never seen so many. How long have they been a problem?"

Donell turned slowly, expecting to see a gun, but, no, just the man standing there, serious about what he'd just asked.

"You worried about fish? **Now?**"

"I'm interested."

"I don't know, fifteen years maybe. They good to eat, but them fins, you're right, they kill a man. I heard tourists brought the damn things from somewhere. Or they come in through the blue holes; them holes deep. Some say they go all the way to China. You believe that?"

Ford said, "Would anyone?"

"Some do. The old folk, they say monsters live down there, come and go as they please. Lusca is one, a giant octopus or dragon. Chinums is another."

Ford, talking more to himself than Donell, said, "Fifteen years ago—that's when the Atlantis Hotel finished its sea aquarium. The timing's about right."

"For dragons?"

"Lionfish. They don't belong in this hemisphere. What I mean is, they started showing up in the Keys about five years after that aquarium opened, probably earlier here. I bet it's not a coincidence. Yesterday, I paid a guy to let me walk around the aquarium plant. They pump in eight million gallons of seawater a day; an open, raw water system. There's nothing to prevent fertilized eggs, even immature fry, from being vented back out to sea."

"Fry?"

"Baby fish. I'm surprised no one's made the connection before."

"Oh . . . yes, they got thousands of them at the Atlantis. Rare fish of all types. The missus and me, we go there and gamble sometimes. But, sir, the reason I come back was—" Donell extended his hand and used the flashlight to show the earring.

"Thanks," Ford said, taking it. Didn't say another word until he was in the plane and had handed over the cash. "Do a good job, maybe we'll work again sometime."

"Landing in West Palm, sir?"

The biologist nodded, and flew away; no lights—just charcoal wings visible when the plane banked.

———

Amile out, he switched on running lights and turned not west toward Florida but east toward a nearby fishing camp. According to the APIS flight plan he'd filed, he was scheduled to clear customs in West Palm tomorrow. There were ways to sneak in under Fat Boy, the down-looking radar at Cudjoe Key, but he'd already taken too many risks for one day.

Andros was a hundred miles long, bigger than all of the Bahamas islands combined yet among the least populated. Fresh water was hard to come by on the vast mangrove flats and salt pans. The land was a limestone sieve. There were hundreds of underwater caves and linking tunnels, more than anyplace its size in the world.

Chino Hole came to mind.

Ford leveled off and followed a glowing chart plotter through darkness to a sprinkling of lights in the distance: Flamingo Cay. It was a private and very expensive bonefish camp owned by a friend, Charles Beckett. The place didn't advertise, and only opened when Charles was in the mood. No need to lure clients. The Beckett family had remained loyal to the British Crown during the American Revolution, so the Windsor family had rewarded them with a massive land grant—much of Andros, and some surrounding islands. Their wealth had quadrupled during Prohibition. They still owned prime waterfront and dockage in Nassau where liquor had been stored and shipped.

Beckett's roots ran deep in the Bahamas. They intertwined with wealth on both sides of the Atlantic.

After he signaled the camp with a flyover, landing strip lights blossomed in an orderly line.

On the ground, he checked his phone and found he'd passed close enough to a tower to receive a text from Tomlinson. Nothing about Gillian Cobourg, but his pal had seen tarpon at Chino Hole. He and the famous fishing guide would continue to explore the area tomorrow.

This was good news.

Ford was in a guest cottage: screened windows, ceiling fans, and a porch built over the water. At midnight, the generator went off. He lit an oil lamp and sat with a book, reading.

What Donell had said about holes reaching through the Earth to China was nonsense, of course. But there was a possibility that karst formations below the Gulf Stream did form a complex conduit, linking Florida with the Bahamas.

Lionfish were on his mind. It had as much to do with Florida as what he'd experienced in Nassau.

Lionfish, with their venomous manes, were natives of the South Pacific and Indian Ocean. In the 1980s, a few Florida sightings had been reported, always attributed to sloppy hobbyists. They weren't a serious problem until the mid-2000s, when they began to show up en masse in the Keys. Now the dangerous exotics had made their way north to the Panhandle and the coast of Alabama.

The Atlantis Hotel had opened its "Mayan Temple and Aquaventure" between 1998 and 2002. There were fourteen "lagoons"; more than fifty thousand aquatic animals and two hundred and fifty species. Most commercial aquariums manufactured their own seawater. Not the Atlantis. They piped it in from the Tongue of the Ocean, six thousand feet deep; a free-flowing exchange between the casino's freakish aquarium show and the sea.

On the table was a chart of Florida and the Bahamas. The timing was right; the complex swirl of ocean currents meshed. Even if there was no underground linkage, fertile spawn and fry spewed by the hotel's unfiltered vents **might** account for what could be a disaster.

Again, he wondered, **Why didn't someone make the connection years ago?**

Maybe they had, and he'd missed it. Ford was pragmatic enough to admit he sometimes deluded himself to bolster his own pet theories. In this case, the pet theory suggested he might find lionfish in a "bottomless" lake in the Everglades.

It was possible. Tarpon, another saltwater fish, had been documented in Chino Hole. Ford could think of no more reliable source than Captain Tootsie Barlow, who'd confirmed what Tomlinson had seen.

He carried the lamp inside. Mosquito netting draped over the bed added a safari touch. Naked, he turned the light low and was getting settled when the creaking screen door put him on alert. The pistol was on the nightstand. But where the hell had he put his shorts?

A towel would have to do.

Towel in hand, he was exiting the bathroom when a woman's voice said, "Don't bother. I've come to thank you properly."

Gillian Cobourg, in a silken robe, stood in the doorway. "I heard you land. You could have at least come and said hello to your patient."

"How's your foot?"

She extended her leg, toes visible through a gauze wrapping. "Almost no pain. A bloody miracle worker, you are. I've been soaking it in hot water like you told me."

Ford said, "Let me get some clothes on and I'll walk you back. We can't be seen together."

"That's what you're worried about? Simple. I'll lock the door." She did; limped inside and placed her flashlight on the table while he finished knotting the towel. "Your friend Charles and his wife are delightful, but they play their cards close to the vest. They said it wasn't your plane, but I knew better. Did you tell them why I'm—"

"No, nothing about you being blackmailed," Ford said. "I'm not sure they would've believed me anyway. There aren't many sisters who would do what you've done to protect a—"

"He's more than just my brother. Billy is a Member of Parliament. You really didn't know?"

"Or care. I'm paid to do what I do."

"Of course, a cold bastard. You try so hard to convince people. I wasn't being noble, if that's why you doubt my story. Some of the things they made me do I **enjoyed**. Self-destruction, the ultimate taboo. A tart's fantasy. Does that shock you?" Staring up at him, she allowed the silken robe to blouse open as if unaware.

He was tempted to ask about Jimmy Lutz. It was no coincidence she'd had a neighboring suite at the hotel, but now was not the time.

"I've done worse things for worse reasons, I suppose."

"Oh for god's sake, please drop the shield. It would break our father's heart if he—"

"Found out his son's a pedophile?" Ford interrupted. "You're right. There's nothing noble about that. Or setting me up to be killed." For a moment, he expected the woman to slap him. "Sorry. It doesn't matter now. You switched teams."

"That's something else I should thank you for. The opportunity. Marion?" She had never used his first name before. "You're wrong about Billy."

It was possible. Hopefully, the truth would be on the thumb drives he had stolen. "The people I work for will be in touch, Gillian. You need to leave."

She stepped closer, face tilted. "Not like this. Please. I wanted to see you again. To . . . make amends. I feel so damn fidgety because of what happened back there. I've never been shot at before."

He back-stepped, hands out to stop her, but let her come into his arms anyway. "Have you been drinking?"

"You tell me," she said, and kissed him. Then again, deeper. "Taste alcohol? That's another reason I can't sleep. This is the first night in months I've gone to bed sober."

"You'll get through it," Ford said. "And, if you don't, think about the consequences. Now, back to your room."

"You don't mean that."

"I do," he said, yet allowed his hands to slide up the woman's ribs to the undersides of her breasts, their softness a warm, expanding weight.

Her breathing slowed, then spasmed. "I like that," she said. Then, her body tight against his, whispered, "It was so unreal when that man started shooting. In a way, my life's such a damn, awful mess, I felt so, I don't know . . ."

"Scared. You're not the only one." Ford, aware that his own breathing had changed, attempted objectivity.

"Please don't mistake me for a well-adjusted woman. What I felt was . . . alive—really alive, and glad to be alive, for the first time in . . ." Her fingers unknotted the towel and cupped him, exploring as if she were blindfolded, while he stood and let it happen.

"My favorite line from **Lady Chatterley**," she said. "Use me."

"What?"

"In the book. That's the line, what she told John Thomas. 'Use me.'"

She leaned to his ear and whispered, "You know damn well I'm using you."

6

The next afternoon, Tomlinson heard his phone ping, and told Tootsie, "It's from Doc. He just landed in West Palm . . . Well, that's what he claims. I'm supposed to meet him on Sanibel tonight."

They were in an old Ford F-150 with rod racks and a **Monroe County Guides Association** sticker on the window. So far, that's all the old man wanted to talk about, fishing on the Keys in the early years. Jimmie Albright, Jack Brothers, Chico Fernandez—all contemporaries. But not a mention of yesterday, or of what Tootsie's father had confessed to in a Bible that had to weigh ten pounds.

Or of Gracie, the missing teenage niece.

Although taking a laid-back approach,

Tomlinson finally had to ask, "Where we headed?" They were on the Tamami Trail driving west, sawgrass all around but strip malls beginning to show. This meant Everglades National Park was behind them.

"Marco Island, so you can picture it," Tootsie said. "Where Deputy Cox and his family caught the ferry that night. I'm not exactly sure where they died, but I've got a pretty good idea. Then I'll show you **who** killed them. Maybe killed Hannah Smith, too—and the name of **that** man weren't Cox," he said as if dangling bait.

Tomlinson didn't expect that but listened while the man continued, "God brings people into our lives for a reason. Ain't nobody else I've shared this with, and I trust in the Lord that's why you're here."

Maybe so. It was strange, the connection they had. This was the first time they'd been in a truck together since five years ago, Key Largo, at the Mandalay Bar, where the First Call Church held Sunday services and sold beer from a cooler. Tootsie had been going through a rough patch. In the space of a year, his father had died, his wife died after a stroke, and squamous cell skin cancer had forced the famous captain into retirement.

That was the hardest blow of all. Jim Beam and depression might have finished the job, but a mutual friend had asked Tomlinson to intervene.

The two were an unlikely pair, a legendary flats guide and a boat bum Buddhist, yet they'd hit it off. Establishing a rock-solid anchor is the first step to surviving emotional chaos. The right anchorage varies from person to person. With Tootsie, it was religion. Two days a week for almost a month, they'd attended services of some type. Tomlinson was a poor role model when it came to alcohol, yet he'd cut back on that, too, until, thank god, a local preacher had befriended the old man.

With his hand out the window, feeling the air, Tomlinson inquired, "By the way, how's ol' Reverend Scott doing?"

"Wouldn't know. He didn't like it when I started drinking again. Liked it even less when I told him maybe God had a hand in what's happening—like I was blaming the Lord. Truth is, I think the preacher's scared."

"Of what?"

"After you finish Albert's confession, maybe you can help me figure it out."

There was nothing to do but sit back and let the story unfold. They stopped near the bridge into Marco, with its view of the island's northern point. On that August night long ago, J. H. Cox, his wife, and two children had been lured onto the ferry that crossed to the Isle of Capri.

It was mostly swamp in those years but was now wall-to-wall homes.

No one would ever see the Cox family again.

Next stop, a mile north, on Collier Boulevard, where mangroves framed both sides of the road. A few days after the deputy disappeared, locals had reported a terrible odor coming from a pond to the west.

The pond was dragged; nothing found.

The first page of Albert Barlow's confession had included some of these details, but what came next was new info. They backtracked to within a mile of the Barlow cabin and turned onto a dirt road.

Tomlinson recognized the area. "This is where I hiked to the lake—that path that's chained off. There's a bunch of old train cars in there. People lived in them, I think, but I couldn't figure out who would—"

"Chinamen," Tootsie said softly. "Just men at first, then whole families." His demeanor had changed with the terrain. He'd become aggressive with a quiet edge, like the hunter he'd been all his life. "This is where the man brought them—some anyway—the ones he didn't kill after taking their money and dumping their bodies at sea. The rest, he rented out as slaves."

"Chinese immigrants? What a heartless son-uva . . . But it wasn't your—"

"No, t'weren't Albert. There's a lot he told me before he died; things he should have confessed to God—terrible things. But that's not who I'm talking about." He reached down, and the long-barreled revolver was suddenly on the seat between them.

"God A'mighty, what's that for?"

"Watch your language," Tootsie said. "This here's a Colt Peacemaker that Albert owned. I don't travel this area without a gun. He lived back in here a ways—not Albert, the man who did all that killing. His name was Walter Lambeth. You ever hear it? The Chinese called him something else. The Bird Man."

"The what?"

"That's what they called him, and the name stuck. Doesn't make much sense, I know. There was nothing birdy about Walter Lambeth. You ever seen old movies of Babe Ruth? He had the same build; same giant head, a nose half as wide as his face. I'll show you a picture when we get back. A few Chinese still lived in those boxcars when I was a kid. They'd burn incense and ring bells . . . wooden bells. I can still hear them. We'd come back sometimes from the Keys before the war."

"Prayer bells." Tomlinson smiled. "That confirms it. They were Buddhists. I saw what I'm pretty sure are prayer flags—just ribbons now—and a ceremonial area. Did you get to know any of them?"

"Not with Walter around. He'd beat the fire out of 'em. Or worse."

Bird Man. Tomlinson thought about that as they made another turn, Tootsie shifting into four-wheel drive on a trail that weaved through cypress. Ahead in a clearing was a rusted boiler from a steam engine. It stood on end, towering above weeds and a jumble of rusting pipe.

"A lot of Chinese worked here—the biggest whiskey still in Florida. Thousands of gallons they made, and the train would haul it north in barrels. Albert and the others called it Mangrove Lightning. They used counterfeit labels and sold it as the real McCoy."

"Corn liquor?"

"Sugarcane. That's a crop that don't grow natural in Florida, but they planted it thick on every piece of dirt around. I can show you these giant pots where they boiled the juice into slurry. More of a rum than whiskey. Chino Hole's just through those trees"—the old man motioned, his window down—"close enough to pipe in good water. They did a crackerjack business until Prohibition ended, and Albert moved us to the Keys. Thank the Lord for that."

"How long after the cypress was logged out?"

"Only a few years, then the village went

bust, too. We've been fighting the feds ever since they took over the railroads, but it's official now. They own most everything, including the lake. Or soon will. Until then, the bastards got no right to set foot on this land."

Tomlinson knew some of the details. "The government's taking over the end of next week, according to Doc. He's doing a fish survey, but he can't start until then. It was in his contract after he won the bid."

"Good luck on that," Tootsie said, more as a warning, then pulled into a drive where iron gates blocked the entrance. "We came the back way, but this is it, the Lambeth place. Used to be an iron foundry with a machine shop. He took it over when the railroad pulled out and the local men—Albert included—were too scared to put up a fuss."

A coral block wall framed the boundaries of the property and the building within. It was a massive metal structure, the exterior red with rust. Windows—there weren't many—suggested three floors, none of which invited light.

"It looks more like a factory."

"They serviced train engines here—see those tracks leading in through them big double doors? Had their own foundry to make parts, but it was all shut down by the time I was old enough to remember much. Yeah, Palmetto Station was quite the town before they repealed Prohibition."

Spanish moss and oaks dominated the area, yet the place had an industrial feel. Welding torches, molten steel, those visuals sparked through Tomlinson's head until he noticed movement in a second-floor window.

"Someone's up there."

"Could be Lambeth's daughter. I've only seen her once and that was years ago. Or a caretaker—I've heard different things. That the feds hired someone on the sly or they're letting her stay 'til she dies." Amused, Tootsie added, "Same as they're doing for me. But at least my kin can take possession. Not her; not any of Lambeth's people."

"What's her name?" Tomlinson asked.

"It's because Walter didn't homestead the property," the old guide replied. "He was a squatter . . . and maybe because she's not right in the head, or so I've heard. Oh, her name? Let me see . . ."

"You know for a fact she's mentally handicapped?"

"Ada, or something simple," Tootsie said. "I couldn't say one way or the other about how she is. The woman was always what you'd call a shut-in. I think she had a relative of some type, too. A son or nephew, I don't know, who stops by every now and again to look after her, and a couple damn big dogs."

"Lambeth's daughter? Then she must be about your age."

"Granddaughter, maybe. No one knows or cares what Walter and his family did. He was an outlaw. You got to understand that. He had a passel of kids. Didn't bother to send them to school, or even church to get baptized, and there was rumors about him knocking up his own girls. Or Walter's sons doing it. I heard his boys grew up even bigger than the old man. Meaner, too, which I can't say 'cause I never seen them."

"A shut-in, huh? That's a hell of a way to live."

"Maybe it's not her. The only vehicle I've seen around here is one of those big bucket trucks the power companies use. Keep in mind, I didn't move back 'til January. I've still got my double-wide across from Sharky's Bar; spend about half my time driving back and forth to Key Largo."

"When you were a kid, you ever speak to any of them?"

"Me speak to a Lambeth?" The question was obviously absurd. "You'll know why when you read the rest of Albert's confession. There, that's what I wanted you to see." He gestured to the rock wall. "You ever try to build a wall patched with concrete?"

Tomlinson, still focused on the upstairs window, saw a pumpkin-sized face appear, then it was gone. "Down syndrome," he said softly. "Is that what people say about her?"

Tootsie was becoming impatient. "Hell, I don't know. Some of Lambeth's kids had that look, but I'm trying to tell you something here. What Albert said before he died."

Again, he indicated the wall. "You need rebar to stack rocks that high or the cement won't hold. But not Walter Lambeth. Know why? I'll tell you. 'Cause he used bones for bracing."

"You're shitting me."

"Human bones. That's what they say. Just you wait 'til the feds tear down that wall. Can you imagine all the legal bullshit they'll have to go through? Some said he boiled off the flesh. Maybe ate it himself or fed it to the workers. Lambeth had different ways of making bodies disappear." The old fishing guide focused in. "Understand what I want you to understand?"

"Yeah. The bastard was a psycho killer." Tomlinson sat back, looked into the man's face, and realized he was serious. "Lambeth actually ate his victims?"

Tootsie, shaking his head, said, "What I'm saying is, this is a bad place. You and Marion need to know that before you go messing about that lake. Even as a kid, we didn't swim in Chino Hole. Fished there, sure. Every spring, tarpon would show up, then disappear come winter. It wasn't 'til I started guiding that I wondered how that was possible."

He put the truck in reverse and continued talking while he turned around. "The Chinese, I remember one saying there were lakes like that in the Bahamas. Tunnels that went too deep for any man. There was a monster he claimed lived down there, kind of an octopus with a lizard head. I don't believe that. But you know what I do believe?"

Tomlinson wasn't listening. He'd drifted off to a zone where veils parted into an unfamiliar corridor.

"If a seven-foot tarpon can find Chino Hole from the open sea, then guess what?" Tootsie shifted into drive. "Any animal that swims can find it, too."

Around seven, Tomlinson said good-bye to the guide and left for Sanibel, intending to enjoy the easy hour's drive. Instead, he found himself drawn to the same wire barricade where he'd parked earlier before hiking to the lake.

Weird, the attraction he felt for the place.

He tried calling Ford as a heads-up he might be late. No answer. After leaving a message, he re-lit the joint he'd rolled to facilitate cognition. He was a sailor, for god's sake, not a swamp stomper, so why was he sitting here trying to summon the nerve to do another spooky recon?

Twenty minutes, at least, he'd wasted. Christ . . . No, it had been an hour, if the clock in his VW van was to be trusted.

He sat back and did the math. The clock was right. Had to be. He'd paid extra for the Deluxe Swiss Alps Touring package—a fridge and an automatic pop-top, plus a folding bed—so all the chronometric options were no doubt first-rate.

The fact was, he was seriously stoned. Okay, then he'd have to walk it off. He got out of the van and slammed the door, determined to look this madness in the eye.

The recon did not go well.

Within the shadows of cypress swamp, abandoned railcars taunted him. The deathless howls of the undead assembled into a single voice; a warning neither male nor female.

The voice whispered, **If you run, he will catch you.**

"Yeah? I'll stick a bumper up his ass," Tomlinson replied aloud. "Catch this," and flipped a bird to the shadows.

He started the van intending to flee via the

main road, Route 29, but made a series of ill-advised turns. The trail somehow led into the same swampy area where Tootsie had shifted into four-wheel drive. Of the many features included in the Deluxe Swiss Alps Package, this option was not available.

The van began to fishtail. Tomlinson accelerated, careful not to over-steer. A brace of cypress trees jumped in front of him—a close call that required a braking technique he'd learned as a delinquent. Once stopped, he again called upon the accelerator for deliverance.

Tires spun; mud flew.

Come on . . . Come on, damn you.

Back and forth he rocked the vehicle, until he knew it would bury itself to the axles if he persisted.

He got out and slammed the door, yelling, "Only a rube would tour the Alps without four-wheel drive. Lying Kraut bastards."

Well . . . it wasn't too bad. What he needed was leverage and something under the tires for traction. Scattered metal waste came to mind. A couple of slabs of limestone would be useful, too. Only a few hundred yards ahead, both could be found at the abandoned foundry, Walter Lambeth's place—if he wasn't attacked by two giant dogs that maybe still lived there.

Was there another option?

Nope.

He dreaded the hike, yet, on the bright side, Tootsie had claimed this was the back way to the place. Supposedly, the main entrance was just off Route 29. Once free of the mud, his limp-dicked van could fly him out of harm's way to freedom.

So be it.

He grabbed a few necessities and set off, wondering, **What other hellish tests await?**

A gust of wind and the odor of rain. That's what awaited. Thunder, at least, cloaked his mutterings when the rust-black building came into view. To the right, the steam boiler appeared tiny by comparison. He crept to the gate, looked in, then trotted on tiptoe past the house to pilfer what he needed.

Every few seconds, his eyes panned along the upstairs windows. No movement; no sounds coming from inside. Hard to be certain because the squall pushed a boiling wind. Visibility was suspect, too. Clouds had drained color from the sunset sky.

Tomlinson felt no bolder but hurried anyway. A chunk of two-by-four went under his arm. This was abandoned in favor of a length of rusted steel. He used it to pry loose a couple of limestone blocks near the base of the wall— then jumped back.

Shit-oh-dear.

Among the rubble was a partial jawbone. A

single canine tooth snarled up at him. Panicking, he grabbed one of the blocks but dropped the pry bar. He knelt to retrieve it . . . then froze because of what he saw through the gate.

A woman had exited the house . . . No, she'd come from behind the machine shop attached to the foundry. A huge woman, shapeless in a baggy sack dress, or misshapen by age and girth. No doubt female. Glossy blond hair, cut short with curls, was as incongruous as the gloves and clodhopper boots she wore.

Tomlinson, on hands and knees, retreated into the bushes to watch.

The woman was dragging something attached to a rope. An ox towing a sled—her struggles were similar. When she was closer, he saw what it was: a bundle of large bamboo poles, all the branches trimmed. By then, she was almost to the gate.

Too late to flee.

He hunkered lower and soon heard, "Hey, hey, good-lookin', what'cha got dah-dah. How 'bout cookin' up dah-dah-dah-dah-dee . . ."

Singing as she worked; a familiar Hank Williams tune. The wheezing lyrics would have been child-like were it not for her gravelly baritone.

The gate clanked open. She struggled past, only a few yards away from him.

"Hey, hey, sweet dah-dee . . . Don't ya' think maybe . . ."

Tomlinson watched from astern the woman's bulk as she continued through the weeds toward the boiler. Wind lingered with her passing. He got a whiff of something foul that heavy perfume could not cover.

Gad . . . what a sad, sad beast of a person. Normally, he would have felt empathy— women considered unattractive by Hollywood standards were, to him, unplumbed treasures. Instead, an involuntary gag reflex vetoed all but the basest of fears.

He lay trapped. Pattering rain swept the trees; thunder boomed as the squall plowed closer. Yet the woman went about her business, loosey-goosey and at ease, as if performing a daily chore.

Perhaps she was.

She separated herself from the bamboo, shouldered the poles en masse and leaned them against the boiler. Spooky, the strength this required. There were a dozen or more, some of the damn things fifteen feet tall and thick as his arm.

A shovel appeared. Still humming, she dug a series of holes around the boiler. Now it was pouring rain. No matter. One by one, she planted the poles so they formed a massive circle. Each was anchored to the ground with wire and a single stake.

A giant bamboo cage—that's what the structure resembled. Housed within was the steam engine boiler.

Bizarre.

When she was done, the woman lumbered toward the gate, indifferent to the storm. Tomlinson cowered as she approached. He heard the clank of a latch, then waited a full minute before risking a breath. When he poked his head up, she was halfway to the house but staring in his direction through a mask of dripping hair.

"Hey . . . Looky there! Ain't you the handsome one," she called while battling a cough—no . . . it was her attempt at a girlish giggle.

Tomlinson didn't want to believe she was speaking to him. He splayed, belly down, hoping to resemble roadkill.

"Aw, playing possum—and flirty, too," she yelled. "Tell you what. I won't let loose the dogs if you promise to . . ." The rest was blurred by a lightning sizzle and thunderous sparks that spewed out of the old boiler.

When he looked up, she was galloping toward the house with the fervor of a woman who'd been spurned, or, perhaps, had suffered a sudden polarizing mood swing.

The zigzag pattern was distinctive. He'd seen it often enough in ex-lovers to know.

He grabbed the pry rod, the block of lime-stone, and hightailed it back through the del-uge and darkness—so dark that what he saw as he neared the van stopped him cold.

The dome light was on. The doors, which he'd locked, were both open wide.

He crept closer. He saw nothing to confirm it, but he knew someone—or some thing—lay in wait, hoping he would investigate.

Tomlinson did an about-face, and reminded himself, **Don't run.**

7

That afternoon, Ford returned to Sanibel Island during a tropical squall. Not by seaplane. The Maule was on the mainland in a private hangar where his old GMC pickup had been waiting. The timing had been ideal for a man who preferred not to be seen coming or going, or even noticed—particularly after the events in the Bahamas.

For this reason, he didn't make inquiries when Tomlinson failed to appear as they'd arranged via text earlier in the day. The mystic boat bum, although usually dependable, sometimes ran amok if tempted by sybaritic needs, not unlike a beagle tracking anything in heat.

No worries.

There was plenty to keep the biologist busy.

He'd been gone four days from his old house and lab built on stilts in the shallows of Dinkin's Bay. There was a stack of mail on the table, and several notes tacked to the screen door. In the lab, a dozen glowing aquariums contained fish, crabs, sea horses, and varieties of filtering species that needed tending to. Jeth, a fishing guide, and a young Cuban girl, Sabina, had done a good job of taking care of things, but Ford was fussy—"methodical," as he preferred to think of it.

The next morning, though, still no Tomlinson. That did worry him. The man didn't answer his cell, nor was his goofy-looking VW van in the parking lot. The upper deck of Ford's house was twelve feet above the water. He didn't need binoculars to confirm his pal wasn't aboard the sailboat **No Más**, or that his dinghy was beached in its regular spot when he came ashore.

Ford began to pace while he called Gillian. As they talked, he went through the notes he hadn't read the night before. One was from Hannah Smith, an ace fishing guide and former lover, who'd been inexplicably chilly for the last several weeks.

He read it again after hanging up: **Pete swam out to my boat, so I brought him home. As his "owner," you should know I was fishing Blind Pass with clients when it**

happened. This was three days ago. If you find someone willing to provide the care he needs, text me, and I'll drop him by the marina. No need to call.

Pete was Ford's dog. Blind Pass was six miles away by water. Half that distance if the dog—a retriever of uncertain lineage—had trotted north on the bike path, then leapt off the bridge. Even so, Hannah's note was downright icy.

What the hell was her problem? Retrievers liked to swim. So what? The dog could wind-scent a soft touch from miles away—that was obvious. Hannah was all legs and dark eyes within a shield of steel when it came to Ford. But an animal? A wet nose and fur brought out the sappiest of maternal instincts.

That damn dog . . . he was probably bloated on steak bones and sleeping on her bed at this very instant.

Never call a woman while angry, Ford counseled himself.

His resolve lasted all of two minutes. Fortunately, as he dialed, the phone buzzed in his hand.

When he answered, Tomlinson's voice asked, "Have you ever been chased by cannibals, then tried to hitchhike through the Everglades at night during a lightning storm? Don't answer. I need a ride."

"Where are you?"

"Within a stone's throw of two rednecks who just called me a long-haired dick smoker. This was **after** they snagged my cash, so, believe me, I'm tempted."

Ford said carefully, "You don't really mean—"

"Tempted to throw rocks, Einstein. God-damn, you're dumb sometimes. Get your butt down here, we've got trouble—**if** you happen to be somewhere east of Fumbuck-all. I'll need a twelve-pack at the very least, and there's a little baggie of weed hidden under your short-wave radio that—"

Ford interrupted, "How stoned are you?"

Click.

Ford was still repeating, "Hello? . . . Hello? . . ." when Tomlinson called back. "I'm sick of that idiotic question. Understand? I'll punch you right in the mouth if you ever ask me again."

"**What?** What did I say?"

"I'm not in the mood, Marion. Pack a bag, kiss the fish or whatever it is your spook protocol demands, then borrow a vehicle with four-wheel drive—preferably a Jeep built within the current century. I need help. As in **H-E-L**-fucking-**P.** How soon can you get here?"

"These two guys, they actually robbed you?"

"Extortion, would be more accurate. Picture

a couple of hillbilly Uber drivers who nixed their basic dental plans. They were kind enough to stop after chasing me into a ditch. Time's money, you know. If they don't get an extra hundred bucks, they've threatened to search my mouth for gold. Trust me, they could use an extra tooth or three."

Ford said, "Listen to me. Take off, running. I mean it. Cross-country. Are they watching?"

"Excellent idea—nothing but swamp and gators in every direction. We're about seven miles northwest of Palmetto Station, a dirt road called Jane's Scenic Drive. Scenic, my ass; there hasn't been a car through here since sunrise."

"Are they armed?" Ford had left the lab and was in his bedroom, packing some items he'd recently unpacked, a couple of them locked in a floor safe.

"You've got to be shitting me. We're talking the **Deliverance** twins, Zeke and his brother, Zeke Junior. Hang on a sec." There was a short muffled exchange before he returned. "Now it's two hundred bucks. I think they're stockpiling cash to buy something warm and fuzzy—a critter of their very own."

"How do they know you're not talking to the cops?"

"After they found a bag of weed on me, and some peyote buttons, we decided the honor system was, you know, the civilized way to handle matters. Jesus Christ, I wish you could hear yourself sometimes . . . You'll need a map, a good one, to find this place."

"How far?"

"A little over an hour, depending on bandits and other insane bullshit I prefer not to list." Tomlinson provided directions, then dropped the sarcasm. "It's been a hell of a night, man. I got my van stuck—I'll tell you the rest later, but that's not the worst of it. First thing I did was hike back to Tootsie's place. He wasn't there."

Ford shouldered a Vertx tactical bag, grabbed his keys, and went out the door. "Keep them talking. If they ask, say your sister . . . No, say a disabled pal of yours is on the way with money. That I'm crippled. It'll put them at ease."

"Did you hear what I said? The front window of Tootsie's cabin's busted, and he's gone. His truck, too. I'm worried about the old guy."

"Keep the hillbilly twins laughing," Ford said. "And one more thing . . . Are you paying attention?"

"Only one of us is, apparently."

"When I get out of my truck, run. I'll scratch my chin, or wave, or something, after I've had a look at them. Like a sign. And I mean **run**."

"Where? I just told you—"

"Doesn't matter. Here's the important thing: when you run, don't look back—and plug your ears."

Tomlinson was trying to convince one of the brothers, Zeke, that the peyote buttons he held were worthless pomegranate seeds, for that's what the cactus buds resembled, miniature pomegranates.

"Then why'd you hide them with all that good weed?" Zeke asked.

Zeke Jr. echoed, "Yeah, why?"

Talking was better than watching these two plink away at turtles and wading birds with rifles, but not much better. The question was asked in a bullying way that was standard for these scraggly yahoos—skinny bastards with tattoos and boney eye sockets. Maybe both weren't named Zeke. Hell, maybe they weren't brothers, but they looked enough alike to be white trash clones; born from similar loins, women immune to stabbings and trailer park fires.

Tomlinson said patiently, "You don't smoke them, you plant them," which wasn't the first lie he'd floated that morning. His most outlandish, yet wisest, offering had been: "If doctors had tested me for AIDS ten years ago, I would've spent about a thousand bucks on condoms. **Most** guys wouldn't see the humor."

Oh, the Zeke twins laughed and laughed, but they, by god, kept their distance after that.

Zeke Jr. grabbed one of the peyote buttons, eyed it, and said, "Can't smoke 'em don't mean you can't eat 'em," and took a bite. "Whew! . . . This some bitter shit!"

Brother Zeke said, "Let me try," and swallowed the other half.

Tomlinson thought, **Let the games begin.**

Two peyote buttons later, the brothers were staggering around, retching near the swamp buggy they'd used to chase him down after sunrise. It was a roofless truck on giant knobbed wheels, with vertical gun racks and a stereo system that wasn't too bad—until they'd switched from country to wigger rap.

Gad, what a grating intrusion into an otherwise miserable, mosquito-hazed morning in the Everglades.

When one hollered, "Turn that shit up!" and climbed aboard to get a rifle, Tomlinson knew the kimchi was about to hit the fan. He began walking backwards, searching for a place to hide.

That's when Ford's old GMC pickup appeared. Turquoise with white trim—obviously equipped with four-wheel drive, a detail that had slipped the Zen master's mind. It fishtailed around a curve, a half mile away on this muddy one-lane trail. Coming fast, sawgrass and water on both sides.

"Hey . . . looky there. Is that your sister? She ain't got no money, driving a wreck like that." Zeke Jr. had to study the truck through a rifle scope before remembering, "Oh, your buddy, the crippled guy. I forgot. He better have our two hundred bucks. We earned it, saving your ass out here in gator country."

That was their gambit—they hadn't robbed him; they'd rescued another long-haired city boy from his own wandering stupidity. Tomlinson wondered, **How many others have they humiliated—or worse?**

"Put the guns down," he told them. "My friend's a . . . disabled vet. You'll make him nervous."

"Vet?" Zeke said. "Hell, I've owned about a thousand dogs and a hundred head of cattle, and I ain't never had need to pay a vet for nothing. If a man can't take care of his own livestock, he don't deserve 'em . . . Zeke?"

Zeke Jr. said, "I don't think he means that kinda vet."

"Shut up. Throw me down my gun . . . No, dumbass, not the .22. I want my AR."

Now they both had rifles; sighting down the barrels as the truck slowed for an instant, then accelerated, and kept accelerating, the chrome GMC grillwork laden with intent as if to run them down. Onward the truck came, a hundred yards away . . . fifty yards, moving faster; Ford, wearing wire-rimmed glasses, both big hands visible on the wheel.

"Whoa! . . . Dude's crazy. Look at him come." Zeke Jr., from atop the swamp buggy, glanced back as if he might leap for cover.

"Want me to put a round through his tires?"

"**Hell?** Through the windshield, if he don't slow down. Shit, dude . . . he'll stop, just you wait and see."

Tomlinson found himself drawn to the middle of the road to screen his pal from bullets, but the truck did stop—when the emergency brake was jammed to the floor. Wheels locked; the truck spun, bed first, and came to rest a respectful distance away.

"That there's some fancy-ass driving," Zeke Jr. hooted. He was buzzed enough on peyote to appreciate NASCAR artistry, and lowered the rifle.

His brother did not. "What an asshole. Ought to put a round through the bastard's belly," he said, scared enough to do it.

When Ford got out and straightened his glasses, Tomlinson thought, **Uh-oh.** The biologist had zilch for acting skills. No one in their right mind would believe the man was disabled.

"How's that bum leg of yours?" Tomlinson

hollered as a reminder. "All these guys want is their money. Right, guys?"

Ford ignored him and started toward the big-wheeled swamp buggy despite the guns. He wore black gloves, and earbuds on a lanyard around his neck.

Earbuds? This was strange for a man who professed to dislike rock music. Equally strange, in his right hand was what might have been a large can of bug spray except for its brass, bell-shaped cap.

Zeke, tracking him through a scope, hollered, "Show us the money before you take another damn step."

The biologist stopped, rubbed his chin for effect, then continued toward the **Deliverance** twins.

Rubbed his chin . . . ? Christ—only then did Tomlinson remember what he was supposed to do. He pivoted and jogged away but couldn't help watching over his shoulder as Ford raised the metal can, and yelled, "Get on your bellies. I'm not going to tell you again."

Zeke found that funny. "You're a big talker, for a man carrying deodorant. Bring it on, big 'un, while I shoot you in the—"

That's all Tomlinson heard before a dazzling light pierced his head. No . . . it was a high-frequency sound with a razor's edge. The pain—excruciating. He stumbled, fell. When he looked up, his eyeballs vibrated. The sky appeared to melt in vibrato sync with a terrible lancing whine.

Unbearable. He plugged his ears and nearly vomited. Pain ceased . . . or he'd been struck deaf. No matter. He came close to vomiting again before pulling a finger free as an experiment.

Yes, thank god. He was stone deaf.

He got to his feet and wobbled toward Ford. The **Deliverance** twins were writhing on the ground while the biologist calmly went through their billfolds. He glanced up. "How much cash did they take?"

Every word was clear, as if nothing had happened. "I can hear!" Tomlinson grinned. "Say something else—I want to be sure."

Ford, glaring, said, "It doesn't mean much if you don't listen. Get in the truck while I go through their stuff."

They were on Route 29, headed for the Barlow cabin, before Ford revisited the issue. "The next time I tell you to plug your ears—"

"No shit, Sherlock," Tomlinson said. "You don't have to tell me twice. Where do you get these vicious toys of yours? No—don't tell me."

He was reading the back of the "aerosol can" that warned FOR EXPERIMENTAL USE ONLY. IF FOUND, CONTACT DIVISION OF SONIC WEAPONRY, TAOS, N.M., UNDER PENALTY OF LAW.

Ford continued, "I left the marijuana and your other drugs in their swamp buggy. Hid it all in a wheel well for cops to find. Hopefully, they will." He glanced over, pleased by the stricken look on Tomlinson's face.

"Man, that's just . . . cruel. My peyote buttons, too?"

"Especially your damn peyote."

The Zen master sulked for a while, then looked up in alarm when the biologist found the main entrance to the Lambeth property and turned in. "Man, this isn't the way to Tootsie's place. I wanted to stop there first."

"I know how to read a map" was the reply. Ford slowed when the boiler came into view, pulled over by the iron gate.

"Shit a'fire, keep going. My van's another quarter mile, and Tootsie's cabin, you've got to come in from the other way."

"Where's the lake?"

"Through those trees. Seriously, the woman who lives here could snap your neck like a pretzel. You don't even want to think about what might happen if she gets you on the ground."

Ford stepped out and stretched. "Any woman who scares you, I want to meet. I'll be working here in a week, so might as well get it over with. You said yourself this is the easiest access."

"I said closest, not easiest. Damn it, one of Florida's best-known guides has disappeared, now you're suddenly all neighborly; want to pop in and make social calls on Brunhilda." Tomlinson looked over his shoulder, aware his pal was eyeballing the steam boiler that towered up from the weeds.

"I don't see any ring of bamboo." The biologist kicked at a chunk of rock recently pried from the wall. "I don't see any human bones, either. Last night, tell me honestly, how stoned—" He stopped when he saw Tomlinson aim the can at him.

"Don't make me use this."

Ford, smiling, said, "It's empty."

Tomlinson got out and slammed the door. "God, you piss me off sometimes. On the other hand, maybe you're right. Maybe I imagined the whole damn episode and we'll find Tootsie inside having a beer."

8

When Gracie Barlow, age seventeen, heard the distant thunk of a car door, she made a mewling sound and prepared herself to be suffocated—a terrifying sensation when it had first happened but now only numbing after nine days chained inside a cubicle that smelled of rats.

It was always this way when the crazy woman got a visitor. The old hag would rush in, cussing, and insert a tube connected to a pump. The leather cowl on Gracie's face would ratchet tighter as the balloon inside her mouth began to inflate. She would gag, then fight panic, until her nose found a space to breathe air. Beneath the cowl, there was never enough room. A bloody pounding in the girl's head would drum louder, louder, then fade into weary unconsciousness.

Nine days. Six car doors. Not a single utterance had she managed, let alone a cry for help. Lately, when the drumming began, she hoped to pass out quickly and not awaken.

"The gags like you see in movies don't work," the woman had explained the first night. "You gotta cut off most of the air, but not too much. That's where you're lucky. I **know** what I'm about. Not like the Bird Man. That ol' cock 'bout kilt me a dozen times before he got it right. 'Course, back then rubbers was made outta lambskin. If the smell didn't get you, the things would break and suck 'em right down your windpipe. Think about that, biddy. You got it easy compared to what I went through."

Biddy, as in a newly hatched chicken. That's how the woman referred to her, or sometimes "paint slut" because of her tattoos. But never "Gracie," or even "girl."

The crazy woman was, well, crazy, but could be dealt with. The fear she inspired was diminished by exposure and her incessant talking, unlike the rancid odor of her blond nylon hair.

It was different with the man who came at feeding time. Gracie feared him more, not less, as the days passed.

Mr. Bird. That's what the old woman called the man, always said respectfully, or with dread. Or sometimes, when they were alone, she'd use a different name that could only be whispered. The name resonated like the pain he inflicted.

Somewhere outside, a metal gate clanked. The girl prepared herself for what came next, which was the sound of a battery-operated pump. It reminded her of the automatic blood pressure cuff her Uncle Tootsie used back when he still gave a damn about his health.

That sad, stupid old fool.

Thinking of her uncle provided a disconnect while the balloon swelled inside her mouth. She gagged, couldn't help it, then coughed, which only allowed the balloon more space to inflate. **Pssst-pssst-pssst** went the pump while blood pounded in her ears. It didn't cease until her jaws were hinged open wide, which forced her head back to create a narrow airway.

Only then could she submit to a slow, woozy silence that amplified sound. From somewhere far away came a polite knock at the door. Gracie struggled to remain conscious while an unfamiliar voice—a man's voice—said something, all of it garbled except for what might have been her uncle's name.

Yes . . . she hadn't imagined it. "Captain Barlow?" spoken as a question.

Maybe it was the police.

Two weeks ago, if someone had told her she'd

pray for cops to appear, she'd have laughed in his face. Now the possibility keyed desperation. She began to bang her head against the wall, a brick wall braced with antique mortar and stone.

She would soon run out of air. Gracie dreaded it; knew her last thoughts would be laden with remorse. It was the same when she tried to sleep. Shameful snippets always associated with her boyfriend, Slaten, and the shitty things she'd helped him do.

Boyfriend—such an innocent term for a man who'd claimed he was twenty-two but was actually closer to forty. They'd met in January when his camper broke down on Gracie's street. She'd had another fight with her mother and was on her way to work when Slaten, a tall, biker-looking guy with tats for sleeves, had flagged her down.

"You look cute in that uniform," he'd said. "What are you, a waitress? Or selling Girl Scout cookies?"

That night, after her shift ended, they'd gotten high smoking what he said was weed but was different from anything she'd ever experienced.

"Like it?"

They were in the back of his camper by then, parked east of Lake Okeechobee near Palmdale where Route 27 intersects with 29.

"They're awesome," she'd said. Not referencing the weed but pen-and-ink drawings that covered the walls; another stack near a propane stove and sink. Wild goth sketches of Japanese dragons and warriors; women in leather with huge breasts. Gracie wasn't pretty—she'd been told often enough—so sometimes fantasized that she was fierce and striking-looking, with a body like theirs. "Is that what you do, sell pictures?"

"I'm an artist, not a money whore. You've got at least one tat. I can see it from here. You don't know what those sketches are, do you?"

They were tattoo stencils drawn freehand, not the commercial crap you could own from any ten-buck scribble shop between Atlanta and Key West.

"I'm a tattooist. A real one," Slaten had said, and explained the elaborate artwork on his arms before revealing the masterpiece on his chest: a dragon shielded not by scales but by an intricate mosaic of overlapping flames.

Dizzy, hard to breathe—that's how she'd felt sitting so close to the man while he removed his shirt and flexed. "The design dates back to hermit monks in China. Those dudes understood that symbols possess powers, especially this one." He'd puffed out his chest, bragging, not ashamed. "Like magic, you know? It's true, not bullshit. You'll never see another tat like this. I created it myself . . . **by hand**. Do you have any idea what that means?"

He'd used bamboo splinters to open his skin, not needles on a rotary machine, and natural herbal inks. A week spent bloodying himself, pain off the scale.

Power. She could feel it radiating from this man.

"Can I say something that might offend you?"

Gracie had winced, dreading what came next, but what he'd said was sweet. "Whoever did that dolphin on your ankle didn't understand what's in here—your heart. You have a beautiful spirit, kid. Really. And your canvas—Jesus Christ, it's like damn near pure perfect."

Her skin, he'd meant. "And lots of it," he'd added as a compliment to her size and weight.

Slaten had brown-black eyes. They glowed through a veil of smoke. "How old are you?"

"Eighteen."

"The hell you are."

"It's true. My birthday was in April. April seventh. Go ahead, ask me what year was I born."

"Save it for the next bartender, I truly don't give a shit what the law or anybody else says. You ever feel like that? Like fuck the world, you know?"

Oh, yes, Gracie knew too well.

"I want to see it."

"My other tats?"

Standing, coming toward her—a huge man, shirtless, in this crowded space—he'd said, "Your canvas. Skin like yours, I want to see it all, every inch."

Gracie had never experienced intercourse, and this was a mature man, not the pimply boy who'd pawed her bra off after a concert—her only date in high school. The weeks that had followed were still hazy; a sweaty, pounding detachment that had left everything she knew, her home, her mother, and the life she hated, far, far behind.

Slaten was a different universe. Gracie existed there—god knows, she'd done enough nasty shit to prove her devotion. Until ten days ago, when, after visiting Tootsie, they'd come here and knocked on the door to inquire about an unusual type of bamboo that grew in the yard. A bluish Chinese variety. Rare. Yantra, the ancient tattooing design, required it.

The sound of oriental wind chimes that hung everywhere inside the building had caused him to knock louder.

Slaten was into the whole Asiatic spiritual-warrior thing—when he wasn't stealing or hustling to score drugs. Flakka, a synthetic amphetamine, is what they'd smoked that night. After a week on the road, she'd almost gotten hooked but in time had switched to only weed.

Not Slaten. He was a junkie and now he

was dead. Or so claimed the crazy woman, and there was no reason to doubt her.

Guilt, retribution.

In Gracie's last moments of consciousness, the concept punished her with the truth. She had stolen and lied and conspired against her own family.

She deserved to die here among broken mortar and bones.

An iron hatch swung outward. A panel of light floated into consciousness. Gracie refused to open her eyes until the crazy woman said, "I'll call Mr. Bird, you play possum with me. Gotta prove you ain't dead yet. Them's the rules."

The girl nodded, as if eager to make amends, and grunted, "Umm . . . umm-okay."

The balloon in her mouth, deflated now, still tickled a gag reflex, but she could make sounds through the leather cowling, which had straps and buckles and two tiny eyeholes.

The old woman, holding a lantern, stood hunchbacked because she was so big and the ceiling was so low.

"Them was federals at the door. I told you they'd be coming, and you know what that means."

More slowly, Gracie nodded her head.

"They got no right. Never did, never will. Besides, it ain't 'til next week they're allowed to set foot on this land. That's what I told 'em. Ran 'em off, I did, but they'll be back. And you know what **that** means."

Again, Gracie nodded.

"One claimed he's a fish scientist. The other, he's got the prettiest hair I ever seen on a man—darn near got my hands on him last night. Remember me saying how handsome he was when I was settin' bamboo? But they're federals, just the same."

"Hate . . . dem," the girl mumbled.

"Goddamn it, speak up." The woman slapped the girl halfheartedly, then ripped the cowling off after fumbling with the straps. "Don't know why he makes us wear this stinking mask. 'Course, I don't get much chance, since he got a taste for young biddies. Suppose that makes you **special**. Well, it don't."

She tossed the mask aside and slapped Gracie harder, skin on skin except for the duct tape that covered her mouth. "The feds was here 'cause of you, asking about that snoopy uncle of yours. If I'd seen him or we'd ever spoke—as if I'd give a Barlow the time of day." While talking, she inspected Gracie's thighs for menstrual blood, then her neck for signs of attempted suicide.

"Let me see your wrists."

Galvanized chain made bell notes when the girl raised her hands. A second chain, belted around her waist, angled to a bolt anchored in the wall. It was just long enough to reach a bucket that served as a toilet. Next to it was a length of foam rubber on the floor for sleeping.

With the mask off, her eyes began to adjust. The room was tiny, no windows. On opposite walls were iron hatches, one that opened into a room where an antique bellows hung from the ceiling. Slaten had guessed the other hatch opened into a furnace.

"An old metal foundry," he'd said.

The walls were charred black and webbed with graffiti, some in English but most in Chinese. Some scribblers had chiseled frames around their words as if staking rights to the only property they would ever own. This was Gracie's interpretation. A sense of utter worthlessness, they must have felt. She understood.

"Stop whimpering and spread your darn legs," the old woman ordered. "I gotta be sure. You know he hates the mess a girl your age can make."

Gracie withdrew into herself and focused on the wall. There were dates still legible from the 1920s and '30s. Several Chinese symbols were similar to the new tattoos that spiraled down her arms. Dancing letters. A capital **T** with legs. A cross encased in an oblong box. An elaborate 7 with a devil's tail and fringed with lace.

Grace. Love. Hate.

Nothing else existed, Slaten had told her. "There's no such thing as right and wrong, and the whole legal system is rigged. We choose our own reality. It's sort of like decorating a room. Your uncle, that senile old bastard, doesn't care about you. Your mother and the rest of your family, do I even have to say it?"

The world sucked. Life was bullshit. Slaten, for once, was right.

The crazy woman produced a box of tampons from her apron. Gracie flinched but re-evaluated when she heard, "Let me unlock those cuffs so you can tend to yourself. I ain't doing your dirty work for you."

Only the man who came at feeding time had allowed her the freedom of her hands—for his benefit, of course. This was something new. Maybe even an opportunity.

"Thank . . . you," the girl said through the duct tape, then waited passively. The cuffs came off. The old woman turned her back, still within reach. **Hit her . . . Strangle her.** Gracie's mind screamed for action, yet her body wouldn't respond. The woman was old but massive, with a head twice the size of a normal person's. She was over six feet tall with shoulders that her baggy dress could not hide. Close to three hundred pounds.

The opportunity came and went. "Why ain't you opened that darn box yet?" the woman snapped when she looked back. "I ain't gonna nursemaid you. If you think I want to watch that filth, you're nuttier than Mr. Bird."

Gracie took a breath through her nose and shrugged as if apologizing. "Turn around," she mumbled while using a free hand to make a spinning motion.

The woman did it. Waddled in a discreet half circle . . . then suddenly stepped out of reach when she heard a distant banging at the door. Not a polite **knock-knock-knock** as before.

"Damn federals again," she glared in an accusing way. "You best have your toiletry done when I get back."

Gracie watched the old hag duck through the opening and waited until the iron hatch slammed closed before marveling at her good fortune. She'd never been left alone unmasked with her hands free. Her first instinct was to rip off the duct tape and spit out that damn balloon, but she couldn't. Not yet—too risky. Instead, she hurried to the eyebolt that anchored her and ten feet of chain to the wall. The bolt was huge, made of iron; a fixture so old, the floor beneath was stained with rust. But solid. Impervious to anything but a saw.

The girl had tried another way. Using her fingernails and splinters of bone, she'd spent every safe moment digging at the mortar around the bolt. Hours ago, or a day ago—it was impossible to know—it had finally broken free. Well, not free, but loose enough to move if she applied her full weight.

She did so now. Faced the wall and climbed the chain hand over hand, and used her feet like a logger going up a tree. When the bolt was at eye level, she planted her feet, knees bent, then gave a mighty yank.

The bolt came free; mortar showered down when she landed hard on the floor. So hard, it was possible she'd been knocked unconscious and was dreaming when the crazy woman screamed, "What the hell . . . he'll burn you for this."

It wasn't a dream.

Glaring in at her was the old woman.

Gracie gathered the chain and ran to the opposite wall, where there was a smaller iron hatch.

Slaten had been right. It opened into a furnace.

9

When Tomlinson returned to the truck, he said, "That old woman gives me the willies. There's someone else inside that building. Someone in trouble, man. Maybe Tootsie, I don't know, but the vibe grabbed me by the throat. That's why I had to go back."

"What did she say?"

"Nada. Just motioned me away, but not until she did a kind of hoochie-coochie thing before she got to the door. Then slid this under it." With two fingers, he held up a note as if it were soiled laundry. "That's what took me so long. She's slow with the pencil. But that's all she's slow with, I'm guessing."

"Hoochie-what?"

"You know, provocative. Like a dance. What-ever happened to subtle feminine wiles? Cripes, she's the size of a rhino and crazy as ten loons. Have a look."

Ford accepted a note penciled in a child-like scribble. **Com back to nite,** it read.

Tomlinson waited before saying, "Isn't this where you smirk and crack wise about my new sweetheart?"

"I think you ought to call the police."

"Yeah, right. Ask them if they've got Prince Albert in a can while you laugh your ass off." Tomlinson smiled at that until he saw the look on Ford's face. "You're serious."

"Not a nine-one-one call. It has to be a cop who knows we're not crackpots. You said she's stunted mentally? From her note, you could be right."

Ford held the paper to the windshield, then sniffed it, careful not to leave additional prints. "Put this somewhere safe." He started the truck.

Tomlinson, staring, said, "You mean you ac-tually believe me for once?"

It wasn't that. "While you were charming the lady, I took a look at that old steam en-gine boiler. On my way back, I found this." He searched among his pockets, then gave up because he had to shift into four-wheel drive. They were entering cypress lowlands, the van not yet in sight. "It's a receipt for groceries and stuff. Out here, people haul their own trash, and I found it near the gate with a glob of other stuff. Trash that had spilled. It came from **inside** the building. How old do you think that woman is?"

"About two hundred pounds north of sixty," Tomlinson said, and opened the glove box on a hunch. There it was, a receipt from a Shop-N-Go on Marco Boulevard. He did a quick scan, mumbling, "Wonder Bread, chips, Mountain Dew, e-smokes, yada yada yada . . ." Then his expression changed. "Oh Christ. I see what you mean. The woman's too old to need tampons."

"Among other things."

"That crazy old witch." Tomlinson spun around in his seat. "I bet she has Gracie in there. Doc, we've got to go back."

"Who?"

"Tootsie's niece. Man, I told you, no one's seen her in more than a week." He grabbed his phone to dial 911, then realized the biologist was right. "Shit. What am I gonna tell them, arrest an old woman for buying Tampax?"

"You left out some other things—condoms and rolling papers. And who buys two jars of Vaseline at a Shop-N-Go?"

Tomlinson started to reply but decided against it. Why admit he'd purchased weirder items when it was too late to save a buck at

Winn-Dixie? Better to remain silent until the damn truck stopped. When it did, he'd jog back to the house by himself if need be.

"It's an odd combination," Ford said, "but doesn't mean a thing until you put it together. A handicapped woman who lives alone in the middle of nowhere? If anyone's being held captive, it's her. Druggie rednecks like the Zeke twins, plus a girlfriend or two. There's probably a simple explanation, but, yeah, we should call. What did you say her name is?"

"Lambeth. Ada, or something similar, according to Tootsie. He only met her once and that was years ago. Her father was a psycho smuggler who killed for fun and profit. Rumor was, he made soup out of his victims." After a pause to look at the receipt, he added, "On the other hand, e-cigarettes. That's what synthetic stoners use as a delivery system."

"Druggies—that's what I said. They could be living off her disability checks or whatever she's inherited. Old people and women in isolation are the world's easiest targets."

"I don't know, man. I can see her as someone's half-witted dupe, but a victim? Being scared shitless doesn't mesh with that hoochie-coochie act of hers. I think we ought to turn around and have a look."

"There's your van," Ford said. "If one of the Sanibel cops doesn't know someone local to call, try Hannah. Her best friend's a deputy sheriff."

Tomlinson thought, **That's not going to happen.**

Two deputies driving separate cars met them at Tootsie's place. The cabin, with its shattered front window, was empty, but they refused to crawl inside and have a look.

Tomlinson, instead of getting pissed, made himself scarce while the biologist did the talking. The cops circled the yard on foot, then had another parley with the biologist, before they drove off. Finally, it was safe to say what was on his mind.

"Those **clowns**. It's been more than an hour since we left the Lambeth place. Gracie could be dead, or god knows what. Why do they hire guys like that?"

"Because guys like you wouldn't make the cut," Ford replied, and started toward the cabin. "If they did, they'd quit because of the shitty pay, plus it's dangerous and they'd have to deal with guys like **you**. Does Tootsie hide a key someplace?"

"Whoa! No need to bite my head off, man. I was simply making an observation based on—"

"Based on an assumption, and you're wrong."

Ford peered in through the broken window. "They've already talked to the woman. Ivy Lambeth, that's her name, not Ada. They spent close to an hour with her because they were concerned about her mental health."

"Well . . . I bet they didn't go inside the place. That would take too much effort."

"She **invited** them in. One of the deputies said it was like walking into a museum. An old blacksmith shop and foundry with all the antique tools. That's not what took them so long to get here. Did you notice a couple of bad scratches on the woman's face?"

"When she came to the door? Absolutely not. How bad? That alone should've made them—"

Ford held up a hand for silence. "Maybe the lighting wasn't good when she did her dance routine. Or she cut herself after we left. Either way, they got her patched up, took a look around, then apologized for interrupting her day. She has a nephew who works construction and lives with a girlfriend. Twice a week, he drops off groceries to the old gal—and what he buys at a Shop-N-Go is none of our damn business."

"The cops told you that?"

"No, **I'm** telling you. Clowns, my ass. On their way here, one of them tracked down a number for Gracie's mother and he called. It's not unusual for the girl to take off for a week or two without a word. The other deputy called marinas in Key Largo. Around noon, Captain Barlow was seen having lunch at the Pilot House. Everyone on the island knows the man. It's one of his regular hangouts."

"Really?"

"**Really.** He didn't disappear, bonehead. He probably took off because he was exhausted after two days stuck with you. Why I let you draw me into these idiotic situations . . ." Ford shook his head and walked toward his truck.

Tomlinson wanted to chuckle but didn't dare. The biologist was among the most patient and amiable of souls—except for a day or so after returning from some far-flung hellhole, which he always lied about in a snappish way.

Ford was carrying gloves and a towel when he came back. After a sheepish shrug, he said, "Sorry. You didn't deserve that. Tootsie doesn't have a cell phone, and he didn't bother to leave a note. There's no way you could've known."

"Tough trip, huh?"

Ford ignored that. "He still has his place in the Keys, right? Give him a call on his landline so we can break into this place legally."

"Let me re-phrase: how shitty was your trip? This is probably a bad time to ask why you were bopping around the Bahamas with a scion of the Windsor family. I looked her up. Gillian Cobourg. **Lady** Gillian, officially. She's a direct descendant of Henry Locock, the illegitimate son of Queen Victoria's daughter. The scandal sheets loved her until they began hating her. That was about a year ago."

Ford had the gloves on, removing glass shards from the window. "I'd appreciate it if you'd forget the texts I sent."

Tomlinson said, "Don't I always? She's trouble with a capital **T**. You know that, right? Some think the **T** stands for 'traitor.'"

It wasn't until the biologist was through the window and opened the door from inside that he responded. "She was being blackmailed— past tense—but that's between us. Now she's dead. **Officially.**"

Ford got his first look at Chino Hole late that afternoon. So many tarpon rolled on the surface, he shot video snippets to share with a few friends who might delight in the anomaly: saltwater game fish in a landlocked lake that was small enough to qualify as a pond.

The footage was impressive, but sharing would have to wait. No signal in this part of the Glades. It gave him time to amend his list of selected friends. If he included Hannah, she might thaw enough to engage in conversation. Or, at least, bring back his dog.

Women, he thought, giving it the same emphasis men always do when they've been outclassed or outsmarted and made to look a fool. And not for the first time this week.

Gillian came into his mind. She had used him. He knew it, and it wouldn't have mattered if there weren't bigger issues at stake. Her loss. Or his. He was still unsure. Ford wasn't a womanizer, not by his narrow definition, but he'd been around enough to know that Gillian was among the rarest of the rare—visually, sensually, physically. Damaged, true, but so what? It's the inner scars that bind lovers, which can be a privilege or a curse.

During private moments, it was difficult not to summon details of the bedroom hours they had shared. No, not shared. It was precisely as she'd stated: he had used her, she had used him. It was the way the world worked. But, my god, so seldom was the exchange as lush and wet and mindless. Tender, too, at the very end.

That was something else he didn't want to think about. He and Gillian weren't done, nor were certain powerful people who cared about her family.

It was after six. Cypress trees screened a westwarding sun. Tomlinson, presumably, was still combing the cabin for an antique Bible he'd described, and some old photos he claimed were missing. Because Captain Barlow hadn't answered his phone to confirm the items were stolen, Ford had left his truck and his pal behind and gone for a run. He hadn't had a decent workout in days. Never mind the heat and sodden clothes, or the long, wet drive home to Sanibel that awaited. Excuses were for those willing to concede that weakness was their strongest ally.

He started back to the cabin at a good pace, and opened it up as he neared a chain that blocked this sandy lane from a secondary road—then slowed when he heard a bizarre faraway noise. It was a feminine wail accompanied by what might have been two alternating notes on a tuba. **BUM**-ʙᴜᴍᴘ, **BUM**-ʙᴜᴍᴘ, **BUM**-ʙᴜᴍᴘ. Like that, but more frenzied.

The mating cry of a bittern, he guessed. It was an uncommon bird, rarely seen because it was so beautifully camouflaged. Its booming vocals had spawned legends of giant swamp creatures, including the Everglades version of Sasquatch.

Ford was a biologist by profession but a naturalist at heart. He hurried down an embankment into the trees, where boxcars lay abandoned to shadows and vines. Every few yards, he stopped to listen. He heard the noise again as he neared the lake. This time, the wail resembled a distant steam whistle . . . or a woman's rhythmic cries. The tuba notes might have been a man hammering with a wooden club.

A more fanciful image came to mind: two giants having sex, the male pounding a bed into the wall while his partner shrieked in sync. Amusing, were it not for an edge of hysteria that sharpened the sound. Ford felt it on the back of his neck.

The noise stopped. He continued toward what he thought was the source, unconvinced it was a bird. Golden light had settled upon the pond. Waking fish boiled the surface. A hundred yards into a stand of cypress, the foundry and machine shop appeared. The limestone wall was hidden by bushes, but he could see a couple of outbuildings and the old train boiler beyond.

Dogs, Tomlinson had warned, yet there was no barking or the telltale circles in the yard where dogs had been tied. The only oddity came from the largest of three brick chimneys. Smoke billowed from it as if jettisoned by a fan. Why would anyone need a fire in Florida on a June evening?

A cooking fire, possibly. One of the deputies had said the building's interior was more like a museum.

Ford weighed various explanations until he heard: **BUM-bump, BUM-bump . . .** That noise again. He spun around and located the accompanying whine.

He'd been right from the start. It was a bird. Not one but several bitterns calling from somewhere near the lake.

When clear of the trees, he settled into an easy jog, still troubled by one detail that was slow to reveal itself: **a cooking fire shouldn't produce black smoke.**

Tomlinson snubbed out a joint in haste when Ford appeared, and got up from the rocker where he'd been enjoying sunset from the porch. "The Bible was stolen, just like I thought. Maybe some pictures and other stuff, too. I just got off the phone with Tootsie. He's pretty upset but told me not to call the cops. Insisted, in fact."

Ford consulted his phone and sent the tarpon video, then went into the cabin. He returned with the towel he'd used earlier and a pitcher of well water. "They knew what they were after, that's why he doesn't want the police. What sort of thief steals a Bible?"

"Exactly, I'm thinking the same thing. He's afraid one of his relatives did it. Now he wants time to check around before getting the cops involved. The question is, why would a member of the family steal the family Bible?"

Ford said, "God, it's hot," and sat down. He gulped water straight from the pitcher, commented on the sulfur taste, which he liked, then asked, "Has he heard anything from his niece?"

"Gracie might have robbed the place. She's the first one I thought of, too, but not a word from her, as far as I know. Tootsie wanted to drive back tonight, but it's two hours from Key Largo, so I told him I'll stay here or sleep in the van. He'll come in the morning. What do you think?"

"You would've stayed anyway," Ford said, getting up, using the towel.

Tomlinson was mildly miffed. "All I meant was, you can bunk in the cabin if you want. I've got plenty of beer and supplies in the van. I don't care either way, but I want you to see something first."

Inside was a box of old photos and newspapers. Whoever had broken in had left the box open in the center of the room.

"This is why I think more things might be missing," Tomlinson said. "They didn't care about this, and similar stuff. It's from the **Saint Pete Times**, August 1925." He pointed to a headline that read

MARCO ISLAND WAR
SHERIFF ENLISTS "NAVY"
HOMESTEADERS ARMED

"But this they wanted. I found it outside." He produced a photograph in a heavy frame: a man who resembled Babe Ruth and was just as big. He wore a straw hat, and a gunbelt over loose, old-time pants held up by suspenders. "They must've dropped it. It's Walter Lambeth. Tootsie showed it to me yesterday when we were talking. Take a look at the crazy bastard's eyes."

Ford did, then was done with it. "You planned to sneak back and spy on that poor old woman anyway. Admit it."

"Yeah, and look for Tootsie's Bible. You make it sound like a dumb idea."

"It is," Ford said. "That's why you're not going alone."

10

Nights before feeding time, Mr. Bird liked
to set up the Kinetoscope and watch a
movie in the very room where Walter
had killed many males and at least two
females. One of them a deputy's wife, the other
a girl child not old enough to speak her first
words.

It put him in the mood.

The movie, which wasn't actually a movie,
helped, too. The Kinetoscope had been in-
vented by Mr. Edison, who, during the same
period, had a winter home sixty miles north in
Fort Myers. You loaded a stack of photos in the
machine and it projected them on the wall so
rapidly, it gave the illusion of motion. Events
frozen in time came alive again.

Mr. Bird loved the Kinetoscope. He lived in the past. He visited the present only to enjoy what the past could not provide.

The past would always be home.

Walter hadn't known Mr. Edison, but he had met an excellent photographer. This was back when Walter was brewing lightning whiskey and guiding Yankees new to the Everglades.

The photographer, whose name was Julian Dimock, had come with his father from New York. They wanted to fish and hunt and capture Florida's rarities on film. The duo soon tired of Walter's bullying, but not before Julian had taken lots of photos. Some would be published and considered classics. Others would be mailed back to Florida as presents to their guides. How the Barlow family had ended up with so many shots of Walter, Mr. Bird didn't care.

He hated the family as much as Walter did.

Tonight was special. Loaded into the Kinetoscope was a fresh stack of images stolen from the Barlow cabin. He blew out the lamp and clicked a switch. The room blossomed with light, then strobed like a discotheque, while he lounged back and lit a pipe. It was long, delicate, made of ornate brass and ivory, with a vaporizing chamber. A Chinese opium pipe, but the bowl contained a synthetic resin. The drug was called flakka on the street, or khat in North Africa, where it originated.

Opium was tough to obtain in the present world. This was another reason Mr. Bird was always eager to return home.

The Kinetoscope whirred and flickered. On the wall stood Walter Lambeth. He sneered, posing with a drawn revolver, and walked in a humorous Charlie Chaplin way toward a gathering of males and females. They were Chinese immigrants, all shirtless. They waited with heads bowed as if showing off their pigtails and glossy black hair, or waiting to be beheaded.

He froze the frame and pulled the same gun from the back of his pants—a .38 caliber Webley service revolver—and attempted to imitate the pose: a hunter with his trophies before they'd been skinned and mounted on a wall.

God . . . such a beautiful image. All it lacked was impossible detail. The females: was their odor fresh? Had they been branded or tattooed?

Next, an alligator hunt. Reptiles with teeth, slashing tails. Mostly small; a couple that were man-sized. And then a true giant. It resembled a floating tree, both ends sharpened like spears. Wait . . . it wasn't a gator. The shape was wrong. It had to be a crocodile.

Mr. Bird jumped up, froze the image, and lumbered to the wall for a closer look. He admired anything that achieved massive size. Yes, a saltwater croc. The pointed snout, the teeth, were distinctive. During Walter's era, they had been common in Florida. Fewer now, no doubt. It wasn't just the animal's size that interested him. Details in the background caught his eye: a building with only a portion of the roof visible. There were two . . . no, three blurry chimneys from which smoke boiled.

The lens was adjustable. Varied angles helped. When he was certain, his nostrils flared to express pleasure. The photo was taken at the pond, Chino Hole, back when the metal foundry was fully operational.

Did I know you? he wondered. **You were a fool to die.**

Overhead were rusted pulleys. Leather straps hung broken, adorned with cobwebs. That was okay. Walter had gotten along fine with just the furnace and the few tools required to vaporize flesh and bone.

The furnace was almost hot enough now.

He crossed the room to a bellows suspended next to the forge. The bellows was huge, the size of his chest. The leather had cracked, but the brass seals were good. He pumped it several times. Shielded within a brick chamber, flames responded with a roar. Even he needed gloves to bang open the steel hatch. Inside was an inferno so pure, it reflected light like a mirror. Mr. Bird, looking in at his reflected nakedness and tattoos, smoothed an eyebrow, and thought, **The girl will never try to escape again.**

On a table lay Walter's branding iron. One of his slaves, a Chinese artisan, had forged it and presented it to him as a gift. As thanks, Walter had embossed the man's eyes, blinding him with a chop of his own creation.

Chop was a Chinese term for a symbol that represented not just a name but one's being. Lovely, that strange design. A dancing letter **T** with plumage and a beak. Perfect for this young female. She wore a perfect canvas that had already been adorned with tattoos.

The branding iron went into the flames. It would be ready soon.

Mr. Bird was ready now.

Outside the door, iron steps spiraled up to the next floor, where Walter's daughter lived. Or sister . . . or both. Hand on the railing, he bellowed, "Ivy, you lazy toad, it's feeding time. Bring her to me. No chains. Just the mask. She'll need her hands or I'll kill her for screaming. You know how I hate screaming."

The young ones could shatter glass.

Nothing like the baritone wail that was Ivy's reply after a commotion that caused him to charge up the stairs.

"Don't beat me, don't beat me—it ain't my fault," she pleaded.

Gracie Barlow had escaped again.

Half the building's third floor was open to the ground to accommodate steam engine cupolas two stories tall. The only light filtered up with heat from the furnace.

From the first whiff of smoke, Gracie had known she'd be killed if they caught her. Or worse. On his last visit, Mr. Bird had taunted her with horrendous threats.

She'd moved quietly, desperate to find a way out, while the crazy woman's voice raged through the building. Rage transitioned into a series of cries and then a shriek. And then an abrupt silence caused the girl to freeze. Heavy footsteps filled the void. Someone was searching for her. **THUNK-THUNK-THUNK.** Each step louder as the person drew nearer to her hiding spot.

Gracie panicked. Wooden supports crisscrossed the plank floor. Boxes of junk and railroad signage materialized from shadows. Her knee snagged something. She fell beneath a clattering noise. Near her face, bold letters warned DANGEROUS CROSSING.

The footsteps stopped. They backtracked

and stopped again near the stairs to her hiding spot on the third floor. The wooden steps were narrow. They creaked under the stress of an ascending weight. Soon, light from below projected a silhouette onto the landing. Only Mr. Bird's head was that wide.

God help me, please help me . . . She repeated the words as she crawled toward an open area. When she reached it, she understood. There were no cross braces here because the floor ended in a space wide and high enough to house a train engine.

She got to her feet and looked down. Three stories below, a grate glowed with orange embers—a forge of some type. Nearby, steel tracks pierced the sliding doors. There was also what appeared to be a film projector. Strange, the milky light it cast. Above her, suspended from the roof, a tangle of rope was draped among pulleys. The girl's eyes traced the rope's course over a rafter, through more pulleys, then . . . my god, straight down to a platform next to where she stood.

A service elevator, she realized.

Behind her, on the landing, a massive silhouette slid into the gloom and became a hulking shadow. The shadow floated toward her.

Gracie screamed, "I've got a knife, stay away," as she stepped over and grabbed the rope. The rope was thick, as dry as straw. She gave a yank.

Overhead, pulleys banged but the platform didn't budge. She tried a different angle, then swung her full weight on the elevator's rope. As she struggled, the familiar clatter of railroad signage created a buzzing in her ears. Mr. Bird was only a few yards away.

God help me, please help me. She dropped to her knees and began a frenzied search. The elevator had to have a brake or a latch. There was—a pair of **L**-shaped bars with handles. She pulled one, then the other, too terrified to realize she had failed to control the rope. The floor gave way, yet fell only a few feet before a knot snagged. The platform slammed to a stop.

Gracie, unsure what had happened, looked up. Mr. Bird grinned down at her, something in his hand. It was a metal rod. The tip of the rod was capped with leather. Wearing gloves, he removed the cover. Sparks rained from the metal tip, which was molten orange and flat like a branding iron.

"When I'm done with you," he said, "Ivy goes into the furnace. One of you needs to appreciate why you're here."

He squatted and looked her up and down. "Move your hands—I've seen your tits before. Damn you, get your hands out of the way so I can use this. Okay, don't . . . Then how about the eyes?"

The branding iron lanced toward her. Gracie

rolled away and screamed amid smoke and the stink of her own seared flesh. A coil of rope was the only escape available. She found it and jumped from the platform when he tried to brand her again. After her short free fall, the rope snapped taut and she fell. Landed hard but felt okay, except for a massive throbbing blister on her shoulder that wasn't okay. The skin was peeling off—a serious burn. **I need a doctor,** she thought while Mr. Bird yelled, "Ivy! In the foundry room. She's in the foundry room. Grab her . . . hold the biddy until I get there."

The train-sized double doors were nearby but looked unmovable. Gracie ran toward what she remembered as a hallway to the living area. No . . . first there was the kitchen, where pots hung above a woodstove. A second hall branched left and right. She went left, following the sound of wind chimes into a high-ceilinged room that stunk of rats and musty furniture. A lamp on the table showed a few windows, and a front and back door.

She tried the main entrance first. It was locked—an old-fashioned lock that, coming or going, required a key. She sprinted past a staircase to the back door. Same kind of lock.

Gracie, who was in shock, began to panic again. It got worse when she heard heavy footsteps coming down the stairs.

She lurched toward a window. That was her

escape. She'd break the glass and climb into darkness, where the air was fresh. Beside a couch was a heavy ashtray stand that cradled a strange-looking pipe. She grabbed the ashtray and threw the curtains aside.

The window was barred.

Oh my god . . .

There was another window, but not enough time to try it. On the landing, the hem of a baggy dress had descended into view. A meaty hand with a butcher's knife appeared next. Gracie hurled the ashtray at the stairs and retraced her steps to the hall.

The crazy woman screamed, "You got me in trouble, damn little paint slut! There ain't no escape. Think I'd still be here if there was?"

A coughing fit of laughter followed the girl through the halls. The woman's labored footsteps followed, too.

"Found her, Bird Man! She's headed toward the foundry. Hey . . . where are you?"

The man's response echoed through the building: "Waiting for her."

Gracie began to weep as she ran. Ahead, the double doors didn't offer much hope. Or maybe they did. A huge iron hasp held the doors shut, not a lock. She could barely reach the damn thing. On tiptoes, she used both hands to rip the hasp free. She fell, got up, and put her shoulder to the door.

Wheel tracks screeched. The door moved a few inches while the woman's rancid odor invaded the room.

Again and again, she pushed. Soon a space as wide as her arm revealed darkness and stars outside. Never had darkness felt so delicious, yet escape was impossible. Gracie confirmed it with a glance. The crazy woman was only a few strides away, coming at her, the butcher's knife raised.

"I warned you, by god, I did. You asked for it."

Sobbing, the girl flattened herself against the door . . . and then thought she was dreaming when the door glided open. She stumbled backwards and fell into the arms of a man. A large man with wire glasses. He held her close and pointed something—**a gun**—at the woman, saying, "I don't want to shoot you, but I will."

The woman turned and ran with the clumsiness of a bear wearing boots. She disappearing into the hall. The man wanted to go after her, Gracie could tell. But he didn't. She babbled an incoherent, "Thank god. Who . . . who are you?"

No response, but the man asked her name and other simple questions. A flashlight replaced the gun when he checked her eyes. She felt numb, and wondered, **Is this really happening?** Light skipped over her nakedness and focused on flaps of skin hanging from her left arm. "Did she do this to you?" he asked.

The girl shook her head, and whispered, "Uh-uh. It was him."

"A man? He's still inside the building?"

She nodded.

Wire glasses sparked as he lifted her off the ground, saying, "You'll be okay, but you need a doctor. Tomlinson? Tomlinson! Get your butt over here."

From the darkness, a second man hollered, "Someone just ran toward the lake. I thought it was you."

They hollered back and forth about that. Soon a skinny, long-haired man was attending to her while the one with glasses took off, carrying a bag over his shoulder but without the gun.

He'd given it to his friend, saying, "If the woman comes back, shoot a round near her feet."

11

Ford crashed his way to the pond, then circled back quietly. The limestone wall provided a view of the machine shop and a couple of sheds. To his left, cypress trees marked the water's edge a football field away.

He sat and waited, knife in hand. When he was convinced he hadn't been followed, he holstered the knife and opened the shoulder bag. Inside was a thermal scope hybrid with amplified night vision. It was flashlight-sized, with a simple switch, and a lens at both ends.

Ford put it to his eye and focused while scanning the building. Darkness was transformed into high noon through a green lens. This was standard for military night vision. When he activated the thermal sensor, the landscape changed. Heat became a signal flag. It registered as shades that varied from scarlet to pale yellow. The hotter an object, the brighter the color.

Atop the machine shop, only one of three chimneys throbbed a lucent red. Saffron borders around the windows showed where heat escaped. In the distance, Tomlinson paced, still conversing with the 911 operator. His ruby cheeks suggested that he was pissed about something— probably because they had yet to hear sirens. The area inside, where a furnace blazed, was shaded orange. Trees, grass, and other plants registered as passive blue.

Superb quality. The technology was new, pioneered by Nivisys, a tactical optics specialist in El Paso.

Shadow Track, the device was nicknamed, for that was its function.

Ford stood to view the area near the pond. Specks of cinnamon revealed roosting birds. He swung around and found the sheds. Nothing inside. A man's heat signature would have registered through wood.

It's what he expected, because he'd done a thermal search of the area on his way to the pond.

So where the hell had the crazy old woman, or whoever it was, gone? Tomlinson had seen **someone**. It wasn't a matter of trust. The biologist knew it was true. Using the thermal unit, he'd followed the person's footprints until a heavy dew had leeched them of heat. That was near the limestone wall.

Ford backtracked to the wall, seeing his own recent prints as swatches of yellow. He was searching the other side when sirens told him that EMTs and police would soon be here.

He was relieved. He was a biologist, not a cop. This was police work. But then the girl, Gracie, the look on her face, came into his mind, and what had been done to her. The monster he was tracking had melted the flesh off her arm with a branding iron. Wouldn't it be nice to catch the monster before there was a need for Miranda rights?

Five minutes, Ford decided, maybe a little more, were still his. He knew how to use the time. On the way to the pond, he hadn't searched the sheds because footprints hadn't led him there. That's where he was headed, toward the closest shed, when he realized it was sided with iron sheeting, not wood as he'd assumed.

Dumbass. Thermal imaging couldn't pierce metal. He stopped and used the scope to do a more careful search around the door seals. The first shed, nothing. But on the second and largest shed, he noticed a sliver of orange heat leaking from beneath the door.

Someone was inside.

Ford put the monocular away and crept to the corner of the shed. After listening for a few seconds, he used the knife to tap lightly. "It's safe now," he whispered, and waited for the door to crack wide enough for a peek. When it did he lunged inside, buried his fingers in the throat of a man he wrestled outside and slammed him to the ground.

"Make a sound, I'll kill you," he said. Ford's glasses had been knocked crooked, but he could see that he was choking a very large man who was naked, tattoos all over his body. "Hear those sirens? Wouldn't you rather talk to me than a cop?"

The man, bug-eyed, shook his head, meaning he preferred the police.

This made no sense until Ford saw that his hands and ankles were tied, and a patch of tape covered his mouth. The biologist relaxed his grip, but only until he noticed the sloppy knots, and how loosely the rope was wrapped. And only a piece of duct tape as a gag?

"You're a piss-poor actor," he said. "If you were kidnapped, the shed would've been locked, and the knots will tell them the rest." He meant the police, not the ambulance that had just pulled in, red lights popping.

The man grunted denials while Ford produced a bandana and a roll of tape. "Let me show you how it's supposed to be done," he said.

Tomlinson told the medic, who was an intern, "I'm kind of worried about my pal. He's a scientist, for god's sake—no match for the sort of twisted monster who almost killed Gracie. He ran off after the bastard, and there's no telling what might've happened if they met up. Mind if I have a look around?"

"Not until the deputies get here," she said. "A detective, whoever's in charge, they have to okay it because it's a prospective crime scene. Those are the rules."

When disappointed, Tomlinson had the endearing habit of praising those who disappointed him. "Integrity, good for you. One day, I bet you run the whole shebang. Rules are meant to be followed or we're talking total world chaos."

"Why, thanks. I appreciate your attitude."

"Fair's fair. I just hope my friend's not out there stumbling around lost, bleeding, maybe— he's the clumsy type—or trapped inside the house. He's blind as a mole without his glasses."

"How do you know he lost them?"

"It has to do with a theory regarding random phenomena—unless a four-eyed klutz is involved. They might've broken if he caught up with that nutcase. Or, quite possibly, he injured himself by running into a tree. You know how you can't stop worrying about certain people? My friend's the bookish type."

The medic snuck a look at Tomlinson, noting his outrageous hair and the kindest eyes she'd ever seen. "Give me a minute. I'll see what my lieutenant says." She started away but paused. "You gave us your only gun, right?"

"As requested. But you're more than welcome to search me." He threw his arms out to guarantee submission.

The intern chuckled, and walked toward the ambulance, where two paramedics tended to Gracie, who was coherent but in shock. She lay beneath a blanket on a gurney, an IV bag attached. The last thing she had said to Tomlinson was, "Can you get in touch with my mom somehow? I want to go home."

The first thing the girl had said while watching Ford jog away was, "Please don't let him do it. Mr. Bird killed my boyfriend and he'll kill him, too."

Mr. Bird.

Chinese slaves had called Walter Lambeth the Bird Man. The linkage produced a chill, which was silly. Lambeth had died three decades ago. If he hadn't, the bastard would be more than a hundred and ten years old. Tomlinson's faith in the paranormal had few boundaries, but what Gracie's captor had done to her ruled out a vicious old centurion. The burn he'd inflicted was an indecipherable mass of blisters. Other wounds, older wounds, were not.

The young paramedic returned, pretended to focus on her phone, then spoke: "You can't use the bathroom inside, but we can't stop you from using the bushes."

"Huh?"

"That's what I told them. Just be back before the deputies get here. **Both** of you. They'll want statements."

Sirens suggested this would happen soon.

"Oddly enough, I do need to whiz. Very perceptive. If you're married, your husband's a lucky man."

"He was until I caught him screwing around," she replied, then offered a tolerant smile. "Get going. Don't make me look like a fool, okay?"

Woman in uniform. This was an unplumbed demographic that, for decades, had been vetoed by Tomlinson's personal bias. He might've felt remorse had he not been so damn jumpy. He hurried to the back side of the property, where there were shadows, and replayed what had happened before they'd encountered Gracie. He and the biologist had come over the wall and split up, Doc saying, "Watch the front entrance. I'll see what's going on inside."

Stay out of the man's way, in other words. Then, after a series of faint screams, Tomlinson had sprinted around to find the biologist holding the girl. That's when he'd seen a hulking figure exit the building and chug off toward the woods. Possibly, the pond. He couldn't be certain. Nor was he sure who it was. Ivy Lambeth was big enough, but how many old women her size and age could run like a bear?

More likely, it was Mr. Bird. Tomlinson hadn't pressed for details because the girl was hurt and in hysterics, but she had provided a vague description. He was a huge man who wore an ornate robe and a mask she'd described as bizarre. The man had murdered Gracie's boyfriend and assaulted her many times over the days that followed. Tonight he had used a branding iron. The girl had never seen his face, only glimpses of his body. Definitely male.

Until then, Tomlinson had suspected that Mr. Bird and Ivy Lambeth were the same person. He still wasn't convinced he was wrong. Only one hulking figure had fled. If Mr. Bird existed, someone was still in the house.

That's where he went, to the back door, which opened easily. Inside was a dimly lit room with furniture that smelled of decay, the ceiling webbed with strange-looking wind chimes that clattered like glass. Near the stairs lay a broken ashtray—an old floor model on a porcelain stand. It had shattered. On the carpet was a Chinese opium pipe, an expensive one inlaid with brass and ivory. On his knees, he sniffed the bowl but didn't touch.

A chlorine odor told him it hadn't been used for opium. Tomlinson wasn't a poppy devotee, but he had smoked enough to know.

He got up and cocked his head. No sirens. Where were the cops? He got his answer when two silent cars with bouncing blue lights slammed to a stop by the gate.

Damn. Should he split now or risk a few more minutes?

An item on the stair landing lured his attention. He went up, two steps at a time. It was a leather strap with brass studs. A similar strap beckoned from the second-floor landing. Instead, he followed his instincts back down, through a hallway, to a kitchen where there was a woodstove but no fire burning.

His nose took charge after that. It wasn't just the scent of wood smoke that called him. It was a more disturbing odor; an atavistic warning of what lay ahead. A peek through a barred window confirmed that the squad cars contained a single cop each. One was busy on the radio while the other sidled toward the ambulance in typical cowboy fashion. A sort of swagger to draw attention to his Sam Browne belt.

Tomlinson ran down another hall in such a

hurry, he damn near skidded into the foundry room that Gracie had escaped. The sliding doors Ford had forced open were still open, a portion of the ambulance visible. One of the paramedics as well, but only briefly. He pressed himself against the wall and summoned his sensory powers.

Something had called him here. An odor. What was it?

He sniffed while his eyes absorbed details. Suspended from the ceiling was an industrial bellows, antique leather and wood. It resembled a gigantic tick. The metal spout pointed to a furnace, where flames roared within an open hearth. Beyond, on a table, was a weird machine with knobs and a lens. A projector of some type, very old, that cast a frozen image onto a brick wall.

Geezus. A crocodile. A big one.

What the hell?

Certain photographic details nagged at him as if important. It was his nose that finally provided understanding. Coal fires, wood fires, fires of peat and autumn leaves, all carried their unique signature. But none registered with the impact of an ancient, barbaric fuel.

Flames reflected off Tomlinson's eyes when he zoomed in on a source that could be perceived but was no longer visible: burning hair and flesh and the residue of bone. At the base of the hearth lay a swatch of melted nylon hair from a wig. It was blond.

Ivy Lambeth had gone into the flames—or someone wanted to give that impression.

Nearby was a singed swatch of leather binding and a page from the Book of Genesis. The Barlow family Bible had been burned, too.

Tomlinson did an about-face and returned to the stairs.

Ford, sitting in an unmarked car, told the detective, "I understand that asking the same questions over and over is procedure, but I really don't have anything to add. Later, if something new comes to me, how about I give you a call?"

"Just a few more minutes. See, the problem is, sure, details always vary here and there. Two sides to every story, right? But the guy you're accusing of assault—rape, too, sounds like—he tells a totally different story."

The temptation was to respond, **Wouldn't you?** That would have been a mistake. Law enforcement types, even veterans, were quick to interpret the mildest of sarcasm as aggression. For a civilian, no matter what country, no matter what language, the first rule of conciliation was this: never, ever piss off a cop.

Ford asked, "What did he say? Maybe that would help."

"The guy? That's not the way this works. I ask the questions, you answer."

"There's no need to keep his name a secret. He told me it was Slaten, Slaten Johnson, which I don't believe. Slaten, maybe, but not Johnson. He claimed he'd been traveling with the Barlow girl, Gracie, when—"

"Okay, here it is." The detective, whose name was Werner, turned so they were facing. "The guy claims he ran because he was scared. That you beat the shit out of him. No, you taped his hands first, then beat the shit out of him and threatened to leave him on an anthill. How do you respond to that?"

The second rule of conciliation was never, ever lie to a cop—unless you've committed a felony.

Ford said, "He's got quite an imagination. I'm no expert, but wouldn't there be bruises, or cuts, or marks of some kind, on his face? I didn't notice any. Oh"—he tried to underplay what came next—"taped his hands? If that's true, it should be easy to confirm. Wouldn't tape have left residue of some type on his wrists? Even a Band-Aid leaves that sticky stuff when you pull it off. Did he say what kind of tape?"

It was obvious from the detective's reaction that he hadn't checked. "Wait here," he said, and walked to a second unmarked car. In the mirror, Ford could see another detective questioning Slaten, the guy he'd beaten the shit out of, but only after removing the tape he'd used, then the bandana that had shielded the guy's wrists from telltale adhesive. Well, he hadn't actually beaten Slaten—just a carefully placed elbow or knee to keep him talking.

Detective Werner returned and sat without closing the door. On the dash was a mini recorder. He spoke into it, saying the interview was concluded. Date, time, and other particulars were added before he switched it off.

"How about we go for a walk? The guy's a scumball, we both know it. I don't care what you did, but I have to make it all fit when I write it up."

The third rule of conciliation was never, ever confide the truth to a cop after denying guilt regarding a felony.

"I'll tell you anything you want to know," the biologist said. "But I'm concerned about my friend, Dr. Tomlinson. Did he leave?"

"Doctor—**him**?"

"Not a real one. A Ph.D. I didn't get a chance to talk to him before the ambulance pulled out."

"So that's how he managed it." The detective looked at the gate, which was open, then started walking. "Crap. I figured he was related to the girl and that's why the EMTs let him ride to the hospital. We still haven't questioned him, which means he either lied or charmed the hell out of someone."

Thank god. Tomlinson couldn't be trusted with a lie or the truth when the police were involved.

When he and the detective had left portable lights and crime scene techs behind, Ford said, "Slaten claimed he and Gracie were traveling together and they stopped here to buy bamboo. Some special variety. That he had nothing to do with hurting the girl because he'd been locked up in a shed the whole time. That's bullshit."

"Which one?" They were on the back side of the property, where both sheds were visible beneath stars and an occasional strobe of heat lightning.

"I have no idea," Ford said. "That's my point. He was in the house and ran out the back door after we found the girl. You saw the condition she's in. Not just the third-degree burns where he branded her, but the other injuries. She'd been beaten and raped. That's the way I read it, so I went after him when he ran. Wouldn't you have done the same?"

Detective Werner, who could pass as a football lineman, chuckled. "I don't know. He's a pretty big dude. Ballsy, what you did. Then I look at your ears and think, hey, Dr. Ford did some wrestling, and he's got the shoulders to go with it. Okay, so you took him down and beat him cross-eyed. Better yet, you did it without leaving any marks that I could see. Great. But tell me something, just between us, **confidentially**. Which shed was he in when you found him? That would save our guys some time, at least."

Ford's mind transitioned to a safe harbor; a cache of lies programmed during five days at an interrogation course at the Navy Remote Training Site somewhere in Maine. He said, "I told you what happened," and shrugged the way men do when there's nothing left to say.

"I'm asking for your help, Dr. Ford. There's more going on here than you realize. Trust me, maybe I can help you."

Ford wondered what that meant but didn't bite. "I've got a ninety-minute drive home. Like I said, if I think of something, I'll call."

He started toward the pond but the detective blocked his way. "One more thing. You were right about the tape residue. Not even a smidgen. So the asshole either made up one doozy of a tale"—the man edged closer—"or you're really good at this shit. Which is it?"

Ford said, "I just realized what the problem is. Gracie must've backed the guy's story. Is that it? In her condition, you don't really believe—"

"His name isn't Slaten Johnson. You're right about that, too. We ran his prints. He's Slaten Lambeth. Does that mean anything to you?"

"Nothing other than he probably has a right to be here. You're not suggesting I was trespassing when—"

"Don't worry about that. In North Florida, the DLE is working on a string of assaults, robberies—a bunch of shit—and you might have got the guy. The tattoo rapist. You don't read the papers?"

"Was he already a suspect?"

"Along with about a dozen others. Lambeth, or whoever the psycho is, is a pro when it comes to cleaning up a crime scene. So far, it fits pretty good. The guy doesn't live here. He lives out of his van and only comes by when he needs a place to flop. That's what he claims anyway. There's something else. We think he might have put his aunt in the furnace before he tried to get away. Clean, you know? A commercial furnace—old, yeah, but still hot enough to melt pig iron, so you can imagine what it would do to a body."

It took Ford a moment to process what he'd just heard. "Not thirty minutes ago, I saw her. I told you that. She ran off carrying a knife after—"

"All I know is, the deputies found what they

found. A female, or what's left of her. That all has to be checked out."

Werner backed a bit to encourage conversation. "Doc—can I call you Doc?—I don't give a damn what you did to Lambeth. Hell, I'm envious. All we can do is try to put him away for a long, long time. To make that happen? I need the **truth**—including the real evidence I'm sure you did a damn good job of hiding."

12

When news got out that two island-ers had saved a girl's life and helped capture a homicidal rapist, business picked up at Dinkin's Bay Marina. It got better when stories about the suspected Tattoo Killer revealed the girl was the niece of a venerated fishing guide. Fox News shot a remote from the parking lot. CBS came to Sanibel, too, but chose the bird sanctuary as a backdrop.

That was fine with business owners. There was always a lull in tourism around mid-June.

No one was happier than Mack, who ran the marina. T-shirt sales tripled the day after the story broke. He did a booming business—in hats, bait, fuel, and fish sandwiches—as well.

"People have to eat," he told JoAnn, who was helping out as fry cook. "If we run low on grouper, thaw out some mullet. What do reporters know?"

He might have surfed the financial boon through the rest of the month if the two heroes had been willing to cooperate. They had not. Now, after three days of refusing interviews, even a profitable week was in doubt. It was Thursday. Tomorrow, the marina's traditional Friday night party was key. Beer sales alone would make the monthly nut, if those yahoos made an appearance. So what the hell was their problem?

That was the question Mack posed, more or less, when he finally cornered Tomlinson. "Are you crazy? Think of the women you've disappointed, for god's sake. They'd flock here in droves if they saw you on the evening news."

That, at least, got the hipster's attention. They were near the maintenance shed, screened from the parking lot by a fence. This provided time and privacy to think. Finally, Tomlinson replied, "Tempting, man, but I can't."

"Why? The cops told you not to talk? Screw them. What's a cop ever done for you?" Mack knew his audience. He let that fester, before adding, "I suppose they ordered you **not** to come to the party tomorrow night."

Tomlinson puffed up a little. "**Ordered me?**

Man, you know that wouldn't sail. Screw them, absolutely. If I want to be there, I'll—" He paused. "I would be there, too . . . But I don't know, man. What about reporters? You know how chatty I get after a few beers."

"Who cares?" Mack said. "It's not like you have to talk to them. A pushy lot, the whole bunch—especially that blonde from Fox News."

"The blonde?"

"Yep."

"The one with the—"

"That's her. She was here an hour ago with her crew. Said she'd be back tonight." Mack, who claimed to be from New Zealand, shared a Down Under wink. "Have you ever been alone with a newscaster aboard that boat of yours?"

Tomlinson, loosening up, replied, "Sure, but never a Republican newscaster," then laughed because he knew what Mack was doing. "This is a slow time of year, I get it, but there're bigger issues at stake. I just got back from visiting Gracie. She wouldn't mind if I told my story, but—"

"Tootsie Barlow's niece?"

"Gracie, yeah. She'd understand, but people would think I'm nuts to put her personal safety at risk. Doc especially."

Mack said carefully, "What people think bothers you?"

"Don't be silly. I'm worried about her. The guy they arrested for assaulting her isn't the—" He stopped, backtracked. "I don't want to advertise the fact she's still alive; worse, where she is. Let me ask you something, Graeme."

Graeme MacKinley was the marina owner's full name.

"Fire away."

"The cops might be sure they got the right guy, but I'm not. Or even if it was a guy who did all that terrible crap to her."

"I don't understand. You think a woman's capable of—"

"Not necessarily. Could've been a monster, neither male or female. A leviathan of some sort, so, yeah, the TV newscasters would love to hear what I have to say. I get it, man. You really think I should take my story public?"

The marina owner cleared his throat and backed away a step. "Only if you want to be fitted for a straitjacket. What the hell's a **leviathan**?"

"The names vary. My personal suspicion? We're dealing with a demon savage, a manifestation of evil from the past that inhabits whatever corporeal form fits the bill. It's hard to explain. I drew a sketch of it today. If you're interested, I can run back to my van and—"

"Don't bother, it can wait," Mack said in a

rush. He rolled his eyes, patted a pocket, and pulled out the stub of a cigar. "You know, maybe it is smart to keep that story to yourself."

"Think so? I don't know . . . I was just warming to the idea. Wouldn't mind meeting that blonde. She's the one with attitude and the killer B's?"

"All in the eye of the beholder, but why sink to her level? Doc, on the other hand, doesn't give a damn about journalism or politics. He's the one the reporters should talk to. I'd ask him myself, but he's been holed up like a hermit ever since you got back."

Ford hadn't been holed up. He'd been on the move, staying at different places, only returning to his lab when there was work to do.

"There's your answer," Tomlinson said. "I'll bounce it off Doc first thing. You know, subtly; let him broach the subject, then put the possibility out there. Manifestations of energy are mutable. That's a fact of physics."

"You do that," Mack said, and left a smoke trail as he walked away.

Ford's lab was an old house on pilings in the shallows of Dinkin's Bay, just down from the marina where, on this hot Thursday eve, people who lived aboard were buttoned in with AC, and TV screens that brightened the boat cabins along A Dock.

"Air-conditioning will be the death of natural selection," Tomlinson remarked. He lounged in a hammock strung beneath fans on a porch, the lab's screen door closed but the inner door wide to stars and a southerly breeze. "Canned air, canned heat, canned lifestyles. Gad. Pre-death chambers, man. We sprint from canister to canister like lizards diving into holes." Across miles of dark water, beyond the entrance to Dinkin's Bay, condo lights stained the horizon with a milky glaze. That's what he was referring to.

Ford, from inside, said, "Have you ever read the **Nassau Guardian**? It's all tourist bureau crap. Good luck finding any real news. Wait . . . here's something."

"Exactly, man. Insulated from death by life, and from life by thermostats. You ever wonder how much mold and shit we breathe in from random encounters with AC? There are enough demons in the world without manufacturing our own." A moment later, he said it again: "Demons. They're real, man."

The biologist replied, "When you get up for another beer, close the fridge this time." He had found a story beneath a small headline:

RARE SCUBA ACCIDENT
DIVE OPERATOR BLAMELESS

Three bland paragraphs reported that Saudi national James P. Lutz had died after an equipment malfunction while diving Glass Window Reef off Dunmore Town. Lutz, age thirty-five, was reported to be an experienced diver, but authorities suspected that poor equipment maintenance, and alcohol, had played a role.

That was eight days ago.

"Never mind," Ford said, pushing back his chair. "A beer sounds pretty good, all of a sudden. You want yours in a glass? I put a couple in the freezer."

"How can you be so cheery when I'm so damn bummed after my trip into town?"

"It's this riveting conversation . . . Hang on . . ."

In the center of the lab was a workstation: a black epoxy table with a sink, faucets, electrical outlets, and a gas cock for a Bunsen burner. Along the east wall, a dozen lighted aquaria were animated by sea creatures. He stopped to clean an intake filter and noticed a strange drawing lying on the bench.

"What's this?"

Tomlinson had left the drawing there on purpose but said, "I can't see through walls, man."

"Since when? It looks like a Chinese symbol. It has to be yours."

Bare feet slapped the deck, and Tomlinson entered the room. "You haven't listened to a word I've said. When I got here, I told you to take a look at my sketch when you were done at the computer. I just got back from visiting Gracie. Did you hear that part?"

"What's the symbol mean?"

"You tell me," Tomlinson said, then remembered he was speaking to a man unsuited for the Rorschach test. "It's a sketch of the scar tissue left after she was branded. No . . . of my interpretation, because the details haven't taken shape yet. The burn got infected, so she's back in the hospital with the bandages off. She'd never seen it before, and the mirror thing was backasswards, so I hit up the nurses for a Sharpie. Rice paper would have been better, but I made do."

As he studied it, Ford muttered, "Slaten Lambeth did this."

"Branded her, I dunno, man. Maybe, maybe not."

"What's that supposed to mean? The detective I talked to thinks Lambeth did the same thing to at least four girls, mostly around Gainesville. Not with a branding iron, but tattoos. He ought to be shot."

Tomlinson let his pal cool down by saying,

"The symbol, sort of let your eyes blur. What's the first thing pops into your mind?"

"That I don't read Chinese."

"Okay, the second thing. Don't think; ask yourself, 'What am I seeing?'"

"A sloppy excuse for a design. A stamp of ownership; something obscene or humiliating, that would be my guess. On two of his victims, he tattooed **whore**, in Cantonese, on their foreheads. The electric chair would be okay, too." Ford tossed the sketch on the bench. "You've researched it by now. What's it mean?"

"Again, it's my interpretation. The blistering's too bad to actually know for sure."

"Your best guess, then."

"We'll get to that."

"I don't doubt we will. You've been setting me up for something ever since you got here. Mack wants us to do interviews, is that it? No . . . he wants **me** to do interviews. Your feelings are hurt, so you came up with some metaphysical gobbledygook so you can refuse honorably if he does happen to ask."

"Whew! That's pretty damn close, man. You're coming around."

It was an amiable way to postpone the topic until a mellower interlude, which was a couple of beers later. The biologist had his Celestron telescope on the upper deck, focused a few degrees south of the meridian. Saturn was there,

Mars nearby, as was a brilliant star, Antares. Too bright for Mars to reveal its red spot, so they were soon done.

"Okay," Ford said, sitting back. "Here's what you were going to tell me. It's about Gracie, right? She's convinced her forty-year-old boyfriend couldn't possibly have been the lunatic who held her captive. And he certainly didn't murder his beloved old Aunt Ivy by burning her alive. Am I close?"

"One of the cops told you."

"Correct. What I hope is, you don't encourage Gracie to believe there's a possibility she's right."

"That's what I'm afraid of, she might be. Did your buddy say anything about Ivy Lambeth having another nephew? There has to be someone else involved. I can't picture Slaten working construction, or dropping off groceries. That's what the cops told you, right? She was a shut-in, so her nephew came by every week, the one who dropped the receipt you found."

Ford was getting frustrated. "Listen to me. There were only three people in the house that night—Gracie, Ivy Lambeth, and Slaten. You should know, you went inside. They're all accounted for, now that dental records have confirmed it was the old woman. Those smelting furnaces burn hot. As far as Gracie goes, you're aware of the Stockholm syndrome. You know what it does to victims. That's why she feels compelled to remain loyal."

"Did you tell your cop buddy I went inside?"

"He's a detective, not a cop, and a pretty good one. He asked, yeah, but of course I didn't say anything. Fact is, I don't know what you did other than confirm the place was empty. Why no details? That bothers me."

Tomlinson had been going over it in his head, what he'd seen and heard in a building that was a lifeless echo chamber of misery.

"I found some stuff I left for the cops to figure out. Ivy's blond wig, and a page from what I think was Tootsie's family Bible. Whoever tossed it into the furnace was in a hurry, or more concerned with getting rid of the confession written in the back. Did your cop friend say anything about finding pieces of a burned Bible?"

Ford said, "You're holding something back. Sooner or later, you'll let it slip, so you might as well tell me now."

Tomlinson nodded, and gazed into his beer. "Bones. That's why I didn't tell you. Human bones. On the second floor was this god-awful chamber made of old concrete. A wood chamber, I think, to feed the furnace. I found femurs, ribs, and skulls with bits of hair—several, their braids still attached. I think I mentioned

Walter Lambeth and what he did to his Chinese slaves."

"Thanks. I can figure out the rest. You felt some sort of moral obligation, so you gathered them up and hid them, didn't you? Or buried them, maybe. That's why you were gone for so long. The police would've made it known if they'd found human bones. I thought you went in there hoping to find the stuff stolen from the cabin. Geezus, sometimes I . . . No wonder you didn't tell me."

There was another reason Tomlinson had searched the house. He moved toward it, saying, "Put yourself in Gracie's place. She and Slaten had been sleeping together for more than two months. Mask or no mask, she would've known the difference between her first and only lover and a crazed sadist. Not that Slaten isn't a vicious criminal, but here's the thing: a leopard can't change its spots and a man can't change the shape of his dick."

"She told you that?"

"I'm trying to help Tootsie, so she trusts me. Slaten talked her into doing some really nasty stuff—it's family business I can't go into— but, yeah, that's what she said. Mr. Bird—she still calls him that—wasn't circumcised, plus the size thing. Then there's the way she was branded. Here . . ." He flattened the sketch on the table, and got up to turn on the deck lights. "It took a while, but I found a similar glyph of an oracle bone that dates back to the Shang Dynasty. That was more than two thousand years ago."

"A photo of an old glyph, you mean. You had to guess because the skin's not healed yet. You said so yourself."

"Not a guess; I intuited. I don't know the exact meaning, not in an academic sense, but I know what it represents."

"Oracle bones foretell the future, I suppose?"

"And how to control it. Stick with me here, Doc, try to stay open-minded. The Chinese, whether Buddhist or Taoist, embraced the doctrines of karma—including retribution for past actions. Cyclical existence, too, which they called samsara. The future can be changed with the oracle's help."

The biologist wasn't going to be lured into another mystic maze. He held the sketch to the light. "It looks like a number seven drawn by someone on acid. Before you visited Gracie, you didn't—"

"Geezus-frogs, give me a little credit, huh? I agree about the drug angle. That's the only thing that makes me wonder if you and the cops might be right. Slaten almost got her hooked on a synthetic, some junk even I wouldn't try. It's called flakka. They used e-cigarettes usually, but I found an opium pipe in the house, so Mr. Bird, whoever he is, was using. And forcing Gracie to share, which is why her memory blanks."

They talked about that, the possibility she'd been so heavily drugged, she hadn't recognized her own boyfriend. As Tomlinson explained, the effects varied. After just a few hits, some women experienced a euphoric high that peaked in orgasm. Others ripped their clothes off and jumped from bridges because they felt like their bodies were on fire.

"The same with guys, but with a twist if they overdo it. Did you read about the college kid who busted down a door and beat his neighbor to death? They'd never even met. By the time cops showed up, the kid had chewed off the neighbor's nose. Cannibalism, man."

That was enough for Ford. He went inside, after remarking, "I don't have to try the stuff to believe Gracie didn't recognize the man who assaulted her."

That struck a strange guilty chord in Tomlinson. He mulled it over until he understood. He had no right to encourage Gracie's belief that Slaten wasn't her attacker because he himself had never experienced a head full of flakka. By all accounts, it was truly wicked shit. Should he try it or pussy out? That was the question. Usually, the rule was simple in these matters:

when flummoxed by a behavioral decision, never say no before sunrise.

Not when it came to synthetics.

Wicked. His attention returned to the sketch, which they'd failed to discuss. These tangents aligned after a bit and he realized maybe it was for the best.

Why amuse the biologist with a symbol that resembled a demonic bird?

Late Friday afternoon, Mack's hopes regarding the reluctant heroes got a boost when fishing guide Hannah Smith appeared. A June squall had chased her and a couple of clients across the bay while lightning popped behind them.

Everyone liked Hannah, but it was more than that for Marion Ford. Their relationship had ended, but he still loved her, which surprised Mack almost as much as the fact they'd fallen in love in the first place. The biologist was a taciturn guy. Hard to read, but even months after their breakup he'd stand a little straighter, and his smile broadened, whenever the woman was around.

Mack said to Jeth Nicholes, who worked behind the counter when he wasn't fishing, "Something tells me we might have a good crowd tonight. Where'd you put those business cards I set aside?"

"Cards the newspaper reporters left here?"

"The TV news, for god's sake. Nobody reads newspapers anymore. You didn't cancel that extra keg of beer, did you?"

"You told me to."

"Call 'em back and re-order, and get another bushel of oysters while you're at it. Hurry up. I told you to get the smoker going, too, but I don't smell any smoke."

Jeth's stutter had all but disappeared except when under stress. "Take a look out the dah-dah . . . the freakin' window. The wind's blowing it the other way."

It was true, and another source of hope. In June, squalls were a daily event—cloudbursts that drenched the islands but soon dissipated. This storm, though, might last a while. It was pushing a lot of wind. Mack considered the towering clouds, noted their green fluorescence, and hurried outside to the docks, where Hannah was hunched over, tying her skiff.

"Long time no see," he said. "Looks like a nasty one."

"What?" She looked up. "Didn't hear you for the wind. Yeah, I've never seen a squall so thick with lightning. It nearly caught us off Woodring Point."

Good, Mack thought. "You'd be nuts not

to wait the storm out, and the timing's perfect. Tell your clients the first beer's on me, and the food's free if you stay for the—" He stopped when Hannah stood to face him. He stared for a moment at the baggy blouse she wore. "What in the world . . . You're . . . Are you . . . ?"

"In my fourth month." She smiled. "This kid's going to grow up breathing saltwater."

Mack's eyes drifted down shore to Ford's stilt house while he stammered, "Uhh . . . good. Great. That's wonderful news."

"The best ever," Hannah said. "And I know what you're thinking. No, it's not Doc's. You don't know the father."

"Oh." Mack's eyes made a random sweep past a line of expensive yachts.

Hannah noticed. "No one on the island knows him. He's a good person, though. A fine man—someone I met a while back, and it just . . . well, happened."

"Oh," Mack said.

Hannah had an easy way of brushing her hair back that reminded him of Westerns, movies with women who rode roping ponies and could shoot a gun. "Mind keeping an eye on my clients?" she asked, walking off. "It's about time I had a talk with Doc."

13

What Ford told Hannah, the two of them standing on the deck watching the squall approach, was, "I've read that the average lightning bolt is an inch wide and five miles long. It's a strange statistic to remember, I know. But I'm trying to decide whether to try one of the new grounding systems for boats. About half the experts say it's a good idea."

Hannah was interested in all things nautical. "The others?"

"Some say a grounded system actually attracts lightning. Others think it doesn't matter either way. More sailboats get hit, for obvious reasons, but the odds go up for powerboats if it's a cat hull or multi-hull. Not a clue why.

Could be there's a correlation between bottom mass and reduced conductivity."

Science, useful maritime trivia, provided a refuge after she'd told him about her child.

Three times he had asked, "Are you sure?"

Twice she had replied, "Yes," and finally, "Please, don't ask again. I can't say I'm disappointed, but I will say I would've been just as happy if it was yours."

Then they were inside in the lab, which smelled of fish, formaldehyde, disinfectant, books, and barnacles that grew at water level on pilings below the pine floor. The house swayed in the wind. Rain hammered the tin roof.

"I should get back to my clients."

"In this?"

"I don't mind getting wet."

Ford had been tempted to respond, **That's obvious,** which would have ended their relationship quickly—and permanently. He was not immune to bitterness, but dismissed destructive behavior as he might ignore a virus. "Not with all this lightning," he'd said. "How about you call the marina and give your clients an update while I make some tea."

Hannah, with her Deep South roots, had fun with it, asking, "Sweet tea? Don't tell me you finally learned how. That settles it, Doc. I'm not letting our friendship go, no matter what you say."

"Hot tea, I meant. The guy, the child's father, he won't mind me being in the picture?"

The child's father was dead. Hannah wasn't ready to share the truth about that, or who the man was, or how it had happened. "We're not a couple, which I knew going in. Fact is, I don't want to be a couple with anyone. Not now. I should make that clear, too."

The common bond of fly-fishing became another refuge. She asked about the video he'd sent, referring to the place as that "little tarpon pond." "Do you think anyone's ever fished it?"

"Not in a long time. There's an old house nearby, and people who lived there were . . . well, not particularly friendly. I'll be there for a while starting next week, so we'd have the place to ourselves, if you're serious."

Hannah was always serious when it came to fly-fishing. The subject carried them through the squall into a post-rain twilight. She'd left with vague driving directions to Chino Hole after warning him about snakes, particularly Burmese pythons.

Ford had warned her, "Don't mention fishing with me to Tomlinson, okay? He's got this weird thing about you visiting that area. It has to do with old-time Florida, some crime committed way back, and he's linked it for some reason with . . . Well, you know how he is."

That was Friday.

Today was Monday.

Ford turned left off Route 29 and stopped in front of what had been home to Walter Lambeth and his troubled progeny. Police had released the place as a crime scene. The yellow tape was gone, replaced by a barrage of **No Trespassing** signs posted by the federal government.

Ford was surprised. A large parcel of land, including the pond, had officially passed into government hands as of today. But how had the feds taken control of the house so fast? Ivy Lambeth had died less than two weeks ago, and her nephew, Slaten, although in jail without bond, was very much alive. Hadn't the family had the same deal as Tootsie Barlow?

Wondering about that caused him to wonder about the old fishing guide. Barlow had returned to the Keys because he'd come to associate the cabin with bad luck—and no wonder after all that had happened. Ford didn't know the whole litany of events, but the robbery and news about Gracie had pushed the old man near the edge. The final nudge was something that Gracie had confessed to her uncle while still in the hospital.

Tomlinson, who'd left for Key Largo this morning, had been unable to reveal details shared in confidence.

Ford got out and took another look at the

steam engine boiler. Hidden in the weeds lay a massive cast-iron pot and a length of tubing shaped like a swan's neck. All components related to a moonshine still. **Mangrove Lightning**, the Florida version made with sugarcane.

He kicked around the weeds some more and found what resembled chunks of igneous glass. Beautifully smooth, in varied rainbow colors. Nearby was more copper tubing.

Copper was as good as cash to druggies and other thieves. Why hadn't someone stole it?

In a way, someone had, Ford realized. The **No Trespassing** signs were proof.

That wasn't his problem. He'd worked enough small government contracts to know not to ask questions outside his field. Just focus on the assigned task. That's what he intended to do, get his first look at the pond, but as he was pulling away, a heavy truck turned in from the main road. It stopped, backed up, then stopped again.

If not for this, Ford would have driven away. Instead, he paid attention. It was a big white GMC diesel with a hydraulic bucket perched above the cab, the kind used by utility companies and tree trimmers. Only one person inside the cab, probably male, definitely large. The distance was too great to be certain, but the behavior suggested the driver had stopped because he didn't expect to see another vehicle.

Ford stuck his arm out the window and offered a mild wave.

The driver backed to a spot wide enough to turn around, then drove away. No company logo, the windows were tinted, and the Florida license plate was too far away to read.

Wrong address, the biologist told himself, but there was a chance he was being tailed again—by the same porn mobsters who'd tried to kill him in Nassau. The possibility demanded he at least get a license number, so he followed. By the time he got back to the highway, only one distant vehicle was visible, and it disappeared around a curve.

Ford pursued in an outdated truck built to last, not for speed. At the intersection of 29 and the Tamiami Trail, he turned west, because why would a utility truck venture into the Everglades? Sixty miles of sawgrass separated the closest populated area from Miami.

He got lucky. Traffic was sparse, and he soon spotted the truck. When he was close enough, he memorized the tag number, then pulled alongside to get a look at the driver.

Damn . . . the wrong truck. A Florida Power & Light logo left no doubt.

He made a U-turn.

The difference between a lake and a pond, in Ford's mind, was could he land a seaplane?

Not here. Chino Hole was a pond, the size of a small crater. It was a limestone implosion, known in the trade as a collapsed sinkhole. A dive would confirm this, he believed, but first he wanted a look at the shoreline.

Pythons weren't a worry, but an alligator big enough to eat him was. Water moccasins could be nasty, too.

Wearing snake leggings, he set off with a machete. Remnants of a path led him past a stone wall to where cypress dominated the shallows and discouraged access. He splashed ahead anyway.

It was hot on this June morning. The footing was slick. Mosquitoes clouded around despite Ford's long-sleeved chino shirt and head net. After a few minutes, he stopped to study an indentation that arrowed shoreward.

An alligator slide.

This was expected. Gators could be found in any ditch where water collected anywhere in Florida. Other than that, they were no different than most animals. They used they same paths over and over. This one looked well traveled and wasn't unusually wide.

Two more slides lay ahead, then a third, in the space of a hundred yards. It was twice the width of the others, but not massive. To confirm this, he followed the slide until vines impaired visibility. This was nesting season. Stumble onto a female protecting her eggs, she'd lunge and bite, or try to knock him down with her tail.

Ford doubled back and let his eyes settle on the pond. Somewhere in its depths, he expected to find vents and adjoining chambers, variations in current flow, and other elements associated with karst formations. The peninsula's geologic interchange moved in relentless slow motion.

A lot was going on under the surface.

He was already noting data to be used later. Native aquatic plants—white lilies, spike rushes, arrowhead plants—flourished among a few invasive exotics, such as hydrilla, which was a snaking ornamental from Asia, and at least one Chinese tallow tree.

He sloshed toward the tree and saw his first carousel of tarpon. Fish the length of his arm sliced the surface in unison, then were gone. The tree was displaced by thoughts of Hannah and her skiff. There was no place to launch a boat here, although it was pleasant to imagine. The woman was the most eloquent flycaster he'd ever seen.

She was also pregnant with another man's child, he reminded himself, so, **Move on.**

He did. On the opposite shore was a spot that suggested he might be wrong about a launching place. It was a delta of marl that funneled ashore over weeds crushed by something as wide as a boat and as heavy. No gator on Earth could create such a slide, so maybe that's what he'd found, a makeshift boat ramp.

The biologist was a careful man. He looked for tracks anyway while he followed the swath inland but found no sign of man or reptile. Weather was to blame. This time of year, storms cleaned the slate almost every afternoon. He continued ahead, expecting to find an access solid enough for a trailer, but the path petered out. The machete took him another fifty yards, where, through the trees, he saw a junkyard of old railroad boxcars.

Good. That told him there was a road. A skiff the size of Hannah's was too big, but a light aluminum johnboat could be dragged to the pond—if he had such a boat, which he didn't.

He arrived at his truck with the intentions of finding one. By then, he was so hot and muddy, he chose to do a quick mask-and-fins recon to cool off. He swam to the middle of the pond, did a few bounce dives until the bottom vanished in spiraling darkness. It was a satisfying fact to confirm. Chino Hole wasn't just another seepage pit built by landscapers, or shallow depression created by nature. The damn thing was deep.

In Ford's mind, the definitions of **lake** and **pond** changed. Chino Hole was both, and also a **crater**.

On his back, he watched for gators while kicking toward shore. Gulls battled with crows overhead while a great blue heron stalked among cattails. A distant swirl on the surface grabbed his attention. Something big had nearly breached. He sculled upright, using his fins for elevation.

A tarpon? If so, it was a mature fish way over a hundred pounds. Or possibly a huge Florida gar.

If not . . . ? Well, he needed to get his ass out of the water until he was sure.

Several times, he paused to glance back before the bottom was shallow enough to stand. He scrutinized the surface after consulting his watch. Curious alligators, when on the move, seldom stayed under more than a minute or two. A dozen more immature tarpon showed themselves. Dragonflies hovered; an osprey crashed the surface, then struggled off with what looked like a good-sized bass.

Ford's attention returned to the shoreline's finned inhabitants. Later, he would do a controlled fish count, but for now a sampling was enough. He swam up and back through the shallows and made mental notes. Among the eelgrass, schools of small fish—bream, bluegill, crappie, and others—spooked away. Bream— they were also called sunfish—were good indicators of a lake's health. A couple of lunker largemouth bass also indicated the predatory chain was in balance.

In his head was the perverse hope he might see a lionfish. His theory about the Atlantis Hotel aquarium, and a karst linkage to Florida, was to blame. Exotic species were undesirable. He saw none. That didn't mean peacock bass, cichlids, tilapia, and a long list of other exotics, didn't live here. Same with a lionfish or two, but the absence did suggest their numbers were small.

The pond's fringe area was a narrow band of limestone. It was heavily vegetated and dropped off fast. That was good, too. Better for a healthy fish population overall, and better for the flow of resident water.

Enough. He dried off, changed, and got in his truck, determined to find a small aluminum boat. Satellites interceded when he got to the main road. Multiple chimes told him he'd missed some calls. Two from Tomlinson.

"What's the emergency?" he asked when his friend picked up.

"How far are you from Tootsie's cabin?"

"Can't it wait? I need to buy a johnboat, and need to get it done before—"

"Tootsie's not on Key Largo. If he is, I can't find him. Drive to his cabin and call me, okay? I've got a bad feeling about—"

"Come on. We've been through this once already. You said he was expecting you."

"Yeah, he was supposed to drive down yesterday, but I don't think he made it. He's got a trailer home near Marina Del Mar. I checked. It's buttoned tight, even the storm shutters are down, and his truck's not here."

"What did the marina people say?"

"You think I'd bother you if someone had seen him? Doc, come on, man."

"Who'd you ask?"

"The girl behind the counter, and a couple of others. A lot of his neighbors go north this time of year. I'll keep looking while you—"

"Yesterday was the new moon. That means good tides in the backcountry. If you were a fishing guide who had to stay out of the sun, where would you go to talk fishing?"

"The bar at the Pilot House. They haven't seen him either, but I see what you're saying. The poor old dude will be jonesing for the flats."

"What about bait shops? Ask around. His niece, Gracie, did you call her?"

"Doc," Tomlinson said, "just make a quick stop at his cabin, that's all I'm asking. It's a base that needs to be touched."

The biologist made another U-turn.

Satellites didn't intrude again until he was on the porch of the cabin, which, apparently, was the only conduit to the ionosphere for miles.

Tomlinson was calling again, but the signal failed.

For Tomlinson, the yelp of a steam whistle silenced Florida, and the island of Key Largo, shifting time and place. For a moment, it was 1925 in the Everglades again, not Marina Del Mar on this nervous June afternoon.

A second whistle blast kick-started reality. Or did it? He had to wonder, as he pocketed his phone. Puttering into the boat basin was Bogart's tramp steamer, the **African Queen**. The real deal from the movie, not some fake. The British flag was raised, people aboard. She'd been refurbished since her days when dry-docked at the nearby Holiday Inn parking lot.

That was years ago. There, the vessel had been displayed naked to the weather, chained like a beast to a commemorative plaque. A forlorn sight, indeed, at 3 a.m. on a particular weekday eve that was still a treasured memory.

It was the juxtaposition that had thrown Tomlinson.

"The **African Queen**." He smiled. "I drank tequila, got lucky, got sick, got lucky again, and woke up on that boat, all in one short night." He was chatting with the marina's dockmaster. Or the dockmaster's helper. Impossible to be certain without a name tag on the guy's shirt. Tomlinson had stopped him outside the office, where they had clear view of the boat basin and Port Largo Canal.

"The same **African Queen**?" the dockmaster asked.

"Yep. Still have a scar from the wood box. Sharp edges, you know, and there isn't much room aft of the boiler. It's not the only reason I prefer sailboats, but it ranks right up there."

The guy, who had some hipster in him, was impressed. Or bored on this off-season afternoon, when a lot of the blue water fishing machines sat idle. "Wow, that is so very cool. There aren't many men who can say that. The same girl both times or were there two?"

They'd been talking for a while, an easy back-and-forth, because the famous fishing guide's name opened doors. Tomlinson might have shared details under different circumstances but shrugged the question off as indelicate. "Back to what I was saying about Captain Barlow, what did you find out?"

"I got this for you." The guy produced a chamber of commerce map and pointed to a spot he'd circled. "Our maintenance guy has been around forever and he said Tootsie used to keep a tackle shed here"—he pointed—"on Blackwater Sound around mile marker 105. Not a big place, an actual shed like the commercial guys used for storage, but big enough he'd bunk there sometimes after a late charter. The area's real Keysey, so he could get away with it. You know, dogs and pickups, and the roads are mostly shell, like back in the pot-hauling days. Maybe he still owns the place, the maintenance guy didn't know."

"Pot hauling," the Zen master mused. "Yeah, the good ol' days are gone forever."

"I bet you've got more than just stories," the dockmaster replied, which, in fact, was a discreet inquiry. It was the way commerce worked outside the system.

Tomlinson took something from his pocket and shook hands, saying, "Thanks for your help. While we're on the subject, I've got a question. You ever heard of a badass synthetic called flakka?"

The dockmaster's mood did a one-eighty. "Don't even mention that shit around here. You want trouble, try one of the biker bars."

Calusa Bait was oceanside, mile marker 90. Capt. Pete's Bait & Tackle was bayside, near marker 103. No one had seen the famous fishing guide, but everyone knew where he lived. So why not try his double-wide near Capt. Jack's Mobile Home Estates, just south of 104, close to Wet Dog Charters?

It was the Keysey way of giving directions down here in this one-lane country; a coral tail that curved seaward like a meteor snagged by the Gulf Stream.

Tomlinson, not for the first time, thought, **I'd live on the Keys if I didn't know they would kill me.**

The Caribbean Club was bayside, mile marker 104. The outdoor bar, with its Christmas lights and beach, was among his favorites, so better to save it for last.

Next stop, Tootsie's storage shed.

He continued north with the flow of traffic, careful to use his blinker when needed. There was a reason. A van with louvered windows and peace sign stickers was a red flag to cops, and the stakes were higher today.

Damn right, they were. In the back of the van were two boxes draped with red towels, towels being the only funereal garnish he could muster on short notice. To the ancient Chinese, the color red, not black, demonstrated respect.

A baggie of grass could be explained. Not the contents of those boxes.

The map guided him through a grid of CBS homes. In their yards, wooden crates—lobster traps—were stacked higher than some of the jacked-up trucks he saw. Asphalt lanes gave way to crushed shell that bridged him into the mangroves. Parallel to the road, a canal created a tunnel without the guidance of seawall.

He liked that: a utilitarian passage dug for working boats and men with secrets to hide.

Soon, on an open gate a flurry of signs appeared: **Fishermen's Co-op . . . No Trespassing . . . Beware the Gun, Not the Dog, Dumbass.**

Now we're getting somewhere, he thought.

No, he wasn't. Around the bend, he stopped when flashing blue light filled his mirrors. Monroe County Sheriff's Department. The cop, a Cuban-looking guy, took his time getting to the window. He leaned in. "Are you a member of the co-op? This is private property. Didn't you see the signs?"

Tomlinson, in tight sphincter mode, called upon his theater skills to save his ass for the umpteenth time. He remained respectful and articulate, then finally got a chance to explain about Tootsie.

"The fishing guide, huh? You think something happened to him?" The cop seemed genuinely concerned. "Follow me. There's a guy I have to talk to at the co-op. If Tootsie's been here, he'll know, and if he's not, we'll check his double-wide. You know where he lives, right? Since you're a friend and all."

It was a test. An easy one. "I've stayed there," Tomlinson replied. "Near Captain Jack's, just south of mile marker 104. Thing is, I've been by there twice today already. That's why I came to check his storage shed. A guy told me Tootsie slept there sometimes when he was guiding."

The cop couldn't help leaning to see into the van. "I hear he was one hell of a fisherman. A storage shed, huh? We'll find him. Come on." He got two steps before he cupped his hands to the window and tried to see past the louvered blinds. "What you got back there?"

"A couple of joints and a case of beer for later," Tomlinson heard himself say.

The cop was insulted. "You tell me something like that, why? Being cute? It's not. It's still against the law, you know."

"I'm trying to save us time by being honest. Open the door, if you want, and have a look around, but that's all you'll find." Tomlinson, dry-mouthed, had barely got the words out when his cell flashed with Marion Ford's name. "Mind if I take this? It might be about Tootsie."

The cop frowned, then wavered. "Wait here until I talk to this guy, okay?" He ambled toward his car.

When it was safe, Tomlinson plucked up the phone. "Dear Jesus, I just had one of those shit-or-go-blind moments. Where the hell have you been?"

Ford replied, "Waiting for Captain Barlow to sober up after a two-day drunk. Traffic's not bad, so we'll be there in about an hour."

"His cabin?"

"Key Largo. He knows where there's a cheap aluminum johnboat for sale."

14

They were on Tavernier Key, watching tarpon weave among pilings, when Tootsie Barlow said to Ford, "Screw it. Help me grab some rods. We're fishing—but don't tell him. He'll blab to my doctor."

Him was Tomlinson, who had left earlier for Key West. No explanation offered or needed after he'd snapped at them both, "Hey . . . get away from my van. My personal stash is in there."

Ford knew he shouldn't let the old man fish, but he'd never seen a better-looking skiff than the one moored here on Tavernier Creek. It was similar to Tootsie's original flats skiff, nothing like the aluminum job he'd bought that morning. It was an opportunity to fish with a master, so Ford said, "Let's wait until the sun's lower—unless the tide's no good. We'd have to worry about squalls, too, I guess, so . . . What do you think?"

Barlow didn't have to think. He knew. There was something he wanted to discuss.

A little after six, they were staked off Black Betsy Keys where a crevice of sand crossed the shallows. Leopard rays had lured enough bonefish within range that Barlow put down his fly rod and got to it. "You might be the one person Gracie will listen to. She'd be dead if you hadn't jumped in, and she knows it. You know what I'm worried about, don't you?"

Ford said, "The court arraignment. If she doesn't change her story, they might set bail for Lambeth and he'll walk, depending on how much evidence they have in the other cases. Probably keep walking, if someone's dumb enough to post it. Or, is it that other thing?"

"Between me and Gracie?"

"It crossed my mind," Ford said to keep the man talking.

"That bothers me, too, what she and her so-called boyfriend did. I could use it against her, I suppose, tell Gracie I'll go to the police if she helps that prick again. Hate to do it. She's **family**, you know? But her mother's near 'bout had a nervous breakdown." He got up, intending to say more, then realized Ford had been trolling for information. "I'll be damned. Tomlinson didn't tell you what she did, did he?"

"Just that he arranged a meeting and your niece admitted something she feels guilty about. **Confessed**, I think was the word. No details. But if you want me to talk to Gracie, don't you think I should know the whole story?"

The old man needed time to decide. He wore sleeves, fishing gloves, and a face stocking to keep off the sun. He pulled it down to his mouth and studied an area to the northwest. "That squall's got some fire in it, but we're okay for now."

"Every afternoon," the biologist said patiently.

"How do you like her so far?" Meaning this skiff, with its teak trim, wooden ribs, and strakes that breathed in a rough sea. The deck was white, the hull polished jade.

"Impressive," Ford said.

"It's a lot more doodadded up than my old one, but she'll plane on dew and track true as cable. The builder—Willy Roberts—he used to say, 'Until someone brings me a fiberglass tree, I'll stick with wood.' A purist, you know? He made some damn fine boats before he passed. That was in '93. I remember because he'd just started my second skiff, a low freeboard twenty. His son, Myrnice, had to finish 'er up. Now that Willy's grandkids are building boats again, I like to stop by. Makes us both feel good. Say"—Barlow moved aft, still very nimble—"how about we run north? There's another spot I want you to see."

Ford, smiling, said, "Gracie will **expect** me to know, Tootsie. I'm pretty good at keeping secrets, too."

The man's attention turned inward while he got under way, him standing at the wheel, the biologist sitting to his left. A quiet four-stroke Merc made it easy to talk, yet not a word about Gracie until the north shore of Florida Bay, in the mangroves where the water was red as whiskey.

"Do you think she's telling the truth about that guy or lying to save his ass? I should have known the moment I laid eyes on him he's Walter Lambeth's spawn. Bastard. Gracie was a good kid until she met him."

The engine was off, the boat staked within range of a pool where the tide eddied, but no fish thus far. Ford said, "Tomlinson believes she's convinced it wasn't him. Either way, she's wrong. Tell me something. She went missing the day they stopped by your cabin. What did you talk about?"

"This and that. Family, mostly, and the bad luck we'd been having. It wasn't comfortable talking with that overgrown skunk listening in, him sitting there with his attitude and freak show tattoos. I remember thinking that Gracie was nervous, which wasn't normal. Now, since we had our private talk, I understand better."

"You two have always been close?"

"Closer than most uncles and nieces, and there's a reason for that." Barlow backed up to when his niece was a child, saying how sweet she was, fairly good grades, but a big girl prone to pudginess, which was why, years ago, he'd laid down the law with the girl's teachers about no more bullying on the playground. After that, Gracie had turned to him if there was trouble. Her father was a shiftless drunk, either following construction jobs or in jail, which is why her mother had never taken his name.

"Gracie'd call every now and again. I could always tell if there was something wrong, or if it was just to talk. She doesn't have enough tomboy in her to like fishing, but if she saw my picture in a magazine, she got a big kick out of it. Like this one time she was getting her teeth cleaned and the dentist says to her, 'My god, Captain Tootsie Barlow's your **uncle**?' You know, like I was famous. She couldn't wait to call. It meant a lot to her, I think, what with her family situation. But girls change when they get into their teens, so I hadn't heard from her in a year or so, then that first funeral come along. It was February. Us Barlows are spread all over the state, but we're still family when it comes to burying our dead."

He talked about that, a cousin killed by lightning, and an RV fire that took his grandson's wife. Then a month ago, there'd almost been another funeral after his nephew's truck hit a tree—a blown tire, the police were now convinced.

"Gracie came to both but fell off the chart after the second funeral. She acted different, too. The Lambeth guy wasn't there, and she didn't mention a boyfriend, but that had to be it. Is Slaten his real name or did he lie about that, too?"

Barlow waited for confirmation, then continued, "I didn't meet him until a month ago, when the two of them showed up out of the blue. The first time I'm talking about, not the day she disappeared. I almost didn't recognize Gracie because of the way he had her painted up like some . . . I won't use the word. First thing I said to her was, 'Those damn things aren't permanent, are they?' The conversation sort of went downhill from there."

Ford asked about the RV fire and the truck accident, more interested in Barlow's reaction than the details. Then asked, "Why did they stop by twice? Not the reason she gave, but why do you think? That cabin's not easy to get to."

The cabin **was** the reason. Everyone in the family knew the feds would take the property unless one of them made it their legal residence.

On their second visit, that was Gracie's offer: she and Slaten would get married, move in, and even pay a little rent, if Tootsie would convince her mother to sign a consent form. She was underage, but marrying a forty-year-old husband would satisfy federal requirements. A win-win all around.

Except for one thing.

"First time I laid eyes on the guy, I smelled trouble. It wasn't just the tattoos or his age. It was the smooth way he had of making his ideas come out of Gracie's mouth. He'd nudge the conversation this way or that, depending on what he wanted her to say. He tried the same with me. Of course, I didn't know he was a Lambeth at the time, so some of what he said seemed to make sense. They both knew I wanted to move back onto the Keys, so he played that card, and a couple of others. You know, to convince me."

Ford, making eye contact, asked, "Is that why they futzed the tire on your nephew's truck?"

Barlow looked away.

"I don't expect you to answer, Tootsie, but here's what I think happened. Slaten wanted the cabin property for himself, so he tracked Gracie down. Probably took a few days to figure out her habits, and how to work it once he realized she was an easy target for a guy like him. Your niece told him about you, that you're a religious man, or maybe what was written in your family Bible. That's a guess, but Slaten is a sociopath. They have to be shrewd or they don't survive long. He hoped another dead relative would convince you to wash your hands of the whole business, so he duped her into helping. Now he's got something on your niece. And he had something else—your family Bible— until it burned. Did Tomlinson tell you what he found?"

"This morning," Barlow said. "Some worthless Lambeth bastard threw it in the furnace. My god, all that family history gone."

"Slaten did it. He broke into your cabin for a reason. You know it was him, right?"

The old fishing guide suddenly looked older. "Doc, you haven't said anything that hasn't gone through my mind a hundred times. Today, though? This might be my last chance to fish with a fine skiff under my feet. Mind if I just enjoy—" He stopped and stiffened like a setter. "We got a school of reds coming. Look'a there. See the silt? They're working their way to a little patch of oysters uptide, but they'll turn soon enough."

A creek eddied into this shallow pocket circled with mangroves, a glassy drop-off where a spiral of mud exited like smoke. Ford didn't see any tails with black dots, but decided not to ask, **How do you know they aren't bonefish?**

Barlow followed the tangent anyway, which was okay. Enjoyable, in fact, to the biologist, who'd heard stories and learned some subtleties, during three stops on the trip across Florida Bay. Tern Keys, Fan Palm Hammock, and Samphire Crossing—the famous guide knew the cuts, every wheel track; had acquired so much knowledge over the decades that his memory covered the bay like a grid.

Like now, Barlow saying, "Rainy season, reds will follow sweet water 'til their bellies bust. Bones, they want salt. Check your tippet and get ready."

Ford handed him the rod instead. "Your turn. Maybe it'll improve my technique."

"Bushes too tight for you, huh?"

"All I'd do is snag trees."

The old guide cackled like a witch, and went to work when a gang of reds began to forage their way out of the creek. He released a small one, then a ten-pounder, after Ford said, "Show me again."

Spey-casting, Barlow called the graceful technique he used to avoid the trees. Then took a chance by saying, "There's a woman guide out of Captiva, I think, who can teach you better than me. **Florida Sportsman** did an article, so I watched her video on the computer. That woman can, by god, throw a fly."

Captain Hannah Smith. No need to say the name, from the look on Ford's face.

Tootsie did anyway, adding, "I'd sure like to meet her."

Harold Barlow got his nickname when he quit cigarettes and took up chewing Tootsie Pops to get him over the nicotine hump. It was something he seldom thought about, but it came to mind when he threaded the cut south of Eagle Key and turned north toward Little Madeira Bay.

Right here, almost sixty years ago, his career had started, and almost ended. His first charter out of Bud N' Mary's, he'd gotten a last-minute call because they'd double-booked Jimmie Albright, who, even in those days, was a big name in the field. Jimmie, a fine man and a crackerjack angler, had a stellar list of clients, wealthy folks who could make or break a newcomer if he did something really stupid.

Young Harold Barlow had. He'd lit a cigarette just before attempting to bring a big tarpon to gaff—a two-hundred-pounder, his pissed-off clients would later claim. As he was babying the fish in, the cigarette touched the backing. Good-bye, tarpon; good-bye, one hundred feet of primo fly line; and good-bye to a possible world record.

Christ, what a way to start.

Jimmie also had a temper. Him and Jack Brothers ruled the flats in those days, so they'd asked the rookie dumbass why they should risk their overflow if he wasn't serious about the trade.

"I'll never smoke another cigarette in my life," he'd vowed, already chewing one of those chocolate-filled suckers that he still enjoyed, but not as much as a good cigar.

He'd been Tootsie ever since. Not in his head, though. Not always. During private moments, especially sleepless nights, he was still Harold, a hick from the Everglades who'd rubbed elbows with the rich and famous and learned a few things along the way. Blue water or thin, fishing was damn hard work. Clients didn't pay good money to be yelled at or treated like fools. They deserved an enjoyable day, so a smile and a good story could be as important as putting fish in the box.

The biologist, sitting to his left, wasn't an easy audience. Stubborn, too, especially since he'd figured out the truth about Gracie. Tootsie tried anyway, by making himself the butt of the joke regarding his first charter. It went over pretty well.

"I've read what there is about the early

guides," Ford replied, "which isn't much. Tell me how it was back then."

Tootsie did; talked about men who hadn't aged a day in his memory—Buck Stark, Bill Hatch, Cecil Keith, and Earl Gentry—all out of Islamorada or Key Largo at one time or another. The stories flowed easily. Tootsie saying, "Ted Williams, the baseball player, was as good a flycaster as he was a hitter, so he tracked down Jimmie Albright. This was back when folks claimed tarpon wouldn't hit a fly. It was all new then. What the early guides couldn't buy, we had to invent."

Saltwater fly-fishing required different knots, reels with drag systems. Bamboo rods and push poles gave way to fiberglass. Shallow water required a whole different fishing etiquette than blue water. Blast the fish off a man's flat, and the day might end in a fistfight back at the docks.

"There were some doozies. Want to hear about the best fight I ever saw?"

Nope. What the biologist wanted to know was, "I recognize some of the names. What happened to those men?"

The question made Barlow feel depressed. He'd fished and been friendly with actors, sports stars, and politicians, even one American president. The same with some of the others, including Albright, who, late in life, fell on hard times but was too proud to let Ted Williams pay to have his roof fixed.

The baseball player did it anyway.

"They all died doing what they loved," Tootsie replied to avoid the topic. He wanted to get back to stories he'd told twenty thousand times.

"That history needs to be saved," Ford said. "It might give your niece something constructive to do, you and her sitting down with a tape recorder. Better yet, have her write it all out."

Christ, right back on Gracie again. The temptation was to re-visit the subject of Hannah Smith until Ford, focusing on an inlet ahead, said, "This looks familiar. Is that Madeira Bay?"

Barlow was impressed. "Little Madeira, and that cut's the opening to Taylor Creek. Not many sportsmen get back in these parts. You know the area?"

"I wasn't fishing. I was with a crocodilian expert, Dr. Jim Mazzotti. This was years ago. I helped catch a couple, and Jim would mark their scutes and record the markings. We didn't use tags. I imagine some of those crocs are still around. Hope so anyway."

"Saltwater crocs, I've seen 'em in here now and again," Tootsie said, "but the biggest one ever? You'll be surprised."

Ford was. A huge female croc had lived in

Chino Hole, and Barlow claimed to have a photograph to prove it. The picture had been taken days before the animal was finally killed and skinned.

"That was before I was born, but I never heard that she bothered anybody. Crocs tend to be shy. Now, a big gator, he'll track your skiff. Not that he wants to eat you. The smart ones wait until you get a good fish on and then have themselves an easy meal. What that tells me is, there are too many damn boats around. Personally, a gator pulls that stunt, he needs to be put down. To hell with the rules. Think about some kid falling overboard."

The biologist sensed the old guide was opening up a bit. He talked about saltwater crocs he'd seen in Australia and Africa, the differences in aggressive behavior compared to the Florida variety, then circled back to the subject of Gracie. Slaten Lambeth had to be put down, too, or the girl wouldn't live long enough to have children.

Those words hit home, but Barlow didn't address the issue right away. That came later, near sunset, as the tendrils of a squall angled toward them from the northwest. He swept a hand along the horizon, and said, "Back in the day, I used to think this patch of water belonged to me. Every little ambush hole I stumbled on. Fifty-eight years, I fished these flats.

Know what I finally figured out? I don't own a damn thing. None of us do." He nodded to the distant squall. "Us fishermen, we're just rain crossing the bay. That's all. But family, Doc. Family lasts. Or at least it's supposed to. That's why I can't talk about what that girl claimed she did."

Later, tying up in Tavernier Creek, he added, "I don't want to risk any more trouble for Gracie. Let me think about it, okay?"

15

It had been years since a stoner had looked at Tomlinson like he was some pathetic opium wretch, but that's what happened when he asked where to score an ounce of flakka. This was at a biker bar somewhere south of Islamorada.

Next stop, Key West. The street freaks were more open-minded yet still treated him with the tender indifference befitting the walking dead.

"I'm not a junkie, I'm conducting an experiment as a social scientist," he explained to a fetching young woman with green hair.

Her reply: **"Right."**

Geezus, "herpes simplex" was a better opening line, so he played it cool after that. Checked into the Cypress House, went for a swim at Dog Beach, and was back in time for happy hour.

The next morning was spent at May Hill Russell Library, which felt cooler inside because of its conch-pink stucco exterior. Newspaper and public records dated back to the 1800s. He focused on the Prohibition years, particularly those when much of South Florida was still part of Monroe County. Smuggling liquor and "foreign undesirables" dominated headlines, but the Marco Island war had gotten some ink, too.

Finally, he had all the pieces of the story. In 1912, a Memphis advertising tycoon brought his money and big ideas to Florida's Gulf Coast. His name, appropriately, was Barron Collier. Sunshine and the new sport of tarpon fishing were untapped gold mines, so he built hotels, and a railroad to keep the rooms full.

Below Naples was a hundred miles of wilderness coastline. Collier had been a visionary. He bought thousands of hectares sight unseen and extended his railroad south, then went to work building a road across the Everglades to connect the thriving Port of Tampa with Miami—the Tamiami Trail.

Chinese laborers had played a role.

Things had gone smoothly until 1924, when a hundred or so homesteaders on Marco Island realized their land had been bought out from under them. Legally. Worse, for once in their lives, they, too, were thriving, thanks to their boating skills and five years of Prohibition. They were a rough lot, a mix of hardscrabble fishermen, war vets, and criminals on the run. Outsiders, especially representatives of the new land baron, were turned around at the point of a gun.

To get kicked off dirt-poor land was one thing. Abandoning water access to Cuban rum was a **Screw you** deal breaker.

In 1925, Collier played his trump card. He established his own county, thereby legalizing his personal branch of law enforcement. The sheriff, William R. Maynard, was right out of **Cool Hand Luke**, no shit. He carried a six-gun, a bullwhip, and owned a bloodhound. Deputies were handpicked, and Collier's 110-foot yacht augmented the arsenal.

Violence began as skirmishes. An example was a story in the weekly **American Eagle**, August 23rd of the same year. It contained familiar names:

> With his head swathed in numerous bandages, J. H. Cox, deputy sheriff of Collier County, with headquarters at Marco Island, was in Fort Myers Saturday evening for surgical aid.
>
> Saturday morning, he attempted to

arrest Walter Lambeth on a charge of being drunk and disorderly and using profanity, and started to take the prisoner away when he was attacked by a mob of a dozen or more and badly manhandled.

The deputy's coat was cut with a razor until his revolver fell from the pocket, and one man cut him on the face and neck. Many hit him with their fists, and Cox stated to a reporter he would probably have been murdered if his wife had not come to the rescue.

He was seriously but not dangerously injured. His wife and two children traveled with him to Fort Myers for medical attention on Saturday night.

On Sunday, Sheriff Maynard, of Collier County, went to Marco with deputies and his famous tracking hound. While searching for the assailants, they captured a cargo of liquor valued at $1,000 that was said to have come directly from Cuba. Four suspects were arrested, including Albert Barlow, who is a well-known seaman, and is said to have ridden a Ferris wheel with notorious Chicago gangster Al Capone on a recent trip to Havana.

Capt. Barlow is being lodged at the Collier County Jail at Everglades. To date, the whereabouts of Capt. Lambeth is unknown.

Ridden a Ferris wheel? Well, in the words of Hunter S. Thompson, tell the truth and let the facts fall where they may. Certain links jumped out: Chicago, Cuba, Capone.

Walter Lambeth threaded them all, but from the shadows.

Tomlinson's interest moved to human trafficking. A search for a Chinese cemetery, after all, had lured him to Key West. Several stories referenced Cuban- and Bahamian-Chinese, the terms always hyphenated, but focused on the plight of the smugglers, not their human cargo. In the 1920s, an estimated twenty thousand Chinese had slipped in through Florida after completing their eight-year contract with the Cuban government to work in the cane fields. Yet, not one word of description about the immigrants, nor a single interview.

Like Lambeth, the Chinese had existed in the shadows. No wonder they had come willingly into his dark world.

As Tomlinson wound through reels of archives, an interesting pattern emerged. Over and over, history repeated itself—which, in his mind, hinted at the existence of a parallel universe.

News story, September 2010: Five Broward County residents were indicted for an international smuggling ring that brought hundreds of Chinese nationals into the state using fake travel documents. In 2016, a similar operation out of Canton Province was uncovered by the feds.

Stories of smuggling rum, whiskey, and drugs also ping-ponged through the decades.

Good ol' Florida. The peninsula's phallic shape was a metaphor for something, Tomlinson wasn't sure what. One fact was certain: the state had a relentless hard-on when it came to trafficking flesh and sin.

His phone buzzed—a breach of library etiquette. He packed his stuff and went outside to return Gracie's call.

That morning, the girl had signed into the county detention center as Gracie Barlow but exited feeling as if she were Gracie Lambeth because of what Slaten had said after hearing what she feared was bad news.

"You belong to me. Nothing, prison, not even death, will change that."

"'Til death do us part" was a more formal way of putting it. The sentiments were the same. Gracie had never experienced such soaring happiness. She wanted to tell someone, but who? Slaten, the cute gangster in his orange jumpsuit, had warned, "Your mother? After kicking you out, that bitch won't understand."

He said basically the same about her uncle, then showed a jealous side, telling her, "I don't want you talking to that long-haired freak. He's a pussy hound. If he so much as touches you, I'll cut his head off."

After Slaten said it, the smoky look in his eyes had made her skin vibrate. It reminded Gracie of what she'd been missing.

Slaten had been right about her family, but Tomlinson wasn't a threat. **Jealousy?** That was silly—as if she could ever want another man. It put a smile on her face while she crossed the street, rough-looking rednecks and blacks everywhere, oblivious to what she was feeling. Slaten's van had been impounded, so she was in a little rental Chevy, driving east, before deciding, **He's protective because he loves me. Slaten doesn't have to know.**

Tomlinson, when he answered his phone, said, "**Hola**, young princess. How'd the lady shrink treat you today?"

State law provided three months of counseling, which was another reason she liked talking to her uncle's sweet-natured friend. Tomlinson understood. He'd given her a famous book he'd written years ago while in a psychiatric ward.

"Same old crap, so I blew it off. I called and cancelled, just like I promised you if I decided not to go. You won't tell Tootsie, will you . . . ?"

Tomlinson could be trusted. He asked if she

was staying clean, meaning drugs, before she continued on with a bounce in her voice, saying they'd allowed her thirty minutes with Slaten, then got to the fun part. "Guess what?"

"You're pregnant," the man replied gently.

"Wow . . . you're good. I only did the pee strip thing this morning. How'd you know?"

"Lucky guess. I bet you were afraid Slaten would freak out, but he didn't. In fact, I bet he was happy about it, right?"

Gracie, driving with the phone against her ear, was stunned. "How could you possibly know so much? I just left there not—"

"Sometimes things come to me," Tomlinson said. "Don't let it spook you. Not that it doesn't scare me on occasion, but I don't want to get into that. Some people, I have an immediate connection. You're one of them, Gracie."

She liked the way he spoke, as if she had value as a person. "Hey, maybe this proves it. I haven't read a book since middle school, but I'm already to the third chapter of yours. It's unreal, some of the things you say, like now, like you're right inside my head, but my thoughts are already there on paper."

"Tell me how Slaten handled the news," Tomlinson replied.

"That's what I was worried about. A couple of times—this was on trips, usually to

North Florida—he said he hated kids, but you should've seen his face light up when I told him. Know what he said? That we'd always be together. Get married! I'm still in shock, I guess, and that's why—"

Tomlinson knew what was coming. She wanted him to convince Tootsie that someone else, not Slaten, had tortured her and attacked those girls in Gainesville. The arraignment date, she told him, had been set for Friday, only two days away. If the judge dismissed the case, she and Slaten would need a place to live.

"My uncle hates staying in that cabin, and you know it. I'll fix it up real nice, maybe even plant a garden—live healthy, for a change. It would be good for all of us. Would you mind talking to him . . . **please**?"

"The state prosecutor is the one you need to convince," Tomlinson said.

"That's where I'm headed now," she said. "My attorney, the one the judge appointed, he doesn't think the state has a case if I don't change my testimony. And I won't because it's the truth. All those nights I was chained up, I would've **known** it was Slaten. But it wasn't, and I'm ready to swear to it now. You believe me, don't you?"

"What about the girls who were assaulted in Gainesville?"

Gracie, getting defensive, said, "He wasn't even in Florida at the time. Why would you ask such a thing?"

"Tootsie thinks the guy is using you, and—don't get mad, okay?—maybe Slaten **is** using you. Or was. Your uncle thought that, even before you told the truth about your cousin's pickup truck. I'm not trying to be mean. It's important you take a step back and see the bigger picture."

"My uncle could tell the cops what we did, in other words."

"It wasn't a threat. I want you to understand there could be repercussions, that's all."

The girl took a patient breath before saying, "It wasn't Slaten. Seriously, if you can read my mind, tell me. Am I lying or telling the truth about him?"

She was telling the truth, but Tomlinson found it hard to say what he did, which was, "I believe you. I have from the start."

"Thank god someone does. Can you call my uncle now?"

"About the cabin?"

Yes. The girl needed a place tonight because of an argument with her mother.

"You can't stay out there all alone, and Tootsie's gone to Key Largo for a few days."

"Oh . . . damn, yeah, you're right," she said.

"I don't mind being by myself usually, but not there, not after what . . . what we talked about."

Gracie had heard voices, too. It was the first of several connections they'd shared.

"The thing is," she added, "if I get a hotel tonight, I'm afraid I might be tempted to go out and celebrate the good news. Me, **pregnant**. I won't, of course. Promise. I'm just telling you how I feel."

Tomlinson had dealt with enough addicts to know what that meant.

"I'll meet you there a little after sunset," he said. "You stay in the cabin, I'll sleep in my van."

An old article in the **Key West Citizen** beckoned him to Petronia Street, off Duval, in search of a Chinese woman, Natsumi Min-Juan. Two decades ago, she had celebrated her seventieth birthday with friends at her little house on Chapman Lane. If still alive, Ms. Min-Juan would be in her nineties. Well worth a search, judging from the article:

> "Sumi," as she is known, came to Florida from Havana as an infant in 1927 on a boat that tragically sank off Cape Sable.

Only Ms. Min-Juan and three others survived. As a young girl, Sumi worked as a domestic until she'd saved enough money to open her first restaurant on Duck Key. In later years, she was active in Miami's Chinese community . . .

Interesting. Cape Sable, a wilderness of sand and shoals, was north of Key West, halfway to Marco Island, for a boat traveling from Cuba. The woman might be a valuable resource if he could find her—and if she was willing to talk to a long-haired stranger with two boxes of purloined bones in the back of his van.

Formalities of some sort were requisite.

Tomlinson had a long, complex history in Key West. He made a few calls before driving to a Buddhist zendo on Stock Island, a quiet hipster enclave where a female student, who might have been Asian, said, "I haven't visited Madame Min-Juan in a while. May I go with you, Roshi?"

Fate had taken a hand.

The Zen student was Lia Park, from San Francisco and Miami via her job as a Delta pilot. She phoned ahead. They stopped and bought flowers, which Lia carried to the door of a small pink house with chickens in the yard. Once inside, she spoke Chinese before summoning Tomlinson from the porch.

Madame Natsumi Min-Juan, although a tiny woman, possessed the bearing of royalty—a withered countenance that had outlived surprise and fear. Attended by a nurse, she held court from a throne of wicker, although her eyes drifted occasionally to the TV.

"**The Price Is Right**," she confided, "is almost as old as I am."

Bamboo chimes mimicked the sound of her laughter.

They sat in a room spiced with incense while the nurse poured tea. Tomlinson asked questions, which Lia sometimes translated into Chinese if English lacked the necessary nuance. It gave him time to absorb the history on the walls. Amid photos were citations and awards neatly framed. Several were from an organization with the initials **CCBA**. He asked what they stood for and struck gold, but didn't realize it until later when he referenced Key West Cemetery.

"I've spent more time there than most," he said, "and don't remember seeing a Chinese tombstone. It can't be a racial issue. Lord knows, pirates of every shade are buried out there."

"**We** have been buried in that cemetery," the old woman corrected, "but we seldom stay for long." This odd response was accompanied by more chiming laughter.

She explained. Chinese custom required that

the dead be returned to their home provinces. No one was better qualified to expound on the subject than Ms. Min-Juan, who for decades had been active in the Chinese Consolidated Benevolent Association. Since the 1880s, the CCBA had been repatriating the bones of immigrants from Florida to California, and as far north as Alaska.

"Bone houses," she added, "that's where our people were stored in the old days while they waited. It was complicated work, all the permits required, so we shipped every seven years, first to San Francisco, then on to China. Miami and Key West were our primary ports. So you see? There's no mystery. Here, I'll show you." She motioned to the nurse, who returned with a photo and a booklet, the paper so old it flaked.

Tomlinson opened the book, then passed it to Lia. "What's it say?"

It was a guide for field-workers; a step-by-step tutorial on how to exhume, clean, and store human remains.

Lia read from the introduction. "'Responsible workers should follow these steps. Search carefully for graves, and don't be casual about it. Be mindful!'" She shared a smile with the Zen master, before continuing, "'Treat your lost ancestors with the respect that one day will be granted you on your final journey home.'"

The book provided a recovery team duty roster: grave locators, a skilled exhumer, a chief gatherer and scraper, and expert packers to wash, dry, and properly wrap the bones. Of great importance was that the queue, or pigtail, not be separated from the skull.

Lia, charmed by the language, read more. "'Rituals as required by each step are imperative when engaged in a process so fraught with supernatural danger. Do it properly and the spirits of the deceased will welcome you. Fail, and the dangers can be serious.'"

Tomlinson thought, **I nailed this one,** yet wanted to know more before revealing what was in his van.

A photo, an old black-and-white, showed the interior of a brick room where boxes were stacked floor to ceiling. Metal boxes, not large, etched with Chinese glyphs. A bone house.

"The metal was called white iron," Madame Min-Juan said, "but they were actually zinc-coated. Not inexpensive, and paid for entirely by donations. Our volunteers were already experts by the time I got involved. That was"— she had to think back—"in the early 1960s. The work was hard but rewarding. In our culture, there is no higher good deed than rescuing restless bones, or covering an uncovered coffin. As we were taught, honoring the dead is a sign of virtue and respect toward one's elders."

She continued on about traditions, then the process of repatriating bones, her focus on Lia, the young Asian woman, while keeping a wary eye on Tomlinson.

"Along with procedural problems, Florida was difficult for other reasons. Boat captains often kept no records of Chinese who'd paid for transport from Cuba and the Bahamas. If a passenger died, or even a dozen passengers, well"—she shrugged—"they might throw their bodies overboard. Or sometimes dig a mass grave. Smuggling was illegal, of course, so the graves were often left unmarked, which is understandable, I suppose. However, how and why some Chinese died before they even . . . Well, I would say more, but choose not to be indelicate."

Tomlinson put down his cup and saucer. "I read that you came from Cuba as an infant. That you were only one of three survivors after your boat foundered off Cape Sable. Is that how it really happened?"

The woman's gaze sharpened while she adjusted her robe of blue silk. "Why are you interested in such things, young man? Old stories that do not concern you? Yes, about the boat, that's what I have told reporters."

"I think it does involve me, and not by choice. The doctrines of karma and samsara— our cyclical paths—brought me here." He let that sink in for a moment. "In my van are two boxes meant to be delivered to you. I didn't know until just now, but first I want to understand what we're dealing with. I'm a sailor; I know Cape Sable well. In a storm, it's very unlikely an infant could have survived. A boat would break up on those shoals."

Inscrutable—it fit, the way her face became a blank shield. "I was very young, not an infant, yet remember almost nothing. A black night and waves. Men yelling in English. That's all."

"It was an unfair question," Tomlinson agreed. "When you were older, did someone— another survivor, perhaps—tell you where the boat was headed? From Cuba, Key West would have been the logical stop, but your boat continued north another sixty-some miles. Marco Island would have been the next landfall."

"You are very persistent. I've already told you, I have no memory of those events," she said, then spoke to Lia in Chinese. Not sharply, yet her words caused the young Delta pilot to sit at attention.

"Madame Min-Juan needs to rest," Lia said. "She's very pleased to have met us, and wishes us a safe—"

Tomlinson, a Zen master, was also a master at bowing himself out of a room. He returned with a box draped in red, placed it at the woman's feet, then fetched the other. "Until now,

I knew nothing about proper procedures, so I did what I thought was best. These . . . human relics, where I found them, they had to be packed in a hurry." Hands together, he bowed to the boxes. "Sorry about the red towels."

She removed the draping, peered inside, then sat back with a stunned look on her face. "Oh my goodness. Where did these come from?"

"That's why I mentioned Marco Island. I found them not far from there, and I suspect there are more. Probably hidden away, or underwater."

"Underwater?" It was a significant detail, also distasteful.

"It's a guess. A small settlement of Chinese laborers lived near a pond where . . . Well, I'm not sure what happened. This was around the same time your boat sank. I hope you're not upset."

"Extraordinary." She gazed down, seeing portions of skulls, braids attached. "But how did you know to bring them to **me**?"

Lia, on her feet, asked permission to view the contents. The old woman joined her in opening the second box. They had a lengthy exchange in Chinese and made guarded gestures toward Tomlinson. After a bow to Madame Min-Juan, Lia sat and took his hand. "She agrees—you're a messenger. A shaman, possibly. Madame wants to share her story with you—the truth this time. But she is tired. Can you come back tomorrow?"

The airborne Zen student, looking good with short black hair, gave his hand a squeeze. "I'm a little overwhelmed myself. If you need a place to stay tonight, my apartment is small, but . . ." She let the sentence trail off, but the meaning remained.

That damn cabin in the Glades. From Key West, it was a two-hour drive to Key Largo, then another two hours to meet Gracie, all before sunset.

"Gad, how I wish," Tomlinson responded. "I might be able to come back in a day or two, but just in case . . ." He took out his sketch of the brand on Gracie's arm and unfolded it. "Madame Min-Juan, I need your help. Do you recognize this symbol? I believe it's somehow related to a man, a bad man who—"

He stopped because of the look of revulsion on her face. She spoke sharply to Lia in Chinese, then said, "You have no right to bring that into my home. No right! Who are you?"

"Look at me," Tomlinson said, putting the sketch away. "I don't understand either, so look at me and tell me why I'm here."

The nurse was angry, too. "You don't know? How ridiculous. Please leave or I'll phone the police."

He ignored her while the old woman stared at him. Several seconds passed before she nodded, and told Lia and the nurse to leave the room.

When they were gone, she said, "There is kindness in you, I see that. With so few days left, I must embrace the messenger whatever the message may be. Where did you find that sketch?"

Tomlinson had watched the door shut. "Your nurse recognized the symbol, too. I could tell. She doesn't appear to be Chinese, so why was she upset?"

"It's a chop mark, not a symbol. A thing that denotes ownership. The girl was frightened because she's my nurse. She associates it with pain. I've seen that mark only a few times in my life."

"When you were a child?"

The woman looked away, then back again. "Our boat didn't sink. It's a story I made up to avoid the truth." Tomlinson offered his hand. She took it, before adding, "I wasn't rescued, I was enslaved."

"By a man named Walter Lambeth."

Her fingers twitched.

"Then there's nothing coincidental about us meeting. You might find peace in knowing these bones were liberated from his property. If there're more, I'll find them. We'll find them. He's gone now, Madame Min-Juan. The man's been dead for many years."

"Impossible."

"Why do you say that?"

"Because he's not human. That's the message you brought to me. You were sent for a reason, so I must show you." She raised her head to confirm her resolve, then slowly parted the lapels of her blue satin robe to show boney shoulders, withered skin, and ribs. Seared into her left breast was a familiar scar.

"It's the mark of Shue Gwee, the water beast," she said, and looked at the boxes. "In our province, he was called Demon Crow."

16

Mr. Bird couldn't stand jail, so he took flight. He preferred a big white GMC diesel, with its insulated bucket and Altec boom that telescoped fifty feet into the air if the outriggers were set. Maximum load, four hundred pounds—just enough to hold a man his size plus tools.

No one questioned a utility worker. Not cops, or guards at gated communities, and definitely not at a Key Largo trailer park. He did a U-ie at Marina Del Mar, backtracked, then turned left into Capt. Jack's Mobile Home Estates.

Tootsie Barlow's red F-150 was parked beside an older blue truck that had tried to follow him yesterday. Luckier yet, the ragged landscaping included a thatch of bamboo among some dusty banana plants. The bamboo was small, not the big timber variety from Asia—as if anyone here would know the difference. Delighted, he drove to the back of the park, where a utilities area was screened by fencing.

It was Wednesday, a little after sunset. Too late in the day for the nine-to-five clock punchers, so it was ideal for a lineman who pretended to want extra work. He'd used that story so many times, it flowed naturally when needed. Like now, as a shrunken man with a Chihuahua wandered up and tapped on the glass. "Does the whole park got cable problems or just us? My wife says it's the TV, which don't make sense 'cause we got a almost new Toshiba."

"I'm not supposed to repair local cable," Mr. Bird said, "but give me a sec while I call in and check. What's your name and address, sir?" He pretended to write on a service pad. Climbing out was always the best part. The little dweeb's head scrolled upward as if filming a sequoia until his eyes fixated on a tattoo that bridged neck and ear. A huge gloved hand prefaced their introduction: "Nice to meet you, sir. I'm a private contractor, name's Vernon. Vernon Crow. If you keep this between us, I'll do what I can."

He liked the name, had chosen it years ago, and that's who he became when he wasn't inside the truck or visiting from the past.

Vernon often heard voices in his head. Probably from spending so much time caged or chained as a boy. He seldom traveled without Mr. Bird in his ear, or ol' Walter for company, as well as Walter's .36 caliber service revolver. No serial numbers on a gun so old, there was no record of its existence.

The bucket had toggle sticks like a video game. Vernon elevated himself to maximum height. Barlow's truck, and the truck that had tailed him, were still in the drive. A third vehicle, a van with louvered widows, was a recent arrival.

He dropped a few feet and swung the bucket to a terminal box mounted on a pole. At his feet was a can of wasp spray, if needed. It wasn't. He popped the lid to find a sheath of outdated candy-colored wires. He tracked pairs of wires, red and green, to their terminal screws. Many were flagged with names or addresses scribbled on tape. It saved time. Tracking wire was a pain in the ass.

Vernon found the old man's landline. On his belt was a heavy rubber telephone with a dial— a test set, it was called. He clipped in and heard a dial tone. No conversation to monitor, although that might change. He left the test set attached. An ohm meter would signal incoming and outgoing calls.

There was a more modern way.

From a case, he removed a telemetry transceiver. Cell numbers of fishing guides were easily found even after they'd retired. Satellite towers lined the Keys, each assigning cell connections via a logarithm impossible to predict yet possible to intercept with a military scanner.

Vernon knew his shit.

Patience. He settled back and inhaled some primo flake using a vaporizer, binoculars within reach. Whew! . . . His brain coiled into a sharp little lens after the second hit. Trailer rooftops were packed in rows that thrummed. The view improved to the south, where, in a kidney-shaped pool, three couples were banging themselves into a sex frenzy, unaware that a privacy fence didn't mean privacy. Not to a man in a bucket truck.

Oh . . . some of the juicy shit he'd seen.

He had a camera with a 185mm telephoto. **Snap-snap-snap.** The lens served as a transit for a GPS locator. Later, if he felt like it, he would match the numbers to an address and the address to a name. The big-money types seldom wed forgiving mates.

Vernon had to make a living somehow. Mr. Bird could be an expensive guest.

To the north was a line of storms. Lightning was always of interest to a man atop a metal fifty-foot boom. Cloud-to-cloud action accounted for eighty percent of all strikes. It was the other twenty percent that could kill you. Or, properly done, kill someone else; a person you wanted dead.

Vernon's eyes shifted to the piddly little clump of bamboo. It reminded him of a delicious trip a while back. Mr. Bird had accompanied him northbound on Route 27, the old railroad trestle to Palmdale, where the tracks skirted Lake Okeechobee and displaced Route 29 before continuing north. Whistle stops included Sebring, Winter Haven, Ocala, and Gainesville.

Mr. Bird and Walter knew the route well. Walter had been a train-riding man.

Past and present mingled on that trip until they got down to business. The Barlows had been railroad folk. The heirs gravitated like ticks to the black snake artery; probably didn't understand why. Kevin Barlow they'd lured into a field west of Frostproof—a stroke of luck, that one.

A million sizzling volts hadn't done the job. Amperage and a good ground wire had.

Their luck didn't last with Tootsie's grandson. The kid had left the RV on some errand before the squall hit. But the kid's wife had come tumbling out of the blaze like a fireball.

Mr. Bird, in feeding mode, had delivered a few strokes of his own before she died. Walter approved.

Even in the grave, Walter Lambeth was not one to forgive and forget. The property was one reason, but not the only reason. Albert Barlow had had it coming. Long ago, he'd peached to the cops about slave coolies, and other such stuff, to save his own ass. Albert had confessed to other crimes in writing.

Two Barlows down and two to go.

The one Mr. Bird wanted most was the girl, Gracie—Gracie Yum-Yum—with her soft parchment. She was too young and pliant to kill all at once.

Slaten had botched that job. And more.

Vernon was thinking, **If you want something done right, do it yourself**, when the ohm meter signaled an outgoing call.

Gracie almost didn't answer when she saw the caller ID but finally picked up, saying, "Please don't be mad, Uncle Tootsie. I'm so sick of my family being mad at me, I can't take it anymore."

"I'm worried, that's all. You shouldn't be alone. Are you at the cabin?"

No, she was in the slow lane, I-75 south of Naples, where the highway bends east into the Glades. "Tomlinson must've told you the news. I knew he would because I gave him permission—not that he didn't coax it out of me. Mom already knows."

"How'd she take it?"

"What, that her unmarried daughter is pregnant? Pissed-off, disappointed, like I'm the biggest loser in the world. Just like I expected, and I don't care. Now I suppose you're going to tell her what Slaten and I did to . . . you know."

"Nope, not the police, either." He said it again, "I don't want you staying at that cabin alone," then explained that Tomlinson had stopped in Key Largo on his way back from Key West. The man who had saved her, Marion Ford, was there, too. They were outside, talking, so her uncle had taken this private moment to discuss something else.

"Let me guess," the girl said. "If it's about drugs, no, I'm not stoned. It's tempting, though, if anyone else tries to spoil the first happy day I've had since—" She couldn't remember the last time she'd been happy, which caused her voice to catch.

"Are you crying?"

"No!"

"Lord knows, if any girl has a right to, it's you, Hannah-Grace. You got your phone on speaker, don't you? I don't want you driving one-handed."

Only her uncle used her full name in an affectionate, not a threatening, way. She sniffed, and wedged the phone between her shoulder and ear. "Of course I'm on speaker. What do you want to talk about?"

"Just that. You need someone to talk to. A woman. A nice woman who'd understand better. I'm too old, and Tomlinson, he's a good egg and all—I know you two hit it off—but he's, let's face it, a man."

Gracie couldn't argue that. While the tears rolled, she smiled a little.

It was an idea Tootsie had come up with today while fishing with the biologist. Well, it had come to him after Tomlinson had shared the "good" news about her pregnancy. A friend of theirs was a crackerjack fishing guide up around Sanibel, a woman named Hannah Smith. Captain Hannah, Tootsie called her.

"The name's not all you got in common," her uncle continued. "She's in a family way, a couple months along, and she's single just like you. They didn't come out and say exactly, but I got the impression she's dealt with some bad ones herself and always managed to come out on top."

"Bad men, you mean?"

He wasn't targeting Slaten, her uncle was quick to explain. He was speaking about experiences the two women might have shared. "Look her up. There's some videos about her on the Internet. She's pretty, in an unusual way—sort of like you. Tomlinson's the one who pointed that out."

"**Pretty?** No way. He said that?"

"Both of you, darn right. I was thinking, maybe give Hannah a call. You'll be staying at the cabin anyway, and she wants to come down and fish Chino Hole."

"Tomlinson thinks it's a good idea?"

"No, and keep him out of this. This is just us talking. Fact that you're my niece, I'd mention it to Captain Hannah right off. Could be that she'll come on the run, and you two might hit it off. What do you think?"

"It's weird, calling someone out of the blue."

"So what? Invite her down, say, 'My uncle can't wait to meet you.' Let her pick the day."

Uncle Tootsie. He'd had a mean streak in his drinking days, or so her mother claimed. Gracie had never seen that side. The man speaking to her now, his gravelly voice full of caring and fun and light, had been the same throughout her childhood.

"You're sweet," she said, and meant it. "I don't know, though . . ."

"Gracie, darlin', do it for me. Please?"

"I suppose you'll call her anyway, and be pissed if I don't."

Her uncle laughed at that, saying, "Not until tomorrow, I won't. Hang on, I've got the number right here."

G racie Yum-Yum was pregnant.

Vernon Crow wet his lips when he heard that through the rubber phone clipped to his belt.

Was there more good news?

Perched high above his truck, there were a dozen unprotected Wi-Fi networks to choose from. He did an Internet search on Captain Hannah Smith, not expecting much, when he opened a video. The woman, tall with shoulders, was casting a fly rod.

Holy hell . . .

Full screen, he watched the footage again, noting the buckskin smoothness of her skin, long legs in fishing shorts, the heavy lift and fall of breasts beneath a blouse that flowed with her body.

Rip the buttons off, make her howl. Excellent . . .

He hit pause. Pulled the screen close to his face, nostrils wide, and sniffed. Into his head came the scent of flesh and girl sweat.

Vernon shaded the screen. Pause, play . . . Pause again after the camera zoomed in: black hair, glossy as tallow. Female features—lips, face, and jaw—but a masculine sturdiness in her eyes.

Raven Girl . . . That's the way he thought of her because of her hair.

Vernon's coveralls became constrictive when he recalled Tootsie, saying, "She's in a family way."

Pregnant, is what the old fool had meant. There was no belly bulge in a second video, and a Google search failed to confirm it was true. News articles about the woman, however, fanned his desire.

Fishing Guide/P.I. Wounds Wanted Man, Claims Assault

Interesting how the stories varied in detail, yet portrayed her as a nice girl hick who couldn't be pushed around.

I bet she's a biter.

He put his gear away and returned to Earth.

It was twilight. Lightning popped in charcoal clouds and pushed the scent of rain. An ounce of flakka struggled to organize his thoughts. Gracie would be alone tonight at the cabin. A perfect opportunity he couldn't pass up. He would go there and . . . do what?

Watch her. Savor her body from the darkness. Snap some photos. That's all. Not unless the tall one, Raven Girl, was there. It was better to wait a day or two—whatever it took— on the chance of capturing both females alone.

Or was it?

As he wrestled with the decision, the shrunken little man reappeared. No Chihuahua this time. "Cable's working great, I sure thank you. Here's a little somethin' for your trouble." The man hesitated at the sound of a growl that also might be thunder.

Vernon, turning, looked down. "What do you want?"

"To give you this. Sorry, mister, if I scared you."

A huge gloved hand accepted a five-dollar bill.

"The wife thanks you, too. Say, I noticed in the back of your rig you've got some stout-looking bamboo. You use that on power lines? As a non-conductor, like a pole."

A resonant growl, not thunder, was the reply.

The man walked backwards a few steps, then hurried to his trailer.

From the driver's seat of the big white GMC diesel, Mr. Bird informed Vernon, **Don't harvest Gracie until I've tasted the tall one, Captain what's-her-name.**

Then, leaving the park, had to add, **Rig the bamboo first, shit-for-brains. It's better if lightning kills the old man instead of you.**

17

Rain caught Gracie at the Marco exit and followed her into twilight, where a gale awaited on Route 29, a narrow road with signs that warned **Panther Crossing**.

She was jittery to begin with. Now this. The windshield blurred beneath a waterfall. Wipers slashed at a glare that worsened if she used her brights. Def Leppard, from the stereo, was a sustained howl. She slapped the volume lower, and concentrated. Finally, a shell road led to Barlow property, where headlights revealed oak trees and the cabin.

The girl parked, put her face in her hands, and sobbed. She'd never felt so lost and alone. It was after nine. Where was Tomlinson?

A burst of lightning confirmed his van

wasn't there. Shadows crowded into a writhing darkness while rain hammered her into a
panic. Should she stay or return to the safety
of lights and people? A hotel would be nice. A
hotel bar, even better.

Calm down.

But how?

In her purse was an ounce of flake she'd
found in Slaten's laundry bag. Flakka was expensive. It would've been stupid to trash it when
she was so desperate for cash. There was also a
vaporizer. She didn't smoke cigarettes, so packing the thing had been an innocent mistake.

Right.

Gracie was lying to herself and knew it. She
shoved the purse aside and picked up her phone.
Only one bar. She called anyway and nearly
broke down at the sound of the Zen master's
voice.

"How goes the battle, young princess?"

"Where are you?"

"I fell into the Winn-Dixie trap near Homestead. You've got your choice: vegetarian pizza
or swordfish on the grill. If there is a grill. Or
that woodstove. For dessert, how does mango
ice cream sound?"

"I was afraid you'd had an accident or something," she said, and covered the phone to sniff
and wipe her nose.

"Is the power on? Tootsie says it's a problem

out there sometimes. Maybe I should've bought charcoal. You mind checking to see if the stove works?"

"I haven't gone inside yet. How much longer will you be?"

"Hey . . . is something wrong?"

Suddenly it seemed silly to be afraid. "It's raining buckets here, and I don't want to get my bandage wet. Plus, my damn allergies aren't as bad if I sit here with the AC on."

Tomlinson knew the problem wasn't her allergies. "Wait in the car," he said. "I'll be there in fifteen minutes."

Next, he called the biologist for an update. Ford had left Key Largo an hour ago and had booked a room at the Rod & Gun Club in Everglades City.

"That's only, what, less than an hour from the cabin?" Tomlinson said. "Why not stop by? Gracie sounds a little ragged. It would be better if we're both there for support."

"I might have a problem," Ford said.

Tomlinson recognized the flat inflection. All business. "Nothing to do with fish or flora, I assume. Have you run amok with the Windsor clan? I hear they have a dry sense of humor."

A joke. The biologist didn't laugh. Instead, he asked, "What're the sleeping arrangements there? The cabin only has one bedroom, right?"

"You honestly think I would . . . ? If that's

your problem, shallow up, man. Even I draw the line at seducing emotionally troubled girls. Or do you mean—"

"In Key Largo, someone was monitoring our cell phone calls."

"Oh. No shit. How do you know?"

"A friend of the lady you just referenced told me. It was a close cover monitor."

"Lady Gillian—my god, it's true. You've got an in with the—"

"Not over the phone, damn it. Someone within a few hundred yards of the trailer park was listening in. They know where you're headed. Check your mirror—no, never mind. You've probably got those bass speakers booming and wouldn't have noticed anyway."

"Maybe not, but I can name every Buffett song in two notes. Why would someone want to follow me?"

Ford replied, "Like I said, I might have a problem."

The porn syndicate again.

With the windows open, a drizzling breeze caused lamps to flicker on a night that muted sound and fears. Gracie had never been the master of her own space. She liked the feel of the cabin already.

"Sit out there and enjoy your beer," she told Tomlinson. He'd changed clothes in his van and was on the porch, wearing baggy white kung fu pants and a peasant shirt with long, baggy sleeves.

"Mosquitoes," he explained. "Not that they bother me much. I'm actually glad the power went out."

That had happened soon after their arrival.

"There's an extra Coleman, if you want to read."

Nope. The man didn't need light for reading. He claimed to have a couple of books stored in his head. "Even if I didn't, there's more than enough lightning bugs. Being quick on your feet is the key."

Laughter felt less foreign now that she was settling in.

Gracie busied herself in the kitchen, which was tiny, but at least the propane stove worked. While swordfish steaks marinated in lime, she made a butter sauce using what she could find and what was in the bag from Winn-Dixie. Rock salt, chives, a wedge of Spanish onion finely diced.

You couldn't be the niece of Tootsie Barlow without learning how to prepare fish.

She set the table while potatoes sputtered in an iron pan. A towel became a tablecloth. Clunky white plates became china. A candle centerpiece added a formal touch. The rest of the cabin was a mess, so she hustled around doing what she could to make the place livable. She flipped the potatoes and put the swordfish on.

"Ten minutes," she said through the screen door. "You'll want to wash your hands first."

"Yes, ma'am," he replied with a salute.

Weird how a guy his age was so young-acting and fun.

"Smart aleck. What did you do with the ice cream? It's not in the freezer or the grocery bags. I checked."

"All part of my sinister plan, dearie. Play your cards right, I'll invite you back to my place for dessert." He was kidding.

Or was he?

Flattered, that's how she felt, until he explained. The ice cream was in his van, which, unlike the cabin, had a working generator and a fridge. After dinner, they could sit there in comfort.

There was no need to wait for the power company to send a truck.

Vernon parked behind what would always be Walter's house because he wanted to confirm the power was off in the area.

Hopefully, the breaker switch on Route 29 had done the trick.

If it hadn't . . . **Oh hell**.

No way did he want to mess with a primary transformer on lines that channeled between towers stretching from Immokalee south. Not on a rainy night. Not beneath cables thick as hawsers that hissed like snakes. It was an electronic field the width of a highway where ions behaved like caged drunks.

A year in Walter's prison had provided him time to learn a trade. Wiring, installation, then advanced courses. He'd never held a job, let alone taught the subject. But Vernon **could have**. He wasn't an idiot, as Walter often claimed. Not when it came to anything of schematic design such as electricity. The genius in him, he believed, was the result of so many goddamn insults.

Think of lightning as a magnetic tongue. It flicks downward, rapid-fire, searching to connect with a polar opposite—streamers, the ionized channels are called. On the ground, an ionized mate, equally excited, responds with a return stroke that flows upward. It's the return stroke that produces the bolt's flash and thirty thousand killer amps. Voltage was nothing without amperage.

Power lines were manageable, lightning was

not, which was why Vernon had stopped here first, at the place where he'd grown up. He entered through the potato cellar, an access hard to find unless you knew where to look. Up a ladder, through a hatch, was the foundry.

Coal dust, acidic pig iron—a childhood spent suffering Walter's abuse had not dented his love for the smell of fire.

He tested a couple of switches, then followed his flashlight outside. The same secondary feed serviced the Barlow cabin. Power would be off there, too.

Excellent.

Now the question was, should he hike his three hundred pounds cross-country or drive to within easy walking distance? The big GMC diesel was a noisy sucker. There were other reasons not to drive as well. Vernon had to think about it because he dreaded walking past those damn abandoned boxcars. This, too, went back to childhood and some of the crazy shit Walter had done to them.

Them being him and Slaten, and their older brother, plus the old man's grandsons. Or his nephews. Or possibly Walter's **other** sons. What Vernon believed varied with his mood and the passage of time. What he knew for certain was, Walter would've screwed a woodpile on the chance there was a snake in it, so screwing his fat sister, or even his fatter half-chink daughter, was a step up, not down.

As to the truth about their mother, who gave a damn?

Not Vernon.

The abandoned railcars were another matter. Normally, he would've switched off his flashlight and skittered past what he didn't want to see. Pointless in a thunderous squall. Every few yards, lightning hurled the boxcars at his eyes, along with memories.

Walter saying, "Ya'll boys don't go near them wrecks, ya' hear? They padlocked for a reason."

Walter saying, "One time, I catched me a coolie sniffin' around them cars. Know what happened? He got his pecker cut off and stuffed down his throat. No-o-o. T'weren't me that did it. 'Twas a demon the coolies call Mr. Bird."

When the old man laughed, which was seldom, it was because he had told an amusing lie.

After that, his threats were prefaced with, "Mr. Bird will cut your pecker off" or "You know **he'll** be watching"—which was scary to a six-year-old boy even if it was bullshit.

And it was.

Or so Vernon believed until a night when the moon was full. He was twelve and bored stupid. The oldest, Walter Jr., had already been sent to the loony bin, and Slaten, the scrawny shit, was eight and did as he was told—usually, but not this time.

"The demon'll catch us, man."

"Fuck the demon, and Grandpa, too. He can't whip us any worse than he has already."

Vernon had swiped a hacksaw from the foundry, cut the lock, and levered open the door of a railroad car that had lettering on the side:

Sawgrass Clipper

It wasn't gold Walter had stored inside, although his eyes went just as crazy-wild when he had surprised Vernon and used one of the many ankle cuffs inside to chain him to the wall of the car.

Six days he was kept there, then finished his yearlong sentence in the foundry's fire box among graffiti and bones.

Walter saying, "If you run, I'll catch you."

Walter saying, "You can either bleed to death or hold still while I use this iron."

Walter, before his last breath, saying, "Guess where Mr. Bird lives now?" Meaning inside Vernon's head.

Even fifteen years later, Vernon couldn't pause to remember without losing himself in the pain of being branded. Glorious pain. It was an unfolding sensation that had satisfied beyond consciousness and left a yearning scar. The feeling could not be duplicated. Only held at bay by sharing the ecstasy with others.

It had to be fed.

Vernon felt the need to feed now.

He scrambled up an embankment to the road, leaving the abandoned railcars behind. The Barlow cabin was another sodden half mile. Worth it, when he saw candlelight within and touched his nose to a window screen. **Sniff-sniff-sniff.**

Gracie, the odor of her skin, was somewhere inside. He knew it even before she glided into the kitchen, a stack of dishes in hand. She wore jeans, a white blouse with buttons. A rectangle of gauze covered the artistry on her arm.

Vernon's eyes erased it all and saw the girl as she was. Naked. Small breasts fuller, a bump of the breathing unborn beneath her ribs waiting to be enjoyed.

He wanted her . . . wanted them **now**, until a man's voice spoke from the next room, some garbled comment about air-conditioning.

Gracie Yum-Yum wasn't alone.

Vernon ducked through the bushes to the next window, looked in, and listened to Mr. Bird say, "That whore. If the hippie touches her, kill him."

They were at the table, finished with the meal, when Tomlinson leaned back and said, "The AC in my van will be good for your allergies."

Gracie's expression asked **What allergies?** until she saw his face crinkle into a grin. "Sneaky bastard. Okay, I admit it, I was upset when I called. For all I knew, I'd been stood up. **You're** the one who was late." She began clearing dishes, then stopped and focused on the nearest window. "You hear that? An animal outside in the bushes, I think. Listen . . ."

Tomlinson got up and put his face to the screen. "Still raining," he said, and that's all because he didn't want to scare the girl. Someone . . . something . . . was out there, watching. A tangible presence. He returned to the table, where there was a fillet knife they'd used to portion the swordfish steaks. It became a toy to play with while he again mentioned air-conditioning, then said, "All I meant was, it's time for dessert, so the dishes can wait. Besides, that's my job. Camp rules, dear. They're very strict. The cook sits back with ice cream while us peons do the scrub work."

"Not in my house." Gracie said this with a perky little edge, and continued stacking plates. From the kitchen, added, "You know . . . this cabin really could be nice with some fixing up. Most of the furniture has to . . . Well, if Tootsie doesn't object. And this god-awful paint. Give me . . . Give us a month, you won't recognize the place."

She was leading up to something. Tomlinson and the knife joined her while he grabbed a dish towel. "When I talked to your uncle about you living here, I didn't mention Slaten. I guess you figured that out, huh? Tell me about the guy. Not the negatives, just the positives."

"Slaten? I know you're against him. Everyone is."

"I'm willing to listen, if you're willing to tell me the truth. What are his best qualities?"

"As long as you mean it, okay. He's an artist. A real artist. And he's . . . he's . . . Well, for one thing, he's the first man who ever . . ."

"Your first lover," Tomlinson said. "We already talked about that. What else do you like about him?"

"We're in love. What else matters? He's the father of my"—her hand moved to her stomach—"but it's more than that. Slaten's smart. He knows the world's full of bullshit rules, and he treats me . . . well, pretty good, considering how young I am. And he'll treat me even better when we have a place to live."

A delicate topic, and possibly dangerous after what Ford had said on the phone about someone monitoring their conversations. Tomlinson reduced the pressure by asking, "How're these damn mosquitoes getting in?" It was an excuse to lock the screen door and close some of the curtains. Then, at the sink, he turned the subject around. "The first one, I'm talking about first lovers, is always special—for a while anyway. In my case, it was my nanny. The way it started was—"

"Nanny?" Gracie looked up from a sink full of suds. "Like a maid, you mean? You must've been rich. How old were you when—?"

"Not too young to appreciate a great set of tits, or too old to forget the shitstorm that woman caused in my head later. Sonja, that was her name. She'd been screwing my father, turned out, and wanted revenge. Either that or she had a Scandinavian screw loose. Anyway, she'd slip vodka into my OJ, or give me a spoonful of brandy, and away we'd go. The details are a little fuzzy. Looking back, though . . . wow."

"She sexually abused you," Gracie said, grim-faced. "She victimized a child; probably got you hooked on alcohol, too. I get it—another dig at my baby's father." She swung a soapy plate toward him.

Tomlinson, using the towel, said, "I meant **wow** as in I've never looked at a pacifier the same way since. Why so crabby, all of a sudden?"

It was a while before the girl gave in and laughed. "You made that story up."

"Nope. Although I am prone to exaggerate when I'm sober. By the way"—he waited for her to face him—"I'm sober now. So are you. If there was ever a time for us to talk honestly, it's now."

"About what, Slaten? Or the drugs everyone thinks I'm—"

"Both, and anything else," Tomlinson said. "Come on, leave the dishes. Wait until I pull the van up close to the porch, then hop in."

"I don't mind a little rain."

"Curb service," he beamed. "It's the way ladies should be treated."

Gracie liked that. There was no hint of alarm in her face. He palmed the knife, started the van, and waited until she was in the passenger seat to lock the doors and drive away.

"Hey . . . where're we going?"

"The AC takes a while if the motor's just idling. We'll find a quiet spot or turn around in a bit and have dessert."

Gracie had to wonder, **Is he coming on to me?** A week ago, the prospect would have been laughable. Not now. After the talks they'd shared, and the man's sweet, caring ways, she felt a pleasant glow. They were friends, for god's sake. Nothing wrong with that.

Slaten wasn't mentioned again until they'd made a U-turn and parked, with the high beams on, facing the cabin. A couple of deer they spooked explained the noise she'd heard. It made the place feel like home again.

"Tell me about him," Tomlinson said. "Not the sex part, just generally about him as a man. His best qualities."

"Well, um . . ." she said. "He's, uh . . . I don't know, it's hard to narrow it down like that."

"Hell, throw in some sex, too, if you want. I'm all ears."

She chuckled, loosening up a bit, then did her best to lionize a man who had dominated her world by shrinking it until only Slaten existed.

Tomlinson listened patiently to the fantasy she created while noting the honesty of her hands. As she spoke, her fingers moved from her knee to her throat, to the grotesque tattoos on her face and neck. Her lap became an uneasy resting area. Often, a hand lingered on the burn dressing while the other shielded her face.

Finally, she said, "You just sit there and nod. Why don't you say something? I can't tell if you believe me or not."

"I believe **in** you," Tomlinson said, swinging his seat around. "It's too early in the game to believe anything else. How about some dessert?"

She watched him crank the roof higher so he could stand upright, then set out bowls in what was a cute little camper with curtains. "I know what you're doing. You think sugar will help me over the hump. Clear my head so I can think straight. That's why they feed addicts candy."

"Really? No wonder I'm jonesing for mango ice cream. I usually smoke a joint about this time of day."

"Go ahead. It won't bother me. Here, I'll prove it." She moved to a table in the back of the van and opened her purse. From it, she produced a tiny bag of crystals and a vaporizer shaped like a cigar. "This is the last of it. I haven't been high since I got out of the hospital and I don't want to be tempted to use this shit again. It's yours."

An ounce of flakka, Tomlinson realized. "I thought we were talking about Slaten."

"We are."

Before he could slip the baggie into his pocket, Gracie gave a great shuddering sob and fell into his arms. "Please, help me. Slaten . . . I know. Everything he touches is poison, but it wasn't him who kept me locked up. I swear. I can't lie to the judge and say—"

Car lights illuminated the girl's face and spun their shadows to the front of the van.

Tomlinson lunged for the curtains, then relaxed. "It's my friend, Doc," he said. "Better set out another bowl."

18

Ford left his truck running because of an oddity he noticed after arriving, but told them, "I'm going to take a quick look at the pond. After all this rain, water samples should show a spike in acidity. It's all about timing."

Tomlinson's expression read **Bullshit,** while the girl asked, "Why don't you let me fix you a plate first?" It was the polite, Southern thing to do—Gracie, the fragile teen, grounding herself with homemaker protocol.

If not for that, Ford would have suggested she use his hotel room in Everglades City tonight. Instead, he took his pal aside and asked, "Were you roaming around the yard before I drove up?"

"We heard something, that's why I got her into the van. Turned out, it was just a couple of deer. I'm worried about her, man. She's absolutely sure the guy who branded her, and did all that other sick shit, wasn't Slaten. If I understood more about that synthetic drug they use—" He stopped. "How'd you know we heard something?"

Ford produced a small gizmo with a lens at each end. "Have a look."

Tomlinson's eye widened in the greenish light. "Wow. A new toy. Thermal imaging? Yeah . . . Gad, is that—" He lowered the monocular, then tried again. "I can see Gracie through the damn walls. Her shape, like an orange sort of ghost. This isn't the same unit you had—"

"No, it's a new prototype. Check the outside wall near the window."

Tomlinson did. "Sonuvabitch," he murmured. "Is that what I think? . . . No, can't be. It's too big." On the cabin's gray siding was a rosy splotch that resembled a massive handprint. It was where a big man would lean his weight before peeking in.

"It's probably a hole in the drywall leaking heat," Ford said. "Just in case, lock the doors and stay inside until I get back. Better yet, stay in the van with the engine running."

"Hold on, ol' buddy. The whole phone-monitoring thing, you've got me spooked. I'm thinking about Gracie. Is someone after you?"

"I hope so," Ford replied. "If not—" He came close to admitting that Gracie could be right. The psycho who'd abused her might still be on the loose, but that was absurd. "It doesn't hurt to be careful," he added.

When Tomlinson was inside, he set off cross-country.

Vernon knew he was being followed—thanks to Walter. The old man had many faults, but weakness wasn't among them. He'd say, "Any man can't survive out here with just a frying pan and a knife deserves to be eaten."

Not referring to gators or bears, as most would. No, he'd meant killed and eaten by a better man. Walter had a taste for it, he claimed. Particularly Chinese.

It was the way Vernon had been raised. The old man hadn't allowed him off the property, not once, before the age of fourteen. The same with Walter Jr., which is probably why the big, bullying bastard had ended up in the loony bin. Ol' Walter would say, "It's 'cause you're all mental retards and ain't got a birth certificate." He'd say, "Learning electricity don't make you smart, and sassin' back shows just how dumb you really are." He'd say, "Not until one of you punks can put meat on the table and **prove** it."

Vernon **had** put meat on the table. Walter, drunker than usual, had loaded him into a boat, blindfolded him, and stopped after an hour's ride. Sawgrass all around, except for a creek no wider than a ditch, and an island of willows nearby. "Here you go, Ching-Ching," which is what the old man had called him, Ching-Ching, even before leaving him there, fourteen years old, with nothing but a pan, a knife, and matches.

Turned out, Walter, crazy as he was, had a sense of humor. That sawgrass prairie was near a dead-end road frequented by hippies and other loner types.

Food wasn't the problem. Finding enough salt to cure meat was.

A week later, Vernon's nose told him Walter was returning long before he heard the boat. It was the one and only time the old man had shown a glimmer of approval. "By god, at least your knife's sharp, shit-for-brains. Appears you might be catching on."

Like now. Vernon knew **who** was following him. It was the biologist with the wire glasses. The snoopy outsider who'd made some interesting phone calls from Key Largo. Something else was certain: the dude was using more than reading glasses to track him on a night black with rain.

It might have been worrisome, in a sporting way, if Vernon hadn't smoked himself to a finely honed edge. In lieu of crystal, a spoon of cheap-ass bath salts had done the trick. A head full of that shit gave a man coyote ears and vision that could penetrate brick.

No contest.

The guy was a slicker. They all were. Slickers didn't know the secret of moving silently through the Glades. Barefoot was the only way to detect twigs before they snapped, and to gently fold palmettos before they rattled. The slick was unaware that subtle changes in air were important. Moist areas retained odors. A patch of dry upland cloaked them.

The biologist was pretty damn good, though.

Vernon put another fifty yards of swamp between them, then monitored the results from behind a cypress tree. Sound communicated the biologist's confusion whenever he came to a stretch of water. The water didn't have to be deep. It suggested he might have a tracking dog. Vernon knew how to deal with dogs because of the bloodhounds Walter had raised, all of them—the best ones anyway—named Maynard. The name dated back to a deputy the old man had killed after stealing the sheriff's dog, his bullwhip, and his .38 caliber Webley revolver.

In Vernon's head, the story was put on pause while he decided, Nope . . . the biologist didn't have a bloodhound. Even a quarter mile away, he would've wind-scented a dog, conditions as they were. The sound was all wrong, too.

Yet, the slicker kept coming . . . not in a straight line, as before, instead zigzagging from tree to tree in ankle-deep water, which Vernon couldn't see, only hear.

How the hell . . . ?

He would figure it out, and have some fun along the way.

To lose a bloodhound, circle a distraction such as a chicken coop—Vernon had done it as a boy. A cache of old bottles might have the same effect on an outsider, so that's where he headed, an artesian well that bubbled up through a wall of rock. Nearby was a field cellar that had never held a potato, but there were still crockery jars, wax-sealed, that dated back to Prohibition.

The limestone lid normally required several men to heft it. Vernon, buzzed on flake, lifted with his legs and let the stone cover fall with a crash. The result was a distant silence, then a flurry of movement.

Yep. The slicker had taken the bait. No need

to bother circling. He headed straight to the pond, moving fast through the trees but as soundlessly as the loam beneath his bare feet. Then stopped.

Oh hell . . .

The slicker had changed angles. He was cutting him off without pausing to investigate what was in those old jars.

Vernon understood then. Slick wasn't following muddy water, or a scent trail. He was tracking handprints from tree to tree. **Heat.** The biologist was using thermal imaging.

Good for him.

Vernon tasted the air with his nose, and got serious. This was fun; better than playing tag with that ball-less weakling Slaten. It wasn't a game if you went by ol' Walter's rules. Early on, they'd used pellet guns and targeted the other guy's ass. After a year or so, Slaten, being smart, or cowardly, had claimed the old man had told him in private to use a .22 rifle and shoot for the head.

"Load up" was Vernon's response.

He was unbeatable out here. He knew every little hidey-hole, and there were a bunch around the pond. The limestone base was pocked like Swiss cheese, some holes large enough for a man his size. Back in the whiskey-making days, the holes had been used for storage. Later, as a place to punish some perceived screw-up.

"I'm gonna let you soak for a while," in Walter's words.

His favorite was the easiest to access—the Coolie Box, it was called, because gators had used it for ripening meat. Vernon made his way through the trees to the water, leaving hand-prints as he went. He waded in, aligned two familiar markers, and soon surfaced inside a chamber that was so dark, he couldn't see his hand in front of his face.

What he could see were a few stars through a fissure in the limestone, a gap several feet long and a foot wide, that opened to the surface. He poked his arm out as a snare and waited. Snaring game took patience. It gave him time to recall the flickering Kinetoscope and the image of a giant crocodile on the wall. Damn . . . he'd missed some fun by being born too late. The railroad, and cowboys on horseback, and all that legal killing during the Marco Island war.

Unlike Mr. Bird, Vernon couldn't return to the past. The next best thing? Seeing the world through the old man's eyes, acting, reacting, and listening as if Walter were still in charge. And keep doing it over and over until the old son of bitch was gone from his head.

It was the only escape.

The biologist slicker, yeah, he was pretty good. A suctioning of muck, a rhythmic slosh, was the only sound he made as he drew near.

The man took slow, sliding steps. When the hairs on Vernon's wrist felt the lift and fall of water, he unfurled his fingers like a bear trap. Then the biologist was above him, a bulky shadow against the clouds, close enough to grab the son of a bitch's ankle and snap his leg at the knee.

Vernon wanted to. Oh god, did he. After that, it would've been a toss-up—do a gator roll and rip the dude's pelvis off, or take his time and enjoy the kill.

Yeah . . . take his time. That was better. Surface. Track the crippled bastard and **really** hurt him, before doing what Walter had done to Vernon that night long ago when he'd broken into the railroad car.

Use the chains, one on each ankle. Apply outward pressure on the legs as if snapping a Thanksgiving wishbone. Next . . . use the knife.

"Like geldin' a hog." Say it just as Walter had said it, while the branding iron glowed yellow. "You can either bleed to death or hold still while I put **his** mark on you."

Meaning Mr. Bird, who had yet to state his plans for the biologist. Where the hell was he? What had happened to the familiar voice?

Frustrated, Vernon took a chance. He rapped a knuckle on the biologist's ankle as the man slid by. The dumbass didn't even notice. Just stood there, scanning the surface, then turned and damn near stepped on Vernon's hand when he returned to shore. The man kept going in a noisy, indifferent way that said he was done with their game.

Oh hell . . .

Finally—finally—Mr. Bird came into Vernon's head, saying, **You know why.**

Yeah, he did, but that didn't make holding back any easier.

Mr. Bird saying as a reminder, **He's bait until I've tasted the tall girl, Raven.**

It was because of a phone call the biologist had made from Key Largo. No conversation, just a message that read "Let me know when you want to come down and fish. Tomorrow, maybe? I've got a little aluminum boat."

Vernon's hunger for Hannah Smith replaced frustration. He slogged toward his utility truck, thinking about that, how to snatch the woman—and Gracie, too—but also deal with the biologist in a way that would be . . . satisfying.

He was so lost in thought, he was at the back rim of the pond before noticing a green laser dot on his chest.

Huh . . . ?

A laser **gun sight**. Christ, how long had that been there?

Vernon jumped away. The laser dot sailed

up his chest to his forehead. He ducked, rolled, and came up on one knee. The laser beam retracted into darkness. Where had it come from? Hundreds of yards away, he guessed, possibly the top floor or roof of Walter's house.

If so, he was dealing with two people, maybe more. Had to be, because that's when a man appeared from behind a nearby tree and blinded him with a white strobe.

"Get that goddamn light out of my eyes," Vernon hollered. A second later, the strobe went out and left floating sparks behind his eyes. "Was that a gun your partner had aimed at me? I'll stick it up your hind end if you—"

"A **gun**?" It was the biologist, his voice the same as hearing him through a phone.

"While you damn near blinded me. Yeah." Vernon rubbed his eyes while his brain transitioned into utility worker mode.

"What were you doing snooping around the Barlow place? It'd better be good."

"Hold on there, mister, your sniper buddy just put a laser dot on my chest. Why? He's gonna shoot me for doing my job?"

The slicker pretended not to understand, asking, "Does your job include peeking in windows?"

Weird, how calm the guy sounded. Not mad, just curious. Vernon changed tactics. "Wait a minute, you thought . . . Let's not get off on the wrong foot here, sir. The power's out and I'm a contractor sent by the local service provider. If you want, I've got some ID in my truck." The polite approach should have allowed him to move a few steps. It didn't.

The strobe came on again, this time pointed at the ground. "That's close enough. What's your name?"

"Vernon Crow, sir. I should warn you right now, local law enforcement always sides with us in these sorts of little misunderstandings. Utility access rights."

"Good idea," the biologist said, and took out a phone intending, Vernon realized, to call the police.

He growled, and charged.

I f not for seeing a human face, Ford might have thought it was an animal that charged him. A three-hundred-pound feral hog with crazed yellow eyes, or a Montana grizzly. No words, no warning, just a rumble that might have been the ground quaking beneath the guy's speed and weight.

The real surprise was the failings of the tactical strobe. It should've dropped the man within a few steps. The unit was calibrated to scramble synapse function, a dangerous piece of equipage that could cause seizures, even lasting damage to the eyes or brain. Weapon enough to stop a voyeur, or an honest utility worker, which was the problem. Until that instant, Ford wasn't sure who he was dealing with.

Vernon Crow was a freak. When he charged, the biologist reached for a pistol concealed in the back of his pants. Impact occurred an instant later. It was like being hit by a bus. Ford was knocked ass-backwards toward the pond and the gun went flying. Dazed, he rolled, and kept rolling, as Vernon tried to stomp him. When the timing felt right, he shielded his face with his forearms . . . caught the man's big bare foot, and rolled again.

Vernon made a whistling sound of pain and fell with the grace of a redwood. Over many years, and twice-a-day practices, Ford had paid his dues as a high school wrestler. Hand control skills, and the sweaty ballet of hip position, were hardwired. He scrambled atop the giant and used both legs to trap Vernon's right knee. After that, choking the guy into submission— or unconsciousness—should have been simple, methodical.

It wasn't. Vernon defied the principles of technique and gravity by vaulting up on one leg and slamming Ford against a tree—something an elephant might do to rid itself of a pesky rider.

A freak, yes he was, and Ford was no fool. He got to his feet and ran, busting through cattails into the pond. The giant mistook the tactic as fear. He followed. Then, standing in water to his waist, wondered, **Where'd that dumb bastard go?**

Vernon's last conscious memory before being pulled under and inhaling saltwater was the biologist speaking into his ear, saying, "Cross me again, I'll kill you."

Not mad, no longer curious. The slicker meant it.

19

By nine, Ford and Detective Janos Werner were on a guarded first-name basis. Not buddies, still playing the question-answer game, but enough trust established to stray into off-the-record areas, like now, Werner saying, "A marine biologist who carries a compact Sig with custom Truglo sights . . . I'm curious." He shucked the pistol's slide to reveal an empty chamber. "Some might think it's almost as unusual as owning thermal imaging gear."

"If they've got perfect vision, maybe." Ford's attention was on a squad car, where Vernon Crow, from the backseat, was giving him the death stare. Those crazy eyes hadn't wavered since three burly cops had wrestled the giant inside and slammed the door.

Werner released the slide, and asked, "Do you mind?" before testing the crispness of the trigger. "Nice. You had it dehorned, too. Smooth as a bar of soap. Which gunsmith did you use?"

Ford said, "The guy's crazy, you know that, right? He's amped up on something. As strong as he is, I wouldn't trust handcuffs to do the job. Same with the Plexiglas barrier. I'm thinking about the uniforms driving him." After a beat, he added, "The longer we wait, the more likely it is the girl will change her mind."

It was something he had suggested: allow Gracie to eyeball Vernon without him knowing it. This was after Werner had said they couldn't hold the guy for more than a day or two on an assault charge. Ford, because he'd assumed they were awaiting an official okay, was surprised when Werner replied, "You're right. Let's go get her."

"Just like that? You could have done it an hour ago."

"Sure, and had my ass handed to me because I didn't wait for all the info from the national data banks. We ran his prints, license, the VIN number off his truck, everything. Even some piss-poor photos for facial recognition I shot with my phone. I just got the results. The truck is registered to Walter B. Lambeth. Ring a bell?"

Ford looked through the shadows of cypress trees in the direction of the foundry. "Only because a friend of mine is a history buff. Walter Lambeth owned the place. He was an old-time outlaw, probably a murderer. It doesn't surprise me they're related."

"That's not what I'm saying. Vernon Crow, or whoever he is, doesn't exist."

"That doesn't surprise me, either. What's his real name?"

"You didn't hear what I said. Vernon—let's call him that for now—he doesn't exist, as far as the public records go. Unless he came into the country illegally within the last few years, something in the data banks would've popped. With his shit-kicker accent? He's lived here all his life, which he admits. In this nation, you can't live off the grid without leaving tracks, but he, by god, managed to do it."

Ford said, "He's got to be related to Slaten Lambeth somehow. I bet they tag-teamed Gracie. If not her, at least some of the victims in Gainesville. The woman who lived here—his mother, maybe his aunt—she was giant-sized, too. In fact, there is a possibility that—"

"Save the theories for later," the detective said, motioning him to follow. "Officially, I'm taking you back to your truck. Unofficially, I want you along to keep the girl calm. How well do you know her?"

"Not as well as my friend. If it's okay, Gracie would probably prefer—"

"Nope, just you or not at all. You realize she might lie just to get her boyfriend off? If she does, he'll walk on Friday, depending on DNA evidence, and there's not much. Like I told you, whoever it is, he's a pro when it comes to cleaning up a crime scene. Still think this is a good idea?"

They stayed on topic, risk versus gain, until they were on the shell road to the Barlow cabin. Werner pulled over, put his unmarked car in park, and made a show of switching off the radio and dash cameras. "Here's the thing. I believe your story—up to a point. Now I want you to do us both a favor by telling me the truth about one little detail. Something you left out."

Ford's mind transitioned to the behavioral coaching programmed years ago somewhere in Maine. "If I can help, Janos, I will. Ask me anything."

"You do **know** what I'm talking about?"

"I'm not sure."

"The guy, Vernon, he might be a psycho, but he's not stupid. Half an hour, I questioned him, and I think he only told me the truth twice, maybe three times. He claims you had someone with you. A shooter stationed on the roof of the old house. Maybe true, maybe not, but someone put a laser dot on his chest. I'd bet on it. Was it you?"

"I remember him saying that, yeah. Something about a gun laser, and was he going to be shot for doing his job? It was a way to make me turn around. That's the way I took it."

"You're saying he made it up?"

"Until now, I haven't given it much thought. What's the distance they teach law enforcement? A guy twenty-one feet away, if he has a knife, can cut your throat before you have time to draw your weapon and fire. With Vernon, that's what happened: he was at least ten strides away and he was on me before I could do a damn thing about it. Three hundred–plus pounds of muscle. I'm surprised I remember anything after he hit me. Somehow, we ended up in the water, and—"

"Doc," the detective said, "be straight here. You're telling me you didn't notice a laser dot on the guy's chest, him, like you said, only thirty feet away?"

In an interrogation, the most dangerous questions are those that can be answered honestly. The unschooled leap at the truth, which sets off alarm bells. Ford gave it some thought. "I tracked him using night vision, and, you're right, a laser would have lit up the place. It would depend on the timing, I suppose, but I . . ." He shook his head. "No, I didn't see it. You have my pistol. If it had laser sights, damn right I would've—"

"A **green** laser dot," Werner said, his eyes shadowed and watching for a reaction. "You've got all the toys. Green, not the standard red laser. That might mean something to you."

It did—a precision laser shooting system he'd tried recently, thanks to a wealthy friend. Ford evaded by asking, "You're convinced he's telling the truth?"

"That's **why** I believe him. He gave me all the standard baloney—you jumped him for no reason. Poor country boy, out here communing with nature, when a supposedly mild-mannered citizen blindsides him. **Sure.** But when a perp, even a psycho perp, lies about being painted up, he's going to say it was a red laser, just like in the movies."

Ford, for the first time, considered the possibility it was true.

"There's no law against having a friend cover your ass," the detective said. "It would have no bearing on this case. Personally, I'd like to know what the hell's really going on around here . . . **Doc**. Trust me, or not, that's up to you."

The biologist looked at his phone. No signal. "Damn it."

"Someone you have to call? Ask permission, maybe?"

The person Ford wanted to consult was Charles Beckett of Flamingo Cay, Bahamas. He pocketed the phone and shrugged.

"Fine. Let's skip the official crap and you tell me what you're thinking. Hypothetically, of course." Werner opened a tin of Skoal, offered it, then tucked a pinch between cheek and gum to show he was patient and willing to listen.

"If there was a third person," Ford said, "I didn't know he was there. A laser doesn't necessarily mean a gun. Laser pointers are cheap."

"Already defending a total stranger, huh? Is that the way this is gonna go?"

"Okay. Hypothetically." The biologist sat forward, unsure how far to take this. "It would have been a shooter with a long gun. A pistol— a laser sight's too shaky from a distance. If Vernon's telling the truth, the shooter had him dialed in but didn't pull the trigger."

"That's what I'm asking you," Werner said. "Why? I can only think of two reasons, but I'd rather hear it from you."

Ford, sensing a trap, took a preemptory risk. "Four possibilities would be more like it. The shooter wasn't a shooter, just some jerk playing games. Or it was a practice run. And some guys, even with a lot of training, can't do it— or so I've read. They can't pull the trigger on a real person. The fourth possibility is obvious."

"That's the first thing I thought of. Vernon wasn't the target."

There was actually a fifth possibility, but Ford responded, "Could be."

"Does someone want you dead, Dr. Ford?"

"Are you kidding? One's in jail and the other's back there in the car, handcuffed. At least, I hope he is. When I told you Vernon's strong, I mean he's like an animal. I hope you passed that along to the other officers." To ingratiate himself, he referenced the news media, saying their definition of the word **unarmed** was naïve and dangerously inaccurate.

Werner liked that. But, being a cop, had to consider motives before risking an opinion. Was the biologist kissing up or intentionally evading?

It didn't matter. The guy was right.

"I've arrested monster-sized guys so wired on crank, you could put three rounds in their chest and they'd still rip your head off, give 'em the chance. Not that I've shot anyone. But I've been on calls, we used Tasers, batons—everything— the whole non-lethal list, and it doesn't faze them. Just once, I'd love to hand a loaded .45 to a newscaster and lock him in a room with a killer twice his size, later ask him, 'The dude was unarmed, why'd you shit your pants before you pulled the trigger?' Now, back to this mysterious third person. Who was it?"

The lies flowed easily. "No idea. If I had to guess, I'd say it was some jerk playing games. When Vernon turned psycho, whoever it was probably ran off."

The detective opened the door and spit, amused. "Yeah, sure. All right, let's go talk to the girl."

W hen the detective said to Gracie, "Are you ready?" she said, "Yes," but wasn't prepared for the massive gorilla-sized face illuminated by the spotlight. A man, sitting in the back of a police car, squinted with fire in his eyes, seeing her, only her, which is how the moment registered in her brain. She ducked behind the seat while Ford tried to comfort her, saying, "You're safe, they're taking him to jail. Gracie . . . what do you think?"

She couldn't think, couldn't breathe. "Jesus, oh Jesus, I just realized . . ."

"What?"

"He **saw** me."

"That's impossible, I promise. He has no idea who's in this car or why the spotlight's on him. Is he the man who assaulted you?"

The detective, at the wheel, said, "Have her take another look, then we're out of here. Ms. Barlow, your attacker always wore a mask, you said. To make a case, you're going to have to be absolutely certain. What about that tattoo on his neck? Recognize it?"

"Yes," she whispered. There was no mistaking the Yantra artistry—a dragon shielded by what had to be a mosaic of overlapping flames, not scales.

"Even from here? I can pull a little closer, if you want, or I've got some photos on my—"

"No, he'll see me, damn it." She kept her head down and clung to Ford, digging fingernails into his knee. "You don't understand. Not with his eyes, maybe, but he knows I'm here. You didn't see the way he looked at me? It's coming back, some of the details. What he . . . **how** he knows things."

The man who'd rescued her asked, "What about the mask, Gracie? How about just another quick peek?"

"It's him. Jesus Christ, how many times do I have to say it? Now please get me out of here."

The detective said, "I'm convinced," and waited for uniformed cops to screen Vernon's view before pulling away. "Ms. Barlow?"

Ford said, "Let her calm down first."

Gracie, on the floor, sensed the biologist's awkwardness as he patted her back or stroked her hair. His hands were tentative, as if she wore a cloak that might rip. This, more than his touch, helped her rally after a few minutes. "Thanks, I know what you're doing. Sorry I lost it there for a minute."

"You did fine," the detective said. "You'll

have to go through it again, I'm afraid. It'll be easier, now that you know you're safe."

"That's what I want," she said. "Him locked behind bars. I'm not getting out until I'm sure."

"Out of the car?"

"Not as long as he's in the area. You don't understand the way he is. Can you have someone call you on the radio when he's in jail?"

The detective's response: okay, humor her. He made phone calls and drove; took the long way. The cabin porch appeared in the side window, but it was another ten minutes before he put down his phone. "The guy's going through the booking processing now on the assault charge. That should put your mind at ease."

"He's locked up?"

"Even better. There are armed cops watching him every step of the way, and the building's like a fortress. Really, you've got nothing to—"

"Is he at the county detention center? I was there today." Gracie, thinking about Slaten, pictured high, drab walls and rolls of razor-wire fencing.

"That'll be his next stop, yeah. Then, hopefully, a state prison. Look, I need to get to the office. Ms. Barlow?" The detective turned in his seat. "I believe you, so I'm going to book him, but if you don't feel right about it, I'm not going to leave you here. Or if you're still upset and need someone to talk to, I'm obligated to advise you regarding your options. We have professionals who can . . ."

Gracie let the man's voice blur while the cabin took on a fresh identity before her eyes. She noticed details that had gone unappreciated on previous visits: starlight and Spanish moss; a sleepy umbrella of oaks embracing the little house with its chimney and tin roof, which appeared waxen at night. Windows the color of butter; oil lanterns inside, impervious to storms and the failure of modern utilities. For water, there was a well with a hand pump. For cooking, there was a woodstove. Plant a small garden and she'd be free of all her mother's whining insults, independent for the first time in her life.

Tomlinson appeared in the doorway, which added a homey, welcoming touch.

"Gracie? Did you hear what Detective Werner said about a facility for women?" The biologist's concern was evident.

She answered, "This is where I live. My family's property. Of course I'm staying. You told me the truth about those . . . about **him** going to the county detention center, right?"

The detective began to reassure her until Ford interrupted. "Janos, wait, that wasn't a slip-up, was it Gracie? You meant Slaten, too.

Both of them. You saw something, or remembered some detail. What?"

The oddest feeling came over the girl, a territorial sense of being on family land and in control. So she responded by thanking the men for their concern, which was the adult thing to do, then said, "For now, I'm glad they're both locked up because, you're right, I need to work out a few details in my head. I'm not sure exactly what, but, when I'm ready, I'll tell you everything I remember."

20

Tomlinson sensed a change in Gracie even before Ford had done a security lap around the property, then drove away, presumably to his hotel. With him, you could never be sure. Since returning from the Bahamas, he had been edgy. There was a reason, as the man had finally explained, the two of them sitting alone in the biologist's truck.

It had to do with the British woman, Gillian Cobourg, and some secret she'd shared with him. Blackmail was at the heart of it, and a politician brother whose computer had been hacked by an international porn syndicate. Ford had the proof—whatever it was—in his possession, so anticipated visitors. No other details had been provided, other than the warning "Keep your eyes open for anything strange."

Strange? Christ, in a ghost town inhabited by a Chinese demon, and the monster kin of Walter Lambeth?

"You'd need a scorecard," Tomlinson had responded.

As to Gracie, she was in full nesting mode when he joined her in the cabin. She tidied up while asking his opinion on colors of paint, whether an extra room or two could be added, and how much it would cost to update the bathroom? Later, after changing into jeans and a white sleeved blouse, she said, "How about some herbal tea and those cookies you brought? I made a pie once, a girlfriend and me, but you'll have to wait until I get some recipes to try that. I will, though. Until now, I never had a reason to learn to bake."

Her eagerness was touching, but it was getting late.

"It's almost eleven, dear. Try to get some sleep. I'll hang out on the porch for a while, then bunk in my van."

Her mood shifted to accommodate. "If you want to smoke a joint, that's fine with me. I can't because of—" Her hand moved to her tummy. "You know. But I won't have a guest sleeping outside when there's a perfectly good couch in here." Then, facing him, she said, "Besides, there's something I want to talk about . . . and, I'll just admit it—I don't want to be alone."

Tomlinson recognized the warning signs, an involuntary moistening of lips that was a precursor to any conscious consideration of right or wrong. It wasn't intentional. The decision could go either way, not that he would allow it to happen. "Sure, whatever you want. Let's sit on the porch."

He lit a PIC coil to discourage mosquitoes and carried it outside. There were two cane chairs and a rocker. The girl needed to pace, so he rocked and listened. What she wanted to talk about had to do with a tattoo on Slaten's chest. "He told me I would never see another one like it, but I did. Tonight. It was on **him . . .** on his neck."

"The guy the cops arrested," Tomlinson said. "I got a look at him. Gad, what a monster. Is he the one who called himself—"

"Mr. Bird, yes. Even without the mask, a man that size, it couldn't have been anyone else. And the way he looked at me—not that he actually saw me, but he knew I was there, I'm sure of it. Does that sound crazy?"

"Nope. Happens all the time, and don't let anyone tell you differently. You don't remember seeing the tattoo before? Maybe the mask covered it. Or body paint, and you said he wore a robe sometimes."

The girl folded her arms as if chilled. "I'm . . . I'm not sure. Tonight brought some of it back. Not all the details, though, and that's the problem. They said the guy goes by the name Vernon Crow, which sort of fits, I guess."

Ford had briefed Tomlinson in private, but had left that part out. "Crow? That's eerie-weird."

She stopped pacing. "What do you mean?"

He wasn't going to tell her about Key West, that Madame Min-Juan had spoken of a demon some believed was more than just a fanciful story. He'd already done some research on the subject, but the girl wasn't ready to deal with what he had learned. "Vernon Crow," he said. "You're right, that's all. It fits with someone who calls himself Mr. Bird."

"They're probably both fake names. What I'm telling you is, Slaten and that man have the same tattoo, which shocked the heck out of me because Slaten claimed he's the only tat artist who can do it. It's an ancient Chinese design called Yantra, and requires a special type of blue bamboo that's sharp enough when it splinters. See, that's what Slaten used instead of a needle because . . ."

Tomlinson listened for a while and decided the girl was avoiding a painful truth. She needed a nudge. He took her hand, saying, "Think back. Slaten lied about why he took you to that house in the first place. Remember the story you told me?"

"The bamboo . . . yes. He pretended he didn't know it grew there." Her eyes drifted toward the floor. "I totally believed him. I guess it's possible he'd never noticed it before. I mean, seriously, who pays any attention to—"

Tomlinson interrupted. "A student of Yantra art would've noticed. What else did he lie to you about? I can list several. His name, for starters. And the way he justified almost killing your cousin when that tire blew. Gracie, you're a smart young woman. Tell me"—his hand moved to the sleeve of her white blouse— "the tattoo you saw on the man's neck, did it resemble what he . . . what **they** did to you?"

"Slaten had nothing to do with it."

"I believe that **you** believe it. But are you sure?"

"Of course, I . . . Oh hell." The girl, suddenly weary, plopped down in a chair and allowed a curtain of brown hair to screen her face. "It's all such a blur. The crazy woman who looked after me, she'd put crystal in my food if I refused to snort or smoke it. I hate that shit; hated it, except for the first time, when Slaten told me it was weed. After that, it just made me sick. Have you ever done hallucinogenics?"

"Oh, I've dabbled a bit."

"You're funny. A lot, huh?"

"More than I should've and less than I some-times wanted." His hand moved to his pocket where there was a baggie of crystal flakes. "You gave me the last of Slaten's flakka, right? Thank god. Some call it Five-Dollar Insanity, 'cause it's so cheap and unpredictable. I've never tried the stuff. Is that what she fed you?"

"I think so. Or bath salts. He knows how to do it, make what he calls synthetic amphet-amines. The first time—we were smoking weed soaked in crystal—it was this incredible soaring high. I remember laughing a lot, and . . . and I felt, you know, almost **beautiful**." Her voice caught. "The two times after that, though, were awful, and it was the same when they had me chained up. Like my skin was on fire. But the worst part was, I truly couldn't"—she had to reach deep to find the words—"I didn't know what was real and what wasn't." She brushed her hair back and looked up with large, dark eyes. "Has that ever happened to you?"

Tomlinson said, "The standard answer is 'Hell yes.' But the truth? Princess, I've done it all, most of it twice, and the truth is, I really don't think so. Even peyote, L.S.D., the really heavy shit, there's always a centering dot of awareness. Five-Dollar Insanity. No wonder you're confused."

"Not just confused, a lot of it I really don't

remember. The crazy woman, I called her. She kept me drugged up and sick, freaking out the whole time I was there. But I still don't think Slaten could've—"

"The woman was Ivy Lambeth," Tomlinson said to remind her of Slaten's real last name but stopped short of saying, **Your baby's aunt or, possibly, grandmother.** It would've been too cruel. But facts were facts. "They killed her, you know."

The girl's manner, body language, everything, changed. "Good. That fat bitch, you think I care? And you're wrong about Slaten. He doesn't know anything about what happened to her. He told me himself this morning."

"Was it after he found out he was going to be a father, or before? Look"—Tomlinson gave her arm a gentle squeeze—"I agree. People we care about sometimes need love when they deserve it least, but there's a reason there's an argument going on in your head about whether to trust him or not."

"I didn't say that!"

"No, but you said he's poison, remember? Now his fall guy shows up with the same tattoo. Gracie, dear, face it—he and Vernon Crow are in this together, and good riddance. You and your baby don't need Slaten to live happily ever after. I want you to believe that."

She tugged her arm away. "I thought you

might understand why my head's so messed up, but you don't. No one can understand unless . . . unless they . . ." She spun around and went inside, letting the screen door slam behind her.

Tomlinson sighed, helpless in the face of the truth. The girl was right. He couldn't possibly understand her confusion without experiencing the drug for himself. Again, his hand drifted to the baggie in his pocket.

No, not while tending to a teenager in trouble.

But soon . . .

Gracie gave up trying to sleep and went to the porch, hoping to recapture what she'd felt earlier, a delicious sense of having her own home. The lights in Tomlinson's van were on, blinds drawn. The hum of its little generator and AC competed with a chorus of frogs. She watched until movement behind the blinds confirmed the man was awake, then crossed the yard and knocked.

He beamed at her through the window and opened the sliding door. "Come in out of the bugs. Hurry up."

She hadn't anticipated being chased inside by mosquitoes, but it was okay. She'd sort of hoped it would happen, the two of them alone, in a space that was furnished more like boat than a camper. "This won't take long. There's something I want to tell you. It's about Slaten."

"Oh?"

Tomlinson's baggy shorts, no shirt or shoes, was the way a rapper might dress. She liked the way he stood there, loose-limbed, and funneled his hair back with a scrunchie, then, with a quick loop, made a ponytail that hung over one boney shoulder. "You were right," she said. "I won't be safe if he gets out of jail. The detective gave me his phone number, and I'll call him tomorrow."

"If Slaten gets out, you mean."

"Yes."

"**Oh.** That's big . . . Have a seat." He motioned to the table where, earlier, they'd eaten ice cream.

"No, really. I saw that you were up and decided to tell you. Like, so I won't change my mind later, you know? Otherwise, I would've gotten dressed instead of wearing just an old robe and sweatpants." She pulled the lapels tighter around her neck, adding, "So . . . that about does it. In the morning, I'll try to make pancakes. What time do you get up?"

Was the man laughing at her? If so, it was in a kindly way, not mean. "What's so funny?"

"Us. All mankind, from sea to shining sea."

"I don't get it."

He waved it off as unimportant and waited until she was seated to return to the subject of Slaten. "Did you remember something specific or is it more of a feeling? The detective will ask. Cops are big on details when it comes to building a case."

"It was something that came back to me tonight. I don't . . . I'd rather not say, if you don't mind. It's not that I don't trust you, but I . . ." Gracie felt herself choking up. She suddenly felt like an absurd little girl who was shy around adults.

Tomlinson slid into the booth and framed her face with his hands. Maybe as a prelude to a kiss, a real kiss, which is what she hoped he would do, but he only kissed her on the forehead. "I'm proud of you. Both those screwheads belong behind bars. Your uncle will be relieved, so I'll let you tell him, okay? Now I'd like you to do me a favor." He indicated a bench seat that had been pulled out to make a bed. No sheets, just a blanket and pillow. "Why don't you curl up there and get some rest? I'll pull the courtesy curtain. I've got some stuff to do on the computer anyway."

"I'm not a child," she responded. "You didn't let me think this through. I'll have to tell the detective anyway, so I might as well tell you."

A couple of key details blurred by drugs had

emerged. The man who'd repeatedly raped her **did** have an intricate tattoo on his neck, possibly a dragon, but sometimes he did not. On those occasions, "Mr. Bird" wore a leather breastplate.

"He had to cover his chest for a reason," Tomlinson suggested, which was a gentle way of saying **There were at least two men.**

"I can't be a hundred percent sure I didn't imagine it. Maybe that's why I wouldn't let myself remember . . . especially after Slaten seemed so happy when I told him about me being pregnant."

A more chilling memory fragment dated back to her first night in Slaten's camper.

"We were all smoked up, then switched to wine, and I got so sick the next morning, I'm surprised I remember anything at all. And I didn't until I saw him, the guy the cops had me look at. He . . . It was . . ."

"Vernon Crow," Tomlinson said, helping her along. "What about him?"

"His head. The size of it, and his face reminded me of a gorilla. That's when I remembered. Slaten had been talking about money, or how rich his family was. Bragging, like maybe he would inherit it. That got him on the subject of a cousin or maybe a brother, I'm not sure, who was off in the head, so they kept him locked up. Like at a facility, I guess."

"Did he mean crazy or mentally handicapped?"

"I don't know. Then something about their grandfather wouldn't let the boy leave the property for years because he was dangerous as any animal and as strong as a gorilla. That's when it came back to me, what he said—an albino gorilla. I thought he was joking, you know? Like something he'd seen in a movie until . . . until tonight when the spotlight . . . And there was something in that man's eyes that . . ."

Gracie looked at him, then looked away. "I knew it then. He and Slaten have to be related somehow."

She broke down. Tomlinson pulled her to his chest and let her sob. Tears receded until later, on the bed, he covered her with a blanket and turned to close the curtain.

"You don't have to go."

"Oh yes I do."

"Why? Am I that unattractive or is it because of them, what Slaten and the other one did to me? I feel shitty enough as is."

He sat, tucked her in, and patted her foot. "You've got it all wrong, Gracie. I'm the problem. I don't trust myself, if that makes any sense. So help me out by backing off the pheromone throttle a tad. Okay?"

"Huh?"

"Pheromones."

"I heard you, but what do you mean?"

"Sensuality, that spark in your eye, girl. One of us has to be strong and I'm a damn poor choice, believe me."

That got a smile, at least.

21

With the camper lights dimmed, Tomlinson sat at his laptop and opened a file he'd created before leaving Key West. **Demon Crow**, it was labeled.

The name, just looking at it, created a vortex of air that sharpened sound, even imagined sound. Twice he got up and opened the van's louvered blinds to peer out into a benign darkness that had a spooky campfire tinge.

A bottle of Corona beer over ice helped.

He read for a while, then checked on the girl. Her rhythmic puffing confirmed she was asleep. Once again he sat in the forward captain's chair and reviewed passages he had copied. Several were from **The Diamond Sutra**, a

centuries-old manuscript found in the Mogao
Caves of Dunhuang, China. Other notes had
been gleaned from the **Tibetan Book of Spells**
and articles on Chinese mysticism.

As a Buddhist, he took care to approach the
writings with the seeking spirit of a Bodhi-
sattva. **Do not cling. Strive for awareness
without striving.**

He read:

> In the spring heart of time exists a reptile
> who is also a bird. Shue Gwee, the Water
> Beast, he is called by those who fear his
> true name. The name can be syllabled but
> never spoken without consequence.
>
> He is known by the mark of Demon
> Crow.
>
> The crow demon roams between the
> light of moon and sun, and on the grayest
> rim of dawn. Unsuspecting victims are
> dragged into caves or underwater and con-
> sumed. He takes possession of their souls,
> which is why he is immortal, and travels
> the centuries with a hundred eyes . . .
>
> Not all receive his mark. Those who
> do carry it for eternity.

Tomlinson's focus shifted to the girl, then
back to his reading. A different source:

The process of spirit habitation is known by the Chinese symbols 替身. They literally mean to "replace one with the other." The Bird Demon returns to life in the victim's body and constantly seeks new souls to inhabit. He mimics their aspect and manner but, for sustenance, must consume human flesh. Woe to his victims for their bones will suffer in the Ten Courts of Hell . . .

The Ten Courts of Hell was Buddhism's version of the Inferno's basement floor.

Tomlinson got up and closed his laptop. Holy Cripes—Demon Crow was like Dracula on steroids.

This problem required serious thought.

He lit a prayerful sprig of incense, a ceremonial touch, while he mulled the situation over. Walter Lambeth, almost a century ago, had been host to a demon. The demon had survived by switching to a younger host or hosts. It was crazed nonsense to all but those who had experienced a paranormal psychotic event.

Tomlinson carried the scars.

Walter Lambeth and his legacy were as real as Florida history. There was no telling how many people the old son of a bitch had defiled. Madame Min-Juan understood the enormity of what had happened. Tomlinson would help her return those lost souls to their homeland, but there seemed to be a more pressing issue. Something he'd just read:

Not all receive his mark. Those who do carry it for eternity.

Shit-oh-dear. If this was true, it was Madame Min-Juan who was in the gravest danger, and possibly Gracie, too.

The revelation required action.

Under the sink was a mini cupboard. Among the cleaning items was a can of cleanser that was actually an insulated safe with a screw top. He removed a baggie of weed and rolled a beautifully tapered joint while an internal debate ensued.

The ancient seers, even the best of them, used the grimmest sort of moral extortion to stress a point. A favorite example was the claim that Hell was the only reward for adultery. Tomlinson had disproved that notion a thousandfold. Evil, on the other hand, had an energy source that could conjure truly horrific punishments—demonization, among them.

Occasionally, Tomlinson had to rein in his Catholic upbringing with a quick reality check. He did it now and the results were not encouraging.

These were dark waters, indeed.

A rhythmic similarity in the names came to him then: the Water Beast . . . the Walter Beast.

Interesting.

He went to the curtain and peeked in at the girl. There were things he'd forgotten to ask her, the most important of which concerned the brand on her arm.

From the shadows, the girl sensed it, and her voice reached out. "I was hoping you'd come back. I was having the nicest dream, then I heard something, or maybe that was part of it. Anyway, I woke up. What time is it?"

He sat on the bed, and they talked for a while. When it seemed okay, he asked, "How's your arm doing?"

"I haven't seen it since it started to heal. The nurses make sure I don't see the scar because the doctor said I shouldn't. Does that sound screwy to you?"

No, it sounded sinister, but he replied, "Listen to the experts unless your instincts tell you otherwise. Oh, I meant to ask you, I have a question about bamboo, something I saw once."

"Is this a tricky way of talking about Slaten?"

"Only if what he told you about bamboo helps me figure something out. A while back—it was at night—I watched someone plant a bunch of giant stalks in a circle. Only, they weren't planted, because the next day they were gone. Is weirdness like that something bamboo aficionados do?"

The girl sat up and felt around for a light switch. "Stop it," she said. "You're talking about the crazy woman. Why do you do that? If you want to ask me something, just ask."

"Sorry," Tomlinson said, and switched on a reading lamp that showed the girl, in a white tank top, her pale shoulders and arms a-swirl with tattoos, black ink on white parchment. "You're right, it was her, but I was trying to change the context."

"Change the what?"

"I lied to you, in other words," he said, "and ended up pissing you off anyway. So what's new in my world? I told you I couldn't be trusted."

The girl chuckled and sat straighter, feeling his eyes on her skin—a misjudgment that caused him to hand over her robe, which she pushed away. "Stop treating me like an adolescent, okay? The bamboo, yeah, she told me about it, as if I gave a damn. Is that why you really came in here?"

"I'm interested, and I'm running out of ways to apologize."

"You're funny, know that? I like you."

Tomlinson stopped the game playing. "You're a valuable young woman, Gracie. Get your health back, and when your baby's old enough to climb around on my boat, bring a hammer, because that's what you'll need to keep me away. Until then"—he gave her a wise, warning look—"let's stick with the bamboo."

"Okay. Geeze. Those disgusting wind chimes in the house, she made them out of what she called lightning glass. She—I don't know how it worked exactly—she'd run a wire from the top of a bamboo stalk to the bottom and bury the wire in sand. That's what she told me. It had to be sand."

"I'll be damned. Lightning rods."

"I guess. She'd do it afternoons before a storm and show me these wormy-looking glass tubes the next day. It has a name, the stuff, but I can't remember it."

Fulgurite. He'd seen the jade-like shards on a long-ago beach in Tahiti. Tomlinson was charmed by the primitive elegance of the technique. "Take a stalk of bamboo, ground it with wire, and lightning melts the sand. It's hard to believe someone like her would care enough to bother."

The girl pulled the blanket to her neck. "I don't want to think about it, what she . . . I haven't told anyone this, but, for the first few days, I was afraid she was really . . . you know. Him. Because of her size and all. I was wrong. I'm not going to tell you why I'm sure, but I am." She shuddered, and settled back on the pillow.

"Gracie, I'm sorry. I should've waited to—"
He stopped midsentence, and said, **"Oh damn."**

"What's wrong?"

"Lightning rods. I just got a terrible vibe—
your cousin was killed by lightning, right? And
that RV fire . . . Geezus, the same thing could
happen to your uncle. Hang on, I've got to
make a couple of calls."

He hurried toward the front of the van, pausing to politely draw the curtain.

Tootsie, after grumbling about being called so
late, said, "You damn near gave me a heart
attack. Nothing good happens after midnight, and I figured it had to do with Gracie.
As long as she's okay, it don't matter, I guess.
What time is it?"

Tomlinson said, "I want you to do something for me. It was storming there when I left
and I'm worried that—"

"It's still pouring down, so what?"

"Any lightning?"

The old man had to clear his throat while
rain hammered the roof of his double-wide.
"What the hell you expect? Another squall blew
in from the ocean side. If you're not drunk,
Reverend, open a fresh bottle 'cause this sorta
business can wait 'til morning."

"Don't hang up, man. Just hear me out."

Tootsie listened for a while, before saying, "That's just flat-ass crazy. Of course I got a patch of bamboo. Name one place on the Keys that doesn't." A moment later, he said, "I'm standing here in my skivvies, half asleep, and you want me to do **what**?"

"Just take a quick look outside. Doc said there was someone near your place this afternoon monitoring our phone calls."

"What's that have to do with my bamboo? Hang on there . . . Monitoring. You mean like listening in? And him a fish scientist. How could a scientist know something like that?"

Tomlinson said, "Trust me, he's usually right about this sort of thing. I've got a bad feeling, Tootsie. Please? I'll explain the rest when you're sure I'm wrong."

"Wandering around in a storm is a hell of a way **not** to get struck by lightning, that's all I have to say. You might as well hang up, 'cause I ain't calling you back 'til morning."

He slammed the phone down before Tomlinson could respond.

At Tootsie Barlow's door was a hat rack where there were white rubber boots and foul-weather gear. He put on a jacket so old, the plastic flaked, and carried a flashlight outside. After a few seconds, he was soaked anyway. Rain blew past in waves while the sky sizzled, a flashbulb effect that stunned the eyes with verdant foliage, yellow and green.

A shaft of light flicked a nearby palm and stopped the old fishing guide in his tracks. A bullwhip snap of thunder was simultaneous. It took him a second to get moving again.

Damn . . . That was a close one.

Yeah, buddy, but not the closest. Many times in his career, he'd experienced the same breathless instant of uncertainty, not sure if he'd been struck dead or not. Of all the squalls over the decades, the worst to ride out—no, the stupidest—was the time a client had hooked a possible world record tarpon on 12-pound tippet and refused to relinquish the rod. More than an hour, they'd followed that fish, while rain and fire poured down from the sky, one bolt so near, they'd felt the shock of the strike through the hull yet heard no thunder.

No one believed them, of course, when they made it back to the dock—same with their tale about electricity melting the leader.

By god, it was true. There were many strange things he'd witnessed that were difficult to believe if a person hadn't spent a lifetime on the water. The bay, the Gulf Stream, and open sea, were particular about who they shared their secrets with.

Years later, however, a client who was also a scientist had confirmed the story was true, explaining, "When lightning strikes, the explosion is a shock wave for the first ten yards. It's only after that that it becomes an ordinary sound wave."

In other words, you never hear the bolt that kills you.

Tootsie slogged against the wind to the clump of bamboo, already convinced that Tomlinson's story was baloney. The flashlight painted a frail beam among thrashing stalks of green. He looked them up and down . . . blinked a couple of times, then looked again. Had to crane his neck because in the middle of the stand was a stalk twice as tall as any bamboo he'd ever planted.

What the hell . . . ?

He wiggled his way into the clump for a closer look. The flashlight found the base of the stalk—damn thing was as thick as his ankle, and it stood free, not rooted to the ground.

This was unusual.

After wiping rain from his eyes, he confirmed something else he saw: a strand of heavy-gauge copper wire that ran toward his trailer. He had to back free of the foliage to follow the wire to its terminus, which was a copper pipe that fed propane to his stove—exactly as Tomlinson had predicted.

Fear. It tickled the back of the old man's neck like static electricity.

Oh Lord. This caused him to remember an important detail. Something else his scientist client had said was "Seconds before a strike, people often report that their hair stands on end."

Tootsie was running toward the safety of open ground when his rainy, thunderous world exploded in a flash of silent light.

Tomlinson returned to the bed, and closed the courtesy curtain, as Gracie asked, "Is Tootsie okay?"

"Stubborn as ever. I just hope I'm—" He stopped, reluctant to upset the girl. "I always get a little paranoid when I'm stoned. Not that I am, but your uncle probably thought I was."

"You're worried," she said, "I can tell. Why won't you talk to me about it?"

The man, with his boney bare chest, chewed at a strand of hair, then shrugged. "It's nothing that can't wait until morning. Get some sleep, okay? The driver seat reclines, so don't worry about me."

"Tommy?" Gracie had been wanting to call him that for a while. "Would you . . . would you mind holding me for a bit? I'm not scared. I know the crazy woman's dead, and that Slaten and . . . **him**, the other one, they're both in jail. In fact, I've never felt safer in my life. It's just that I—"

"You're restless?"

"More like a lonely feeling, I guess."

A bittersweet smile on his face, Tomlinson said, "Scoot over."

For half an hour he lay with his lips near her ear, whispering small blessings, his voice too soft to hear, until he thought the girl was asleep. She wasn't.

"Where are you going?"

Done with lying, he responded, "To smoke a joint. Need anything?"

"Yes, but apparently that's not gonna happen tonight. Would you mind grabbing my purse? It's in the cabin on the bed. No rush. It's nice and cool in here with the AC."

Barefoot, he went out into a summer night, the shadows wild with throbbing fireflies while he used the lighter. Man, he needed those first two hits. Then a third, the smoke finally curling into his brain that was already eager for more.

Inside the cabin, he paused and sniffed the air, alerted by some imagined oddity. Through a window was the VW van, its windows dim, the silken engine purring on idle. Nothing unusual about that.

He returned to the task at hand: finding Gracie's purse. This required a lamp to be lit—and another cookie, while he was at it. The weed had blurred the cerebral edges, putting him in munchies slo-mo. He searched the bedroom, and found Tootsie's long-barreled revolver, nothing else, then looked under the bed. That's where he was, on his knees, when the van's headlights swept the window, the driver already shifting into second, then floored the accelerator.

"Sonuvabitch."

Tomlinson said that many times while he ran in pointless pursuit, then hit a patch of sandspurs. The damn things pierced his feet like tacks. Limping and hopping, he turned back to find Gracie's rental car locked, and two of the tires flat. Which was okay until he realized her purse, where she probably kept the keys and her phone, was gone. A frenzied search proved it had been stolen.

The situation got worse. His cell phone, and everything else he'd brought, was in the van, including his shoes. The cabin's wall phone hadn't worked all day but had at least made static noises. Not now. It was dead. Someone had cut the line.

No . . . not someone. Some **thing**.

"You son of a bitch!" Tomlinson screamed the words from the porch, then challenged the stars with the forbidden name. "Demon Crow, Demon-fucking-Crow. If you've got the balls, here I am." From the yard, added, "Do you hear me, Walter Lambeth? Come get me!"

Carrying Tootsie's long-barreled revolver in a bag, he set off, limping, toward the demon's lair . . . or the main road.

Whichever crossed him first.

22

Mr. Bird couldn't abide jail or an insane asylum, so he took flight. He preferred big diesels to the tin can frailties of a Volkswagen van, although the camper had already provided options that were useful.

A bed: Gracie Yum-Yum, with her ankles, wrists, and mouth taped, lay there making pathetic cat sounds.

Later, on a mattress of foam, not a blanket on the ground, it would be feeding time.

The hippie's cell phone GPS was on the dash: they drove in darkness on a one-lane shell road, headed northwest out of Palmetto Station, taking the backcountry route into Collier County.

Walter had hunted this road as a boy. Walter had fed scrap body parts to gators. Mr. Bird knew the rutted hazards well, but only the GPS could provide a record of the hippie bastard's recent travels and his favorite destinations.

He scrolled through the list.

Hmm. **Dinkin's Bay, Sanibel.** An icon indicated it was home. Excellent. No need to search for a "Dr. Ford," which is how that dink detective had addressed the biologist.

Ford and the hippie were neighbors. Vernon had harvested this detail from their phone calls.

Mr. Bird yearned to bury his thumbs in the slicker's eyes and pluck them out, saying, "You've never experienced thermal vision until now."

The branding iron would provide an education.

Trouble was, the biologist wasn't easy prey. Vernon had learned this the hard way. Maybe the slicker was home, maybe he wasn't. Walter, who'd fed a family and his chink slaves via woodsman skills, had a philosophy about that:

Use the right bait, dummy, then hide your ass in a tree stand. Hunting on foot is for fools.

The phone had a touch screen. He scrolled until he found "Capt. Hannah." A star icon provided her address, an island on Sanibel's bay side connected to the mainland by Pine Island Road. She was probably asleep at this hour, so easily surprised.

Walter knew those backcountry islands. He'd

done business there in the '20s after the railroad was built to bring rich tarpon sports down to catch tarpon, a fish that was no damn good for eating. On the trip back north, the same sports had turned a blind eye to boxcars loaded with whiskey. Why not? It was making many of them richer.

Walter had salivated at the name Hannah Smith.

Mr. Bird, at the wheel, remembered the woman as she was now through Vernon's eyes: Black hair glossy as tallow. The buckskin smoothness of her skin, long legs in fishing shorts, the heavy lift and fall of her breasts beneath a blouse that flowed with her body.

The biologist had the hots for Captain Hannah. Could be, he was the one who'd knocked her up.

Bait. Two for the price of one. No . . . four, because both women were pregnant.

He was thinking that, imagining the possibilities, when a sudden thunk in the back of the van caused him to look over his shoulder.

Damn little redneck biddy. She had wrestled herself off the bed onto the floor. He checked the mirrors, even though he'd yet to see another car, then pulled over. Moths swirled in the high beams. The van creaked beneath his weight. He towered above the girl and watched her eyes widen, then glaze.

"You got some tongue on you, I forgot," he said, referring to the tape she'd managed to push from her mouth. "Anxious to use it, are you?"

The girl made a wheezing sound in an attempt to speak but only managed a bawling noise that might have been "Ple-e-e-ease don't."

God, he loved the way terror melted a human face into a waxen death mask. It was a moment to be savored. He did, took his time, before saying, "Make you a deal."

The girl nodded eagerly.

"Tell me what you know about this woman fishing guide, Captain Hannah."

Gracie was so scared her memory froze. "Huh?"

He repeated the name. "Think she might be up for a threesome? Better answer me. You know what happens when I get mad."

"Okay, okay . . . I'm trying to think." She cringed as the man's expression changed. "Wait . . . I remember now. The woman, the guide—my uncle told me about her. Yes, I think she would. Hannah, she's . . . I find her very attractive."

"You do, huh? My, my, my, I just learned something new about my little Gracie Yum-Yum. You might be worth keeping around for a while. Does she live alone?"

There was only one safe answer. "By herself, yes. I'd really like to see her again."

The man's expression read **Lying bitch,** but he said, "Ain't that sweet, you two so close and all. Probably 'cause you're both in a family way, huh?" He watched the pain those words caused. "That's excellent. That's what I wanted to hear." He dropped to his knees suddenly, his face poised above hers like a dog about to bite. "In that case, you won't have no problem telling me where she lives."

The heat from his breath made it impossible to breathe. She felt herself teetering, unhinged, unable to voice a lie.

The man she thought of as Mr. Bird straightened to his knees, amused. In his hand was a cell phone displaying a map. He touched a star on the map. While the phone calculated distance and directions, he said, "Don't worry your pretty little head, I got her address."

That was it. He returned to the driver's seat. Not another word for a mile or so, until the van swerved abruptly and stopped. "You see that? Goddamn swamp buggy pulled right out in front of me," he said. Not mad but interested. "No lights, either. Are they broke down or"— the van moved a short distance and stopped again—"stupid bastards won't let me pass. They ain't cops, if that's what you're hoping. So let's see what these here boys got worth sharing."

He got up and grinned at her. "Gracie Yum-Yum ain't for sale, but maybe we can barter."

alter had dealt with hundreds of these piney woods hard cases, weasels with more bluster than brains. Vernon and Slaten, the same thing, although it was Vernon who'd carried the heavy load when roaming the Glades as boys.

Him being so big and smart and all.

Mr. Bird channeled that knowledge as Vernon sized up the pair of gizzard-thin rednecks who'd stopped him, seeing in the headlights they were ugly enough to be kin. One sat atop the buggy, with its giant knobbed tires, gun seats, and a gun rack. The man held a rifle. The other, a bandy-legged rooster type, carried an axe and wore a puckered smile as if about to crow.

"How ya'll doing tonight?" Vernon called, stepping out of the van so they could see who they were dealing with.

Oh-h-h-h shit. That was their first reaction. Next came surprise—they'd been expecting someone else.

Who? he had to wonder.

"You boys have engine problems? Happy to help, if I can. Say . . . I get the impression we've met before."

"Well, sir, we was thinking the same thing. That van sure looks like one owned by a friend of ours. A sorta hippie-looking dude. A Yankee. Don't reckon you know him?"

Vernon thought, **Witnesses,** but said, "Hell yes, I know that weirdo freak. Don't tell me he cheated you out of money, too? Why you think I'm driving this piece of junk?" He ambled toward them to show how at home he was out here in shit-kicker land.

"Cheated you, huh? Ain't that a coincidence. That tough guy friend of his, the one with the wire glasses—you know him, too?" Rooster, doing the talking, used the axe as a leaning post, while the other stood and shouldered the rifle.

"Boys, let's be straight here. How much they take you for? Look"—he waved them toward the van—"I'm not greedy. There's something in the back should cover your losses. Come on, have a look. If you like what you see, let's say we share fifty-fifty, then you can do something for me."

The scrawny one with the rifle jumped down, saying, "What'd he say, Zeke?"

"Deaf bastard, you don't gotta holler," Rooster replied without looking away. "Mister, I like a good trade, but it'd better be real good. Depends on what you got. What **we** want might be a bit tougher to negotiate."

What Vernon wanted was every goddamn thing they had, including the license plate on the buggy. "See for yourself," he said, and slid the door open, then waited while the scrawny fools bickered about who would get Gracie first.

Diversion was a Walter tactic. With a boatload of chinks, once their money was paid, he might point at the horizon before using a club. Or, in the Glades, during the Marco war, say to a deputy clinging to his wife and brats, "The sheriff sent me to fetch you, that's all I know. **I'll** look after your family."

Vernon took a step back while the men ogled the girl, lying naked, all taped up, just her and her tattoos, poor Yum-Yum's eyes wider than her lips when she screamed.

Even the deaf bastard reacted to that by dropping his rifle.

A rifle butt—handy. It became a bludgeon after he'd forced the men facedown in the sawgrass and stomped them into submission. Light as their bodies were, it took only one trip to drag them close to a gator pool. The swamp buggy, driverless, mashed them into the mud before its tires bogged and stalled the engine.

Not a shot fired.

Bullets cost money. Wood is cheap. Walter Lambeth was a frugal man even when it came to killing.

Vernon returned with what Walter thought of as swag: guns, ammo, a Florida license. A can of camo paint was used to slather the van as if it were a junker.

"I need turpentine," he told the girl.

Not because of the paint. Blood.

His wide, spattered face appeared in an iPhone glow that marked their destination.

23

Hannah Smith heard the chain-driven rattle of a VW van pass by, and thought, **That's odd.** She lived aboard a boat, a refurbished 37-foot Marlow, on an island where people fished or farmed for a living, so drove pickups or normal cars.

Could it be Tomlinson?

Unlikely. It was 3 a.m., according to the clock in the V-berth, which was usually a fine place to sleep. Not tonight. A few minutes earlier, the power had gone off. With it, the AC. She'd been lying there, debating whether to rely on screened windows or try to sleep, despite the heat, on this restless June morning.

When the van went by again, she got up.

Who else would be wandering around the island at this hour?

Tomlinson was a good friend, although closer to her mother, Loretta, who lived across the road in the family house. A brain aneurysm and two surgeries were a handy excuse when the woman wanted to smoke grass, and ramble on about whatever streamed through her mind. The spirit world was a popular topic.

Tomlinson provided what Loretta wanted as well as what she needed: a compassionate ear.

Hannah, in a bathrobe, exited the cabin to the Marlow's aft deck. The sky was black with stars and slow-scudding clouds. A sliver of moon muted lightning in a western squall too far off to hear. The dock her uncle had built long ago wobbled through the mangroves to the road.

No traffic. There seldom was at this hour in the fishing village of Sulfur Wells.

Beyond, atop a shell Indian mound, was a yellow pine Cracker house, with a tin roof and a wraparound porch. Veiled by darkness and screens were ceiling fans and a hammock, where, as a girl, she'd slept on hot summer nights like this.

For more than a hundred years, the progeny of her great-great-grandfather Daniel Summerlin Smith had done the same.

Hannah docked her boat here out of family

loyalty, not because of fond memories related to her childhood. Loretta had been an unhappy, critical parent. She'd had a wild streak, with a taste for married men, and would slip off without so much as a note, let alone bothering to pack a school lunch. And the arguments, my Lord . . .

Lately, though, Hannah's feelings had softened. She was four months along and would soon experience the difficulties of motherhood for herself. If there **were** difficulties that could exceed the love for a child.

Hannah doubted it. Never had she felt so glistening and alive. Morning sickness had ended weeks ago. Aside from a few tender private areas, and a sudden distaste for coffee, nothing had changed but her optimism.

Four months along was the best of both worlds. She could still work and fish; and wear normal clothes, unless she wanted her tummy to show.

Sometimes she did.

A decision about that had to be made before sunrise. She was meeting Marion Ford to fish a hidden spot he knew in the Everglades. A lake called Chino Hole. As an enticement, the biologist had promised to introduce her to a man she'd heard about all her life—Captain Tootsie Barlow, one of the greatest flats guides in history.

"He offered," Ford had told her on the phone. "He wants you to meet his niece, Gracie. You heard what happened to her, but, what you don't know is, she's . . . uhh—"

"She's pregnant, too?" Hannah had guessed to rescue him from awkwardness.

Not that she needed an enticement to visit. The opportunity to fish a pristine lake loaded with tarpon was enough. She would take a couple of Sage pack rods and a box of newly tied flies. That wasn't all, of course, as she'd mentioned on the phone.

"What about dangerous critters? The way you describe the place, it sounds pretty wild."

"Alligators, of course, but I didn't see any big enough—"

"I'm talking about pythons. After what happened last winter, nobody knows better than me they're dangerous. They've darn near taken over the Glades."

Irksome, the man's naïve laughter, although some would have read it as confidence. "I'll bring snake repellent," he'd said, then changed his mind. "What am I saying? You're the most self-reliant person I know. You'll bring your own."

It was his way: risk a mild joke, then apologize with a compliment that fired confidence, and sometimes a blush.

Marion was an unusual man. Thinking his

name produced an inward smile, albeit bitter-sweet. She had been in love only once in her life—with him. Maybe still was. It didn't matter. She had wanted this child even before she knew it, so Ford's solitary lifestyle, and his secrecy, had eliminated him not as her one hope for a kindred mate, but as a father.

With Hannah, her child would always come first.

From a distance, the chain-drive clunk of the VW van shifting gears drew her attention. She started down the dock to investigate. Near the mangroves, a squadron of mosquitoes forced a retreat. Her body had adapted to the bites, as most do, except for tender areas such as ankles and behind the knees. She swatted her way into the cabin, and saw the time. First light was in less than three hours.

Heck with bed, she thought. She would dress for a day in the Glades, stop at Perkins for breakfast, then doze at their meeting spot until Ford showed up to lead her the rest of the way.

She was at the end of the dock, loading her SUV, when headlights rounded the curve and a Volkswagen van cruised past at idle, then sped up. Hard to make out details in the dark, but the peace symbol stickers under the brake lights looked familiar. She waved and hollered. The van followed the next curve, and it, and the sound of its engine, were gone.

Strange, the feeling that came over her. Not fear, exactly. More a prickly awareness of something not quite right. She returned to her boat, and, after arguing with herself, decided there were a handful of people she could call anytime, day or night. She tried Tomlinson's cell and got voice mail. Rather than leave a message, she sent a text, asking if he was in the neighborhood. Ten minutes later, still no response.

Her sense of unease climbed a notch. She called Ford.

The biologist, although a methodical person, kept odd hours. When he answered on the first ring, the relief she felt was greater than anticipated, or cared to admit.

"I feel like a fool calling you so late," she said. "Did I wake you up?"

"It's early morning, not late," replied the stickler for accuracy. "I hope you're not calling to cancel our fishing trip. Is something wrong?"

"I've got a question," she said, and explained about the van. "I'm not sure it was his, but, seriously, what are the odds of seeing one like it in Sulfur Wells? I tried calling him, then sent a text. That was a while ago and I haven't heard back."

Ford said, "That's all?"

"Okay, I'm being silly, but it seems strange. Doesn't it to you?"

"Tomlinson's not a morning person, unless he starts at midnight. I doubt it was him. He's looking after Tootsie's niece at the cabin I told you about. At least, that's where he's supposed to be. You are coming to fish?"

"I was just leaving when the van drove by. Doc . . . I could've sworn it was his. The same bumper stickers, everything. Are you on Sanibel or in the Glades?"

Ford was in his truck, lights out, watching an airstrip where a turbo Cessna had just landed. "I'm staying at a hotel. I don't understand why you're leaving there so early. We're meeting in Ochopee around seven, right?"

"Maybe I should wait and see if he drives by again." Hannah was now at the aft cabin window, looking out. "I'm sure he'll call when he sees my text. I don't know why I'm worried." She waited through a long silence. "Marion, are you there?"

Ford said, "I was just thinking . . . Yeah, call the police."

"Don't make fun of me."

"I'm not. You've got good instincts, Hannah. You're alone on your boat, and your mom's alone in the house. I should have taken you more seriously when—"

"Loretta's with her bingo friends."

"You're by yourself?"

"She's on a church trip to the Magic Kingdom.

Now you're scaring me. Is there some reason you—"

"We'll get an early start, that's all," Ford said. "Leave now, and text me when you're on the road. I'll meet you no later than six-fifteen. Oh, and Hannah?"

She knew what he would say before the words were out of his mouth: there was nothing silly about trusting her instincts.

"I learned that the hard way," she replied.

In the boat's cabin, under the settee couch, was a lockbox she'd opened while packing. She took out a buckskin brown Galco holster. It was soft as glove leather, designed to be concealed inside the pants, or beneath a jacket or shirt. She hadn't planned on wearing it because of the strain it might put on her tummy. Her lightweight khaki slacks were already snug, yet the holster felt okay once it was positioned inside the small of her back.

In a shoulder bag loaded with fishing gear was a small 9mm pistol. It was a gift from her late uncle, Jake, who had been a Tampa detective until a couple of bullets had forced him into a safer line of work.

Hannah popped the magazine, and locked the slide back above an empty chamber. The pistol was fifty-some years old, custom-made with a fluted barrel of burnished nickel-plated steel. On the handgrips, in red, an archaic

Scottish word was stamped: DEVEL. It had taken some research to find out it meant to "smite" or "knock asunder."

Like Marion Ford, Uncle Jake had had a mysterious side.

She holstered the pistol, the full weight of it, and experimented with how it felt sitting or walking. A further test was stepping up onto the dock, where she texted Ford: **Leaving in 5.**

The magazine dug at her ribs when she descended into the cabin, so back into the gear bag it went. After a final look around, she was closing the bag, ready to leave, when a voice called her name from outside, and said something too faint to hear.

Hannah went toward the door. Seconds later, she heard it again, a frightened voice, saying, "Are you home? I need help."

She looked out, then threw the door open and ran toward a girl, who stumbled from the mangrove shadows and collapsed before she reached the dock.

24

What Gracie wanted to do was warn the woman, scream her name and tell her to stop, phone the police, instead of rushing to kneel beside her in the shadows, then cooing, "What happened to you, sweetheart?"

Too late. From behind, Mr. Bird grabbed Hannah's hair, slapped a hand over her mouth, and slammed her to the ground. He was furious after circling the area three times before realizing Raven Girl lived on a boat.

Gracie couldn't watch after that, so turned away, until she heard the woman say, "Mister, touch me again, you'd better kill me. I won't quit until you do."

The courage that required gave the girl a

boost, but only made him madder. "Oh, I will, I will. When I'm ready." Then drew a big fist back . . .

Gracie averted her eyes. She wished she'd covered her ears.

After that, the woman, Hannah Smith, went silent, except for breathing and an occasional gasp.

"Fetch the tape, girl."

Gracie did.

"Go aboard the boat and get her purse. Make sure you get her phone and keys, too."

She did.

"Now hop in her car and lay them rear seats down so you two ladies have a place to stretch out."

She did that, too, fumbled around in the woman's SUV, moving fishing rods, inflatable life jackets, and other gear to make room. Some of the light stuff, she tossed up front, because movement wasn't easy—her right arm was taped to her side and her ankles were hobbled with rope.

Something Gracie also did was hide a fillet knife in the back of the vehicle, inspired by Hannah's show of bravery. She'd found it in the boat's galley and managed to slip past while Mr. Bird was busy rolling the woman in a sheet.

"Calms them down, makes 'em easier to

lift," he said to someone, not her or the woman. Speaking as if an invisible person watched from over his shoulder.

He'd been doing that a lot since abandoning the van at a dump site in the mangroves. There, he'd argued with himself about setting the van on fire, then ended by muttering, "Ching-Ching, you ain't got the brains of a toad. Cops see flames, they'll figure it out. Step aside, unless you want your throat cut." The thickest redneck accent had won out.

Mr. Bird's redneck rages were the worst. They put Gracie in robot mode.

"Climb your butt in there so's I can tape you right."

She did, crawled into the back of the SUV and lay next to Hannah, choosing the passenger side, where the knife was hidden under carpeting.

"Damn it, sit up so I can do your hands."

The girl had been through this enough to know how to angle her wrists so the tape appeared to be tight but allowed some movement.

"Now your mouth."

Same thing, if she let her jaw drop open before the first wrap was pulled tight.

"Hey . . . what hell's going on in that head of yours? You ain't cried or pissed me off by screaming. Something tells me you're being tricky."

Her body tightened when she felt the weight of him over her, searching for something in the car's dome light.

"You must like my new jail outfit, huh? Or did you miss me? Answer, goddamn it. I bet you missed our special times."

Gracie, eyes closed, replied with an affirmative mewling sound.

"Lying bitch."

The hatch door slammed closed; then they were moving. Shadows streamed past the windows. Soon, on a smoother highway, came streetlights, and panels of light from cars passing in the opposite direction.

The woman, Captain Hannah, was conscious. Gracie sensed it from the way the woman braced her body for curves rather than roll, slack-muscled, like a corpse. The sheet lay loosely around her, her face exposed except where tape covered her mouth and part of her nose.

Using an elbow, Gracie nudged her, and watched one glittering eye blink open. The girl reached over and, using a fingernail, scratched the tape away from the woman's nose to provide more air.

Hannah's head turned in the darkness. She nodded imperceptibly, aware of the man's eyes in the rearview mirror.

"How ya'll doing back there, Yum-Yum?"

The girl's grunt, two syllables, resembled the word **okay**.

The man used a Bic to relight his opium pipe, and exhaled. "How about you, Raven? That's what I call you from now on, 'cause you ain't no captain. There's never been a captain that compares to me, man or woman. How you getting along?" The SUV slowed. Through the side window, a crimson light blinked green. They were moving again, accelerating up a grade, into the occasional wind wake of an Interstate. "Goddamn, you Smiths are stubborn. Ya'll never change . . . ANSWER ME."

The woman, staring into Gracie's face, sent a signal. The girl responded on her behalf with a quizzical grunt to hide the truth.

"Still out, huh? By god, that'll teach her for sassing me. Long as she ain't dead, I don't give a damn. Us three is going on a trip. You never been anyplace like it. Yum-Yum, you like to ride horseback and drink whiskey? I've about run out my string in this shithole you call a world."

The SUV slowed, swerved, while he re-loaded the pipe with crystal, then flooded the space with smoke that smelled of chlorine. The stereo came on, loud. News . . . static . . . hip-hop . . . NPR . . . a game show, the host saying something like, **Wait, wait, we'll be right back**.

"Fucker. Don't expect me to wait."

Static, loud . . . louder as the driver's-side window dropped open. "Hear that, Raven? **Wind.** That there's what a real captain calls music."

Next, a bluegrass station, so loud the car vibrated.

Hannah wormed closer so she was nose to nose with the girl. Facial expressions, a nod, a nudge with a knee, became forms of communication. It wasn't easy. The left side of her face was grotesquely swollen, a reminder of the danger.

Gracie knew what Hannah wanted. It took a while to muster the courage. With her fingernails and tongue, she levered the tape away from her own mouth just enough to speak in a whisper, her lips to the woman's ear.

"You okay?"

Hannah surprised her by nodding: **Yes.**

"He's insane, we have to think of something."

Yes.

"I'd loosen your tape, but I . . . He'll kill us both when he sees it."

The woman's stony silence meant, **He'll kill us anyway.**

Gracie's courage began to fade. "You don't know what he's like. Maybe . . . maybe he'll let us go. He looks and talks so different than I remember. Could be he'll smoke enough to pass out, and—"

An aggressive nudge silenced the girl. Hannah extended her chin, the message unmistakable: **Loosen this damn tape.**

When Gracie did, the woman immediately vomited—a soft retching sound—then inhaled several filtering breaths. She had a concussion, or worse. Might die, possibly, the man had hit her so hard.

"You need a doctor. Do you understand where you are?"

Hannah knew something inside her head had been damaged. The nausea and strange strobing colors scared her, but she managed to nod in a way that meant **I'm fine.**

After that, they took turns tilting their heads to converse. Short whispered fragments, lips to ear.

When Hannah learned the girl was Tootsie Barlow's niece, their predicament was less confusing but no less dire. She recalled fragments of the backstory. The survivor in her wondered, **Why the hell did he come after me and my child?**

That had to wait.

She struggled to make her mouth work while consciousness blurred. "Where's he taking us?"

Gracie didn't know.

"Does . . . does anyone know you're missing?"

Tomlinson did, but they'd left him at a cabin in the Everglades, no phone, no shoes, and his van stolen. "He's had time to hike to a road by now . . . if his feet didn't give out. I'm worried about him."

It wasn't because of the shoes she was worried. Gracie said their captor had stopped the van after pulling away, then left her alone for fifteen minutes or so. "He could've gone back to the cabin and killed him. Honey, I'm so scared."

Hannah whispered, "Calm down," but felt dizzier after what she'd just heard.

Tomlinson . . . dead?

The girl sniffed, and repositioned her head. "There's something I'm almost afraid to tell you. He's so damn strong, I don't know if it's even possible. I . . . I hid a knife. A knife I took from your boat. It's here, somewhere near my knee, where the carpet pulls up."

"Get it."

"Are you sure?"

"Get it. **Now.**"

It took a couple of quiet minutes for Gracie to squirm her body around and find the thing. When she returned within whispering distance, Hannah, fighting to remain conscious, told her what she'd been reluctant to reveal.

"Cut my hands free. I've got a gun."

Over the years, Mr. Bird had used many hosts to savor many victims. Few were worthy of his ancient branding mark. The girl, a teenage biddy, hadn't been chosen, but try to teach idiots like Vernon or Slaten the difference between **delicious** and **deathless**.

Old Walter, as raw as he was, understood. Only men without a conscience were trustworthy. Morality was such a spidery web of lies that—

Hold on. Movement in the mirror interrupted the buzz he was enjoying. He sniffed, and watched the females converse, unconcerned, until something metallic caught a flash of light.

"Pit stop," he announced, and swerved onto the shoulder, the headlights showing cattails and a canal dug by dredges that were also used to build the road back in Walter's day. "You girls go ahead and piss anytime, anywhere you want. This ain't my buggy."

He made a show of yawning, got out, then rushed around and threw the back hatch open. "What the hell's going on in here? Move your asses, come on."

Gracie, hands and ankles bound, hit the ground like a sack of spuds when he pulled her out. His eyes skated over her body and saw nothing other than that she'd chewed through the tape again. Nothing unexpected about that.

It was the same when he yanked the sheet off Hannah, but he wasn't done once he saw that she was awake.

"Look familiar, do I? I should. This ain't the first time we met. I done kilt you once, almost a hundred years ago."

The woman glared at the crazy man through her one good eye.

"My god, your face looks like someone pumped it full of goo. But still a feisty li'l vixen, huh? Hurry up, now, roll over . . . Better yet, sit up and let me pull that shirt off. I'm dying to see what's under there."

Hannah, staring, said, "Lay a hand on me, you might."

The expression on the man's face asked **What the hell's that mean?**

Her lips felt numb. She had to wet them to say, "You would've found it anyway," and lifted her shoulder to reveal the knife because it was the only way to avoid a more thorough search. "Must'a fallen out of my tackle box. Don't think I wouldn't have used it, I would've. But at least give me credit for cooperating."

Goddamn. Ol' Walter would've eaten this woman up with a spoon.

The man palmed the knife, felt its weight, then touched the point to her belly. Beautiful, the expression of horror this produced. "You got some chili pepper in you, girl—and that ain't

all, from what I've heard. I **like** that. Two play-
things rolled into one. Get it?"

Hannah hyperventilated while the man
laughed.

"Why, look at you. Seems I finally got your
attention. Now shift your ass a little . . . that's
right, on your side, and let me see your hands
are still taped good and tight."

They were.

Satisfied, he lifted Gracie like a sack of
grain, tossed her into the back, and slammed
the hatch closed. They were driving east again
on the Tamiami Trail when the first low pla-
teau of sawgrass appeared beneath a horizon of
stars.

Back in Walter country.

Another ounce of crystal freshened his pipe.
Smoke plumed from his nose. Mr. Bird returned
with his recollections to instruct Vernon, not
just to entertain. Over the decades, he'd found
only one ingress and egress to this part of the
world. Otherwise, he would've balked at coming back, but, goddamn it, the pond, Chino
Hole, was his only conduit home—home to
the past.

He had come to hate the present as much as
he despised them all: the Barlows and Walter
Lambeth, and their crazy retarded kin.

This would be his last trip.

On the stereo, country twang replaced

bluegrass, the bass speakers booming. Music so loud and sweet, it was impossible not to sing along.

"Hey, hey, good-lookin', what'cha got dah-dah. How 'bout cookin' up dah-dah-dah-dah-dee . . ."

Grinning, Vernon blew smoke rings at the dash . . . then yelled, "Sheee-it!" when, out of nowhere, a man stepped onto the highway, waving his arms. A tall, skinny man with a ponytail, not young, not old, more like a hippie holdover from another time who'd decided, **Screw hitchhiking, I'll flag down a car.**

Familiar, the man, as his face blurred past.

The SUV swerved, braked hard, and bounced to a stop after a hundred yards of weeds and gravel. The hipster, a bag over his shoulder, reappeared in the rearview mirror. He was running barefoot on asphalt.

Vernon realized, **It's Gracie's boyfriend.**

Mr. Bird whispered, "I'll tell you when to kill him."

25

When Hannah texted from her boat **Leaving in 5,** Ford had been mildly irked.

He'd asked . . . no, he'd told her to let him know when she was safely on the road. The difference between **leaving** and **left**, as he knew, could span a lifetime.

That was an hour ago. Since then, not a word. If there wasn't a pressing need to be where he was—sitting, with lights off, in a hotel parking lot—he would have gone straight to their meeting place. It was a shed-sized post office in Ochopee, another lost village in the Everglades.

Hannah's cell went to voice mail. A text sent twenty minutes ago remained unanswered. Ford rarely delighted in using what some in the business referred to as privileged access, but he didn't hesitate to use it now. He typed a code into a satellite phone. A robotic menu led him through more security measures and finally to a human voice.

"I need a GPS track, South Com quadrant," Ford said, and provided Hannah's cell number.

"Level, sir?"

Standard triangulation was usually good enough, but not out here in the Glades. "Keyhole aspect," he said.

"Aye-aye, sir," was the reply. "Active or a pin locator?"

"Full on, and keep it running," Ford said, because . . . well, why not? He would have done the same for any of his friends, or so he rationalized.

Somewhere high overhead, orbiting sensors began to interlock and probe. The phone's screen changed. It showed the peninsula of Florida, then rocketed earthward to a ribbon of Interstate that was I-75. A pulsing saffron dot showed that Hannah was in a vehicle southbound, not far from the Fort Myers exit.

This was reassuring. She had been delayed or had made an early stop for breakfast. Fort Myers was more than an hour from Ochopee, which gave him time to finish some unfinished business.

Weird, though, that she didn't answer her

phone. Or, maybe she'd switched it off accidentally—it made no difference to the orbiting sensors.

Further proof was available. He touched a series of buttons, and said, "Real time."

The screen changed again. Now he had a live view of I-75 from five miles above: flowing headlights, traffic sparse, at 4 a.m. He tapped the saffron dot. The camera zoomed. He watched until he was satisfied that Hannah was in her own vehicle or one very similar—a dark-colored SUV.

After that, he felt better.

It was 4:05 a.m.

At 4:35, curtains in a ground-floor hotel suite brightened. Ford had been ready for a while. Torqued onto his 9mm Sig was a Thompson sound suppressor. Clipped to his belt was a military stun device, and he wore surgical gloves. Before getting out, he used a tiny six-watt laser to fry the building's security camera, then walked to the door. Within, a shower hissed, a toilet flushed. The odor of coffee mingled with morning summer air. He placed his hand on the doorknob. And waited.

It didn't take long. When the knob turned, he slammed the door open, saying, "Don't make me shoot," while his eyes moved in sync with the pistol, seeing a bedroom, bed unmade, a kitchenette, and a table where two carry-on bags were packed, ready to go.

The man they belonged to stumbled back in shock. "Hey—easy, now. Shit. What you want?" Next came a look of recognition. "Goddamn . . . it's you."

Ford knew he was being tailed but had been unsure who it was until now. He swung the door closed without taking his eyes off Donell, the Bahamian constable he'd bribed on Andros. "Are they blackmailing you or are you just stupid?"

"I can explain, man, give me a chance. You don't think I'd—"

"Answer the question. Are they paying you?"

"Well, depends on—"

"Goddamn it, Donell, I need to know who I'm dealing with. If they've got leverage on you or your family, then—"

"No, man. This strictly business." The Bahamian, regaining some composure, lowered his hands long enough to straighten his collar. "If a better financial opportunity come along, yeah, could be I'm interested—if that's what you're asking. We both professionals, gotta look out for ourselves. Ain't that right?"

"How much?"

"Money? Man, that's personal. Paying me,

yeah, but not to kill you, if that's what you're thinking. I don't do that kind'a work. They sent me to recover what you stole from a gentleman in our fine city of Nassau. I believe you know what I'm referring to."

The Bahamian had mixed a lie with the truth. Ford played along. "The thumb drives."

"The very same. Must be valuable to a certain party."

"If that's all they want, we might be able to work a deal. The technology's too good these days. Turns out, the stealth drives, they self-destruct if the wrong sequence is entered. My buyers backed out; now I'm stuck."

"Oh? Strikes me, that there's a good selling point when discussing the matter with friends of mine. Got all three?"

"In pristine condition. I'll want something in return, of course."

Donell grinned. "See? This how the world works. Okay, now let's hear what that is. Mind if I put my hands down while we . . . ?" He waited for Ford to nod before doing it, lowering his arms, and moving to establish his personal space. "What you're wondering is, am I some pimp flunky or actually part of the operation we're discussing? That's the question you could've asked right off, and saved us waving guns around."

"They send executives to do this sort of shit? Come on, Donell."

"If I didn't trust you, man, I wouldn't bother sharing the realities of the situation. We very careful, when it comes to security. Of who does what in our particular line of business."

"Oh, you've proven that. Tell me about it. What sort of business?"

The man's smile faded. "This a test? I don't care much for being called a liar. The movie business, we'll call it that." In response to Ford's cold stare, he added, "I ain't one of the prissies buys that shit, but, as I said, money is money."

"If you didn't do it, someone else would, right?" Ford waved the Bahamian back a step, and bolted the door. "Pretty risky, coming to the state that wants to extradite you. Must be important. You're a vested member; have a professional interest, I suppose."

Donell's ego liked that. "Why hire if you got the desire? Dealing with you, it's a job I wanted done right. That's why I'm here personally."

"Your boss approved, huh?"

"Those in executive positions, we do what we have to do."

"Call them," Ford said. "Call your partners and put them on speaker."

"Huh?"

"You heard me. Where's the special phone you use?"

Donell's eyes involuntarily started toward the table before he caught himself. "In my pocket, where else?"

"Which bag?" Ford asked. He shifted the pistol to his left hand, and dumped the contents of the smallest bag on the floor. A blue Gresso satellite phone landed next to a shaving kit. "Russian-made," he said, and kicked the phone within Donell's reach. "I know better than to guess at the password. Call your people, tell them I have what they want and we'll make a deal."

The man exaggerated a show of patience. "Come on . . . it ain't that easy. You **know** that. Let's stop this foolishness, my brother, and—"

"Quiet. Someone's coming." Ford motioned to the window while reaching for the stun device on his belt. When Donell turned, fifty thousand volts dropped him to the floor.

First, Ford confirmed the man wasn't choking on his own tongue, then went through the bags. By the time he was done, Donell was conscious and his muscle spasms had ceased.

"We're going for a ride," Ford said. He helped the Bahamian to his feet.

East of Route 29, almost to the village of Ochopee, Ford turned right through **No Trespassing** signs onto a shell road. A mile and a couple of turns later, the headlights panned across a turbo Cessna, nose angled toward stars. He beeped the horn, three shorts and a long—the letter **V** in Morse code.

A light in the cockpit came on. It blinked three times in reply—a short, a long, a short—the letter **R**.

R for "ready."

Handcuffed to the door, Donell was ready, too.

"Call them," Ford said.

"Already told you I would, but you gotta promise me, man. We got us a deal, right?"

"Depends on how convincing you are," Ford said while he typed a code into the Russian satellite phone. "Go ahead. You know what to say."

They'd spent the drive going over it, back and forth. Negotiations had improved when Donell, on his knees in a ditch, felt a gun on his neck. The man wasn't the major player he pretended to be, but he'd been in the business a while through contacts in the Bahamian government. He was a facilitator and probably an occasional procurer of victims, although he'd stopped short of confessing that.

Ford had recorded it all, as he did the

conversation that came next, Donell on speaker with a man who had an Arabic accent.

The deal offered was this: in return for the thumb drives, the organization would admit through an anonymous source that "evidence" used to blackmail an unnamed Member of Parliament was bogus. The information had to be emailed within the hour, along with details regarding how the material had been contrived.

"Sounds very fair, sir," Donell concluded.

"You're a fool if you believe that," the man said through the speaker. "Is someone pointing a gun at your head? Tell him to shoot, you'll be better off."

Ford took over. "Let's pretend someone did harvest information from the thumb drives I have. You won't know for certain until you get them back. Either way, you lose if you say no. Are you aware that Donell is a wanted man in Florida?"

"Arrest him, hang him, why would I care?"

"Because you'll be next in line, along with your people in the Bahamas. Chances are, the prosecutor will cut a deal with Donell in return for everything he knows. How's my offer sounding now?"

"We know where you live, Dr. Ford. That's exactly how it sounds."

"That brings us to a worst-case scenario. If

you refuse, let's say someone **has** harvested data from the stealth drives. Every name, every government official, involved with your business will be made public. How many countries do you operate in?"

There was a long gambler's pause. "If such names exist."

"If," Ford said.

"You could go ahead and do that anyway. What sort of guarantee do I have?"

"Only one that I know of. Hands off Gillian Cobourg and her family, or I'll come looking for you myself."

"Such a violent man. Her brother's a pompous fool, and his government's about to fall anyway. In other words, his value is no longer—"

Ford interrupted. "Look, I have a plane waiting to fly Donell to Andros. Do you want the drives or not?"

Less than an hour later, the satellite phone pinged with confirmation: **Information received.**

The turbo Cessna took off into a dark June morning. The pilot, Charles Beckett, from a family forever loyal to the British Crown, wagged his wings in salute, then banked east, flying low over the trees.

Ford didn't notice. He was puzzled by what he saw on his own satellite phone. It was a real-time Keyhole view of Hannah's SUV from a mile overhead. She had stopped on a lonely stretch of the Tamiami Trail ten miles away, car doors open, the headlights bright enough to cast two giant shadows on the gray canvas that was the road.

Why had she stopped? Who was the second person?

He rushed to his truck, hoping to intercept the woman. On the way, he called from his cell. Voice mail. An instant later, his phone buzzed with an incoming call.

"Hannah?"

No, it was Detective Janos Werner. "Sorry to call so early but I can't get ahold of the Barlow girl and figured you might have some numbers for me to try. She's probably not in danger, but, personally, I think she should know."

"What's wrong?" Ford listened a while before he said, "Jesus Christ . . . escaped from where?"

26

Tomlinson recognized the SUV that stopped for him out here in the middle of nowhere. A **Captiva Guides Association** sticker confirmed he was right. But it wasn't Hannah Smith who got out and called, "Need a ride?"

He recognized the bearish baritone, too. The combination jolted his resolve. Death was in that voice, horrors inflicted century after century. The temptation was to flee, not face the enemy he had called down from the stars.

"I'd say yes even if I was wearing shoes," he hollered back in a sweet parody of the naïve. "Where you headed?"

The driver opened the passenger door, reached

in, and switched off the dome light. "Can't go no-where 'til you get your ass in the car. Hurry up."

In the refracted glare of headlights, Tom-linson got a glimpse of two bodies bundled in the back of the SUV before a massive face loomed over him. Moths, bewildered by the light, feathered the face with scurrying shad-ows. He took a chance by asking, "How you doing tonight, Vernon?"

The driver said, "Name's Walter, shit-for-brains," and that's the last thing Tomlinson heard before a numbing blow knocked him into semi-consciousness.

Mr. Bird was impressed. Never had a victim seen through flesh and bone to perceive the power of Walter's darkness within. It put him in a redneck party mood. Hungrier than ever.

"How you doin' back there, ladies? Got us a passenger, we do. Yep, the real McCoy, with the prettiest hair you ever seen. He's carrying a bag with an old-time pistol in it."

Gracie was bawling again. "She keeps vomit-ing. I think she passed out. Tomlinson . . . are you okay?" She'd heard his voice.

"Never mind about him. She breathing?"

"Sorta, but—"

"Then shut the hell up, we got your boy-friend for company." He reached over, slapped the hipster's face—not hard—to see if he was playing possum. "What's your story, bub? Back there at the cabin, you got any idea how close I came to dousing your lights? Good thing I saw that wheel gun in your hand. Colt Peacemaker, ain't it?"

Tomlinson had been listening for a while, aware that Hannah was behind him, tied up or unconscious, Gracie was alive, and near hyster-ics. They were headed for the foundry, probably, or Chino Hole. It was time to do something; fight or get off the pot. He sat straighter, wiped blood from his nose, and said, "You tell me."

Gracie cried out, "Tommy, get help, run!"

"Keep your mouth closed, girl, we're talk-ing." The driver glanced over. "Tell you about what?"

"Albert Barlow's gun. I found it in the cabin after you took off with my van. You missed some of the good stuff, Vernon, when you robbed the place."

"Walter, or Captain Lambeth," was the reply. "Say it. Say my name."

"Look . . . **Walter**, why not let the girls go? Tell me what you want and—"

"It weren't Albert's gun. Here"—he lifted the Colt by the barrel and held it near the dash—"see the initials? A tinhorn deputy named

Johnny Cox carried this until he was bull-whipped 'til he cried. Him and his wife and brats all there, watching. Albert didn't have the stomach for such things, so he run like a rabbit—but only after stealing what he could. This Colt being the best of it, which is why it goes back in the bag for safekeeping."

Tomlinson said, "August 1925, the Marco Island war."

Rumbling laughter accompanied, "By god, a man who knows his history. Could be you're right about those dates."

"You're not sure? Walter Lambeth would know exactly when it happened." Tomlinson waited, but no response. "Tell me something. What's it like? For you **now**, I mean. Do you hear voices, or do you really believe that sick sonuvabitch is still in control?"

"**Bitch**? Pretty strong word for someone not fit to judge pigs."

"He was a monster and you know it."

Vernon's head pivoted as if on a turret. He was thinking, **Finally, some asshole worthy of Mr. Bird's brand.** "August, maybe that was the date. I can sure as hell tell you how the wife and her brats died. Albert told 'em some lie about leaving on the train and carried 'em across from Marco on the ferry. You know the area?"

Tomlinson replied, "There's a lake near here.

You . . . **he** cut their throats and let gators do the rest. No . . . a croc. Or they went into the furnace like he did to his Chinese workers. Which was it?"

Amazing, this skinny old hippie. Vernon said, "Ain't you the cat's whiskers? Whoops— hang on to your seat." He turned onto a rutted road that was familiar, the foundry and Chino Hole not far ahead. "What happened was, the Chinamen, burning their bodies and all, that came later, after . . . Well, it was what Walter did to the woman that night that made him different. At the time, deputy's wife, she was—"

Tomlinson interrupted before he got out the word: **pregnant**. "I know the rest. If Walter was proud of something like that, he deserves to burn in Hell. What, you're his son, his grandson? Maybe you listened to those stories at Grandpa's knee, but why do the same sad, sick shit over and over again?"

Vernon looked over and grinned. "Keep doing it 'til you get it right. It's something he used to say. Drive a stake through his heart, turn him into gator shit, that's what it would take."

"Take to kill him?"

"He said that, too. The man had a way of laying eggs in your head that hatched. You didn't know ol' Walter."

"I'm not so sure," Tomlinson said, his

attention on the Colt Peacemaker, which was in the bag on the floor, driver's side. Mounted on the dash was his own damn cell phone, a GPS map aglow. Two more phones were on the console, one of them probably Hannah's. Atop a clutter of boating gear was a ceramic opium pipe that explained the stink of chlorine. "What're you smoking?"

The driver's eyes sparked. "Oh, something real special." Steering with his knees, he filled the pipe with crystal, lit it, puffed, exhaled. "Or do you like whiskey? I got a stash hid away near here."

"Both," Tomlinson said, and took the pipe. Smoking was an excuse to sit back, relax, and drape one arm over the seat. His fingers found Hannah's hair, warm skin . . . no movement. Crusted blood, a slick area—dear god, maybe she was dead. He inhaled, coughed a cloud of smoke, and kept coughing. Acidic sparks assaulted his frontal lobe. The sparks burrowed and traced a delicate veinery through his head into the cortex mass.

"It ain't smooth, but she gets the job done." Vernon grinned while Mr. Bird observed and considered options.

"Flakka?" Tomlinson sputtered.

"Bath salts plus a touch of flake—my version of what they called Mangrove Lightning."

"What **he** called it, and this sure as hell isn't whiskey."

"It's better, way better. Pure flakka don't hold a candle. Take another hit, but don't hog it all."

Tomlinson did. Tears flowed. His brain ballooned with a delicious, hellish heat. One more yank for good measure. "Wowie, Lord," he muttered. "After a couple hits—is that when you hear his voice?"

"Whose? Oh, him. Yeah, Walter loves this shit, which, I admit, sort of confuses me sometimes as to who gives the orders. You know? Hey . . . careful, slick." Tomlinson had intentionally fumbled the pipe during the exchange. Vernon retrieved it and used the lighter again, puffing hard, aware of what had almost happened. When the smoke cleared, both phones were gone from the console, but the bag was still there on the floor.

Tomlinson pretended not to notice. Waited for his turn with the pipe, and double-pumped the next hit to show good faith. His senses blazed with a feeling so raw, it couldn't be defined. Nor could it be slowed. It was an expanding euphoric need, like hunger, but with a seething edge.

A third, then a fourth hit, breathing the smoke deep, brought understanding. Rage, he realized. A teetering madness was flooding in behind his eyes. He battled for control, using mental tricks learned from bad L.S.D. This shit was **nasty**.

Voice lower, he handed the pipe back, saying, "Slow down, dumbass, I want to savor this."

"Dumbass?" More rumbling laughter— ha-ha-ha. "Hey, boy, that there sounded like something the old man would say. You trying to piss me off?"

"No, I'm trying to picture the way it was back in the day."

Vernon glared, while Mr. Bird whispered, **Do what he says. We'll put him in the pond.**

The glare faded. "Enjoy the view, makes sense. Another bowl, this whole place will come alive. Horses, a bunch of chinks lined up with their coolie caps and ribs showing. The six a.m. from Immokalee's due about now. I love hearing that train whistle."

Tomlinson, his arm draped over the seat, fingers stroking an unresponsive Hannah, nodded. "Thought you might."

Streaming toward them through the windshield, the first gray rim of morning showed a roofline through the trees where sparks spiraled skyward. A chimney.

"Uh-oh."

"Uh-oh, my ass. Pass the pipe, slick."

"Are you blind? Your house is on fire. Either that or someone's there."

"Naw, it's the crystal kicking in. You know how to stoke a furnace? That's where we're headed. There's a special room with ankle chains for the females. What do you think—chain 'em, have some fun?" Vernon, channeling Mr. Bird, watched closely as he added, "It's what some would call a permanent commitment."

Tomlinson reemerged from a secret haven in his head and made eye contact. "The way I feel, I'd chew your leg off and pretend you don't have balls."

"My leg, huh? Whoo-ee, I like the way you think. Want a taste of those two, do you?"

"If it's just you and me, I'm about two hits past overdue. Immortal blood lust and cannibalism, oh hell yes. If you want me to say it, I will—I'm ready for the mark of Demon Crow." He spoke as if in a daze, then appeared to awaken. "Hey—why are we stopping?"

"Hop out. There's something I want you to see."

Vernon's voice had changed. Tomlinson wasn't happy with the timing, but he had to do something because the drug was winning control. He pointed vaguely. "Over there? Looks like a cop."

When the driver turned, he lunged and grabbed the bag. Shit, no weight to it at all.

When he looked up, there it was in the dome light, the long-barreled Colt aimed at his face.

"Get out of the goddamn car or I'll shoot you where you sit. Hell . . . I'll do it anyway just for lying."

Click-click—the sound of a hammer ratcheting. Tomlinson threw up a hand, opened the door with the other, and rolled away from a deafening blast.

In his mind, a voice called after him: **If you run, he will catch you.**

G racie could only lie there, listening. A single gunshot . . . a yowl of pain, a slamming car door, then the panicky sound of men wrestling in the brush, or running away.

"Hannah, wake up . . . Come on, you've got to help me."

The woman stirred. She exhaled, a moaning sound, while her feet and arms twitched, not unlike a dog running from a dream.

Blessedly, the dome light blinked off. It had been painful to look at the woman's damaged face.

"Can you hear me? Nod if you understand."

A slight nod in the darkness. Or was it imagined?

Gracie had nearly chewed Hannah's wrists

free but another bout of vomiting had interrupted. That was many minutes ago. Since then, the girl had worked desperately to free her own hands, but quietly. Not now. She pulled her knees to her chest, got one bare foot between her wrists, and used leg strength to push. The damn tape stretched . . . stretched a little more, which gave her hands room to move, but it wouldn't break.

Exhausted, she scooted closer and nudged the woman. "For god's sake, wake up. I need the gun. Where'd you hide it?"

The lashes of Hannah's right eye might have fluttered.

"Oh thank god . . . you can hear me. Pull your hands apart . . . You can do it, I promise. The tape was about to break when you got sick again."

BOOM. A second shot, not far away, interrupted.

"Oh shit, honey, he'll be back soon."

Gracie contorted herself until both feet were between her wrists, then extended her legs as if trying to lift a massive weight. The tape refused to break, but it stretched enough so she could thread one foot through, then the other, as if stepping through a rope.

Finally, her hands were in front of her. In a frenzy, she freed her ankles, and was gnawing at her wrists, when she realized it was more important to have the gun. "Hannah, I need to roll you over. You gotta help me . . . Honey, try to move your arms. You're too big for me to move by myself."

She lifted the woman's shoulder and struggled to roll her on her side. Hannah coughed, babbled something, and began to struggle, still dreaming. The thread of tape on her wrists must have parted because one elbow went limp. The momentum rolled her onto her back again.

Gracie, in tears, was yelling encouragement when, through the rear window, she saw movement beneath a channel of stars that marked the road. A silhouette . . . someone large . . . a man, possibly . . . approaching, moving slowly toward the dark SUV.

"Oh god . . . it's him." She crouched low, her forehead against the glass. "He's coming . . . The gun . . . I need the goddamn gun. Or . . . wait. Where'd he go?"

The man, if it was a man, had vanished. The girl spun around, aware of what would happen next. He would do what he'd done before, shock them from an unexpected direction, drag them out of the car, and . . .

"Hannah . . . I've got to get help. Please wake up or I'll have to . . ." She hugged the woman's leg and shook it. "I'm so sorry!"

Gracie scrambled over the driver's seat, cracked the door enough to slide out, and used her hip to close it quietly. Screaming insects dominated the darkness, where, among trees on the opposite side of the car, movement again caught her eye. A shadowed form appeared . . . shoulders . . . a human head that caught the breeze like moss . . . and vanished.

She set off through the woods in the opposite direction, walking . . . walking faster. Behind her, bushes rustled. She began to jog toward what she hoped was the main road, then sprinted blindly when a branch behind her shattered beneath a terrifying weight. The ground was soft. A maze of protruding cypress knees offered a clearing in the distance. She tripped and broke her fall, hands taped, outstretched, then was on her feet again, splashing through a pocket of swamp. Remnants of a rock wall nearly tripped her again. On one knee, she paused to listen. Tunneling toward her from the darkness came the sound of heavy feet in slow pursuit.

Oh dear god.

To her left, visible through the trees, was an elevated area of straight lines and rectangles. She knew it was a jumble of abandoned railroad cars. Ahead, to the right, a silver sheen marked the pond. On the other side, hidden from sight, was the hellish building she'd been held captive, but the main road was there, too.

The girl, duty-bound to the child within

her, made a bold choice. She went toward the water, careful about the footing. The ground was muck pocked with limestone pools, some knee-deep. She was wading the rim of the pond, when a sudden breeze seemed to whisper, **Gracie . . .**

An echoing quality suggested the wind had filtered up through striations in a nearby ledge.

She stopped, aware of an unseen danger, then screamed when a massive hand grabbed her ankle from below.

27

Mr. Bird, before taking flight, had advised Walter Lambeth, **Prepare to die.**

That's what he longed for: ol' Walter and his kin, the idiot sons and half-breed daughters who carried his mark, to vanish from the present so they would no longer stain the past.

It was his only escape.

This was not something Gracie Yum-Yum would understand. But she did understand when he clicked his teeth near her ear and said, "Call your boyfriend. Yell his name loud and convince him it's safe. I've got a score to settle with that skunk—he disappeared on me."

Shivering, wet in the darkness, she did it. Hollered, "Tommm-linson," and wanted to warn him, **All he's got is a knife,** but her courage failed before she was dragged down and scolded.

"Not just his name, shit-for-brains. God-damn it, that he's safe and you need him. It's feeding time. Remember what that means?"

The whispering voice was so different in this tepid chamber that stunk of rot. Beneath the water, huge fingers explored her body. They intruded and applied pressure while the girl stammered, "I . . . I remember."

"Then make him understand. Tell him to move his ass, and keep yelling until he's in the water. You ready?"

Again, her body was turned. She was lifted. Gracie's head breached an opening in the limestone that framed her neck like a yoke.

"Tommm-linson. Please. I need help!" Over and over, she hollered, afraid to pause even for a long breath . . . then had to pause, startled by something visible only from the water's surface. Staggering toward her was a cloaked figure that, in starlight, she expected to be Tomlinson.

No . . . it was Hannah Smith. The woman's size, her long legs, were unmistakable, but her posture was canted as if favoring her right arm, which hung at her side. Was she carrying a gun?

Beneath limestone, the long silence was no-ticed. Another scolding—or worse—awaited, so there was no time to think. "Run!" Gracie screamed. "Jesus Christ, he'll kill us both if you don't—"

The girl was dragged under, and held under, by massive hands that she clawed and scratched and battled with her teeth. Not until she was semi-conscious, floating faceup, in a chamber that smelled of rot, did she realize that something was terribly wrong with her body.

It was too dark to see, but her fingers understood.

Mr. Bird had used the knife.

Tomlinson was blown away by the flames and voices hammering inside his head. A demon, or the restless dead, had guided him to a railroad coach bearing the ornate name **Sawgrass Clipper**.

No idea why, but here he was, alone, carrying a five-pound pistol. Embossed golden letters on the car provided enough light to take stock. **Finally.** He'd been on the run since Vernon had tried to shoot him in the head. The struggle that followed was a blur, but a couple of details were as certain as the blood dripping down the side of his face.

Vernon was not in hot pursuit, as Tomlinson had believed. This was distressing. If he'd known, he would have ignored the voices and returned to Hannah's SUV instead of trying to lead the crazy bastard away from the girls.

Something else: Vernon had shot off a piece of the Zen master's right ear. His fingers confirmed it. The lower half was a pathetic stub. Cosmetically, no big deal, thanks to his indifference to ego, but the gunshot had rendered him deaf. Gad . . . the constant ringing, combined with flaming apparitions, might have driven him mad had the voices not taken control.

No time for that now—not with Hannah and Gracie in peril. He started back but soon had to heel over, battling stomach cramps. The drug, flakka, had begun another orbit through his brain. In waves, it came, a cyclical heat. With it, an overwhelming anger so intense, he had to employ a remedy from his experimental years in San Francisco: Inhale . . . exhale. Observe from the distance. **Listen.**

Insects, frogs, lit up the sky like sirens. A breeze soughed through the ferns and cypress, while the starry tree canopy remained motionless. It was an illusion. There was no wind—just like the first time he'd visited Chino Hole.

His eyes wandered among the black geometrics of railcars. Emanating from the old luxury coach came a pneumatic rasp amplified by steel walls. Steady inhale-exhale respirations vibrated through the soles of his bare feet and alerted his brain. Something, someone . . . a force was inside the railroad car hiding. Waiting. Breathing.

Pneumatic respirations became a familiar voice, then a chorus that crystallized in his ear.

You came to set us free.

Rage is fear untethered by caution.

"Goddamn right, just try and stop me," he yelled, and strode through the brush to the **Sawgrass Clipper**. The car was huge, the size of a semi. Moving the door on rusty tracks should have required freakish strength. Maybe it did. He used his hands, then a shoulder, and the door skidded, true on rails, wide open.

Tomlinson got a hallucinatory glimpse of what was inside—ankle chains, bits of bone, coolie caps—then was forced back by a lucent spinning wind that arced skyward. The spiral brightened. It sparked a bolt of lightning and cascaded on a comet's path toward Chino Hole. Impact from an uncertain source echoed with the thump-thump-thump of gigantic wings.

Wings . . . ?

Demon Crow. Geezus, had he allowed the monster to escape?

He took off running—too deaf to hear a distant, desperate wail that was Gracie's final plea for help.

Hannah's SUV was empty when Tomlinson arrived. Doors closed, lights off. No cell phones or keys to make use of when he peeked in, only some scattered boating gear.

Christ, he'd been a fool to run off and leave them. He was berating his cowardice when he did hear a voice . . . Hannah's voice. She was arguing with someone, a man who didn't sound like Vernon, but it could be no one else. He sprinted through the trees, leapt the rock wall, then moved quietly, carrying the old revolver in its sack.

Overhead, the sky hissed. The persistent thumping of wings assumed a motorized rhythm while sparks rained down. They twirled and drifted with the lazy indolence of a parachute. Tomlinson's mind skipped back to childhood: fireworks on the Fourth of July.

Darkness was hollowed by an eerie glow that led him closer to the pond. There they were: Hannah, arms extended, hands cupped around a gun, saying, "Damn you, where's Gracie? I'm not gonna ask again. If you haven't figured out who dropped that flare, you should, and do what I say."

A flare? Vernon ignored the showering light and faced her from only a few strides away. He had huge sloped shoulders and a chest that would take more than one bullet to stop. It made him cocky. "Hell, girl, you're about to pass out, and your face is something a rat might eat, but that's all. Think I'll just wait here and let it happen." He stepped toward her.

Hannah, looking woozy, instead of stepping back, said, "Last warning." She spread her feet and crouched.

Shit. Tomlinson ran out of the trees, yelling, "Stop, stop, stop! I'll shoot you myself, you sonuvabitch. Hey . . . look at me. Where's the girl?"

Hannah turned toward the familiar voice. At the same instant, the man charged her and was shocked when she actually did it, pulled the trigger—**ker-WHACK**—but not in time to spare herself a bone-jolting impact.

"Get off her . . . stop this bullshit." Tomlinson ran until he was close enough to square himself like an old-time duelist. He reached into the sack. "I'll do it, by god—look at me, you crazy bastard! Hannah, are you okay?"

Vernon had the woman's shoulders pinned. "She won't be when I get done." He had ripped her gun free and was holding it to Hannah's forehead. From his knees, told Tomlinson, "Drop that Colt or I'll kill her."

It took a drug-addled moment to understand. He meant drop the pistol, a long-barreled Peacemaker once owned by the deputy who Walter Lambeth had murdered before butchering the man's wife and children.

Tomlinson's resolve wavered as a strange new voice came into his head; a voice he did not recognize as Mr. Bird's. A professorial whisper, saying, **Butchered them all, that's right, so pull the trigger. You know who he really is. It's him—Walter.**

Hannah began to struggle beneath Vernon's weight. He slapped her hands away and hollered, "You don't got the balls. An old wheel gun like that, you're more likely to hit her than me. If you want to see Gracie alive again, slick, you got no choice." His head, pumpkin-sized, turned in the gilded, cascading light.

Christ . . . it was true. It was the same face in the photo Tootsie had shown him, broad nose and cheeks like Babe Ruth. All that was missing was an old-timey straw hat and suspenders.

The voice whispered, **He split them women open like quail, their babies, too, and put them in the furnace. That's what Walter does. He'll never stop unless you shoot him.**

Tomlinson blinked the voice away, took a breath, and tried to focus on what was real. "Where's the girl?" he hollered. "If you prove she's still alive, and get the hell away from Hannah, you can walk out of here. I'll give you an hour's start before I call the cops."

"How dumb you think I am?" Vernon was getting tired of dealing with the hippie, and this pissed-off woman who wasn't nearly as pretty as

Raven Girl casting in the videos. "You're running out of time, slick, and so's your girlfriend. She's drowning, if you give a damn."

"Gracie? You sick excuse for . . . Tell me where she is!"

The voice whispered, **She's already dead,** while Vernon gestured toward the shoreline. "There's a special place I got her hid. You want to see her, better drop that goddamn Colt. She ain't got long, but that's up to you. I'll give you to the count of five."

"Wait, this is crazy. Look, man, no one has to die. Why don't we—"

"One," Vernon hollered.

Tomlinson squinched his eyes closed, opened them, and peered down the barrel. His hands were shaking.

Do it, the voice urged.

The Peacemaker's hammer clicked back as if by an invisible thumb.

"Two."

The pistol's rear sight floated beneath his eye and framed Vernon's chest. The vicious voice continued to badger. Tomlinson blocked it by allowing his senses to probe something inexplicable: a single dazzling green eye had appeared in the cypress gloom that hugged the pond.

"Three."

The blazing eye emitted a beam of light, thin as a laser. It panned the water, attached itself to

Vernon's chest, then moved to Vernon's forehead and painted a third eye. In a drug haze,
Tomlinson noted the purity of its color, a radi-
ant celestial green, and decided: **A sign!**

His finger cupped the trigger. His finger
tightened.

"**Four**, dumbass. Oh hell, I'm gonna kill her
anyway, so—" Vernon scrambled to his feet,
extended the pistol, then was jolted backwards
by a puff of wind . . . or the blazing green eye
that had leapt to his knee.

"Sheee-it!" he yelled. He looked down,
shocked to see a shard of bone and black seepage. His eyes moved from Hannah to his
shattered knee. "You bitch. Didn't even feel it
when you shot me. By god, I'll—" He raised
the pistol.

Tomlinson pulled the trigger—**BOOM-
BOOM-BOOM**—three times. Smoke billowed from the barrel.

The last thing Mr. Bird would ever say to
him was, "Shit-for-brains, you missed."

"Fuck you, Walter" was the reply. Tomlinson remained fixated on what was happening,
ready to fire again.

Vernon staggered back as if on wooden stilts
and turned toward the pond, unaware of the
green eye on his temple. He managed several
Charlie Chaplin strides before seeking sanctuary in the water. He splashed, facedown, pulled

himself along the bottom, and swam toward the cypress gloom, dog-paddling, not kicking much.

The blazing green eye blinked off. A shadow emerged from the cypress. The shadow glided into the water, and continued to glide, carving a soundless wake on an intercept course, Vernon still unaware.

Tomlinson walked toward the slow, inevitable collision. **Crocodile,** he thought. Vernon, from the way he jolted upright in shock, then screamed, possibly feared the same. He went under, came up, then was taken down again in a thrashing frenzy.

After that, all sound was blotted by a low-passing helicopter. The helo pivoted sharply, and was circling back, when a searchlight spotted Hannah, standing, waving her arms.

A voice boomed from the chopper's PA system, "This is the United States Coast Guard. Cross your arms if you activated a maritime EPIRB in the area."

Hannah did it: formed an **X** with her arms. The emergency transmitter she'd activated was on the life jacket that Gracie had tossed to the front of the SUV while making room.

"Wave your arms if you need immediate medical attention."

Tomlinson, on the run, waved, too, then tended to the woman while they waited for the chopper to find a clearing in which to land. There wasn't one, but distant sirens told them help was on the way.

"I think I'm okay, I'm just so worried about Gracie . . . and my baby." Hannah, fingers on her abdomen, said variations of this many times yet refused to break down in tears. Tomlinson remained positive, and, buoyed by her bravery, pretended to ignore the drug horrors still going on in his head. What was real, what was a monstrous illusion? The girl had been right about that. It was impossible to differentiate— except for one nightmare that came true.

During a lengthy search, the helo made another pass. On the turn, its spotlight revealed Marion Ford slogging down the shoreline, the body of Gracie Barlow limp in his arms.

Questions from the chopper's PA were ignored. The biologist spared the girl indignity by telling Tomlinson, "Take her into the woods and find something to cover her with. They're shooting video. It's required on a mission like this."

My god . . . the horror of what a knife had done to Gracie's stomach. Tomlinson battled nausea, and whispered inaudibly, while Ford ran to Hannah, who managed to stand and allow herself to be taken into his arms. "Oh, Marion . . . please tell me she's not—"

"I was an idiot not to figure it out sooner,

I'm sorry." He took out a small flashlight and winced at what he saw. "Turn your head so I can have a look."

"Maybe you're wrong."

"I'm not."

"Oh god. Where'd you find her? I don't understand why you're here. There was a man. I shot him. Now I'm afraid he might come back and—"

Ford said, "Get that out of your head. You didn't shoot him and he's never coming back. Maybe this will convince you." He produced Hannah's phone in a waterproof case. "It was in his pocket."

She stared. "Then . . . you must have . . . Did you . . . Are you sure he's—"

"Don't ask. We need to get you closer to the road, then I want you to lie down, okay? An ambulance and the police will be here soon. I called a detective friend after I found your vehicle and saw . . . well, what I saw in the back."

Vomit, a spattering of blood, and coils of chewed duct tape were enough to convince Ford that he had to act fast and possibly from long distance. Two laser-guided acrylic darts had shattered when they shattered Vernon's knees.

The last thing Ford said to Hannah before she was wheeled into the ambulance was, "Your baby's going to be fine, and everything else can wait. We'll have plenty of time to talk later."

He hoped it was true. The woman's slurred speech, and the concern on the faces of the EMTs, caused him to wonder.

None of this was shared when he found Tomlinson, but he did say, "You're closer to Captain Barlow than anyone. It's better if he hears about Gracie from you, so you know what you have to do."

The sun was almost up, and it was several calls later before they learned why the famous fishing guide didn't answer his phone. The dockmaster at Marina Del Ray shared the grim news. Tootsie had been struck and killed by lightning outside his double-wide on Key Largo.

Tomlinson finally gave in and wept. "I should have never told him to go out in that storm. Tootsie warned me, this is a bad, bad place. Doc, please don't do it. Your cop pal said the same damn thing—don't go back in the water."

True, which is why the biologist was hurrying to get into his scuba gear before a police dive team arrived. It was a way of burning time while awaiting word about Hannah, but there was another motive.

"No choice," he said. "You were right. There's something big down there."

Maybe there was.

Ford returned to the same shallow grotto

where he'd found the girl. He had left her killer there, the man's head wedged in a crevice until a deeper, safer spot could be found. But, when the murk cleared, a flashlight confirmed that the body of Vernon Lambeth was gone.

Where? Ford surfaced and scanned the pond. Nothing to see but strobing blue lights above the tree line. He cleared his mask and explored the shallows thinking he'd returned to the wrong chamber, but there was the only one large enough to conceal a three-hundred-pound man.

No need to panic, but an underwater search seemed prudent. For twenty minutes, he cross-hatched the area. Aside from a mild carom of downward current, there was nothing to explain what had dislodged a body from a chamber roofed with rock.

That was okay. If Lambeth was found, much of what the coroner saw could be explained, or evaded with lies. The insane sometimes fell and shattered their knees. Homicidal killers sometimes drowned.

Ford returned to where he had started and poked his head into the chamber for a last look. A column of sunlight breached the limestone striations from above. He augmented visibility with an LED flashlight. The combination revealed something he hadn't noticed before, and shouldn't have touched. But he did.

"The skull of a prehistoric crocodile," he told his pal after surfacing, then described the animal's incredible size while he took off his gear.

Tomlinson stared at the crater called Chino Hole and nodded, saying, "**Finally.** They're all free."

28

The day Hannah Smith was released from the hospital, Ford drove her home. They sat for an hour on the deck of her boat, not saying much because, along with a concussion, she had a broken jaw that was wired shut.

Important topics required a legal pad and a pencil. Five pages were filled before he stood to leave. One point was worthy of re-confirmation.

"Are you sure?" he asked.

Hannah had never been confident about her size, or her looks. It took some effort to look into the face of a man who'd saved her life and only nod.

"You're welcome to think it over. What with the painkillers and all, maybe you'll—"

She shook her head no. The decision she'd made was her own.

Ford had a way of smiling that brought to mind a boy who'd rather be alone in the woods than exchange social pleasantries. "May I?" he asked.

She presented her lips for a kiss, then held him tightly for what seemed a very long time, but, watching him drive away, realized, **It wasn't long enough . . .**

The next evening, June 21st, a full moon marked the summer solstice. The Earth's western hemisphere had orbited into opposition, so the bright lunar rim appeared huge when it crested the mangroves of Dinkin's Bay.

It was Thursday, 8:37 p.m. The sun had set twelve minutes earlier. Many of the marina's liveaboards were at Mack's beach cottages, a former nudist colony, watching the solar fireworks, not the lunar drama, when Tomlinson entered the lab carrying a cardboard box.

"I should train that dog to bite anyone who doesn't knock," Ford said. He was calibrating a new spectrometer, holding it up to the light, until he noticed the box. "If you found more bones, I don't want to hear about it. I've never lied to the police so consistently in my life. Well"—he adjusted the spectrometer's focus ring—"not in this country anyway."

Tomlinson was scratching the ears of a yellow-eyed retriever, which was okay until he started cooing, and jabbering baby talk. The dog banged its tail a couple of times, then nosed the door open rather than put up with more nonsense. A heavy splash followed, causing screeching seagulls to rocket past the laboratory windows.

"Wow, you two are in a funky mood today. Wait 'til you see what I brought—and, no, it's not what you think."

Ford, in fact, felt better than he had in a while. His discussion with Hannah was a factor, as were recent plans made to spend a week bonefishing at Flamingo Cay in the Bahamas. He watched his pal place a heavy ceramic jar on the table, the lid sealed with paraffin that had outlasted a rusted wire stopper. "A gift from your friendly **madam** in Key West?" he asked.

It was a reference to Tomlinson's recent work for the Chinese Consolidated Benevolent Association. With the help of Lia Park, the commercial pilot and Zen student, they had reinvigorated efforts to find China's forgotten immigrants, and repatriate their remains for formal burial.

"Could be," Tomlinson said. "A present from the grateful spirits of our newly mourned dead. I was hunting around behind Tootsie's cabin when they—or something—led me to what must be an old root cellar. It wasn't far from the pond, but you wouldn't know the place. The thing's hidden in the weeds, all lined with—"

"Limestone blocks?" Ford interrupted. "Please tell me you weren't nosing around Chino Hole. Not since you got back from Key Largo anyway."

"How'd you know?"

"About Tootsie's memorial service?"

"No, the root cellar."

"I saw it. It's about five feet deep, rock-insulated, and big enough to hold several cases of these things." He hefted the ceramic jar.

"Why didn't you say something?"

Ford had to laugh. "You're unbelievable, you know that? I didn't tell you for the same reason the state put my contract on hold. No trespassing. Not you, or me, or anyone else, until the feds are done. There's no statute of limitations on murder, and the crime scene folks aren't going to buy your story about channeling a family of serial killers."

"Killer," Tomlinson corrected.

"Either way, they'll arrest your ass," Ford said. He didn't want to hear any more theories about the behavior of abused feral children, so he carried the jar to an epoxy workstation and switched on a lamp. "What's in here, you think?"

Tomlinson knew. "You'll need a screwdriver to get that bastard open. I'll be back with some ice and a couple of glasses." At the screen door, he paused. "I heard you drove Hannah home from the hospital. Did she say anything about her . . . condition? Guys around the marina keep asking, especially the women."

"She did," Ford said. "I'll meet you on the deck."

Alcohol distilled from sugarcane, aged ninety years in earthen jars, should have been translucent as rain when poured by the light of a rising full moon. Not this stuff. It was tannin-stained as if dipped from the mangroves.

"Cripes A'mighty," Ford said, making a face. "This shit's awful."

"Gotta let it breathe, man. It'll grow on you. Seriously, it helps if you pretend Prohibition wasn't repealed. Here, watch me." He swirled the liquor and chugged it down. **"Wow."**

He could only mouth the word, so poured another glass while waiting for his voice to return. "Yeah . . . now we know where the name comes from. I sorta like the salty taste. Gives it a margarita flair, you know?" He snapped his fingers. "Limes, man. That's exactly what we need. I'll be right back."

While he waited, Ford stared at the moon and thought about Hannah, and others he knew and had known. Often, he marveled at the day-by-day courage demonstrated by so-called average people, their relentless endurance as well, yet was prone to dismiss those qualities in himself as motivated by doubt, or the fear of failure.

It was time to ask himself the same question he'd posed to Hannah: was he sure?

No . . . but taking action, moving on, was always preferable to inaction. On the other hand . . . ?

The subject was something to bounce off Tomlinson, the social scientist, when he returned with three key limes freshly wedged. "To be or not to be," he summarized. "Where've you heard that before? Man, I've written papers on that very conundrum, so don't get me started."

He launched into the subject anyway and, one glass of moonshine later, was still talking, then suddenly stopped. He sat back. He scratched at his bandaged ear and re-focused on his friend. "Hey . . . does this have something to do with you and Hannah? In the house, I saw your fly rods, your gear, and travel bag all packed."

"It does," Ford said.

"Both of you?"

"In a way. She got good news from the doctors. They were worried about something called placental abruption because of the beating she took. They wanted to be sure; now they are. Her baby's fine."

Tomlinson closed his eyes to savor the unexpected news, then had to wipe them when he got to his feet. "Hot damn—this is something to celebrate," he beamed, then began to pace. "Doc, look, we've been friends a long time. I never thought I'd hear myself say this, but what you should do—hear me out, now—you should get in your boat, haul your stubborn ass over there, and ask that woman to marry you."

Ford **had** asked her. That's why he'd held off until tonight before agreeing to meet Lady Gillian and members of her family for a week of bonefishing on Flamingo Cay. It was their way of thanking him for a job well done.

"I'll think about it," Ford said. He tilted his head back and finished a second drink that, foul as it was, freed him to say, "The worst that could happen is, she'd say no."